ADVANCE ACCLAIM

'Maggie Humm's novel, *Radical Woman: Gwen John & Rodin*, is a marvellous portrait of a singular artist who, even as she fell under the dominant spell of the French master, was stubbornly refining her own vision more or less in his shadow.

The author gives us the creative ferment around Bloomsbury and the Slade at the turn of the twentieth century, in which Gwen developed her craft in the fruitfully competitive hotbed of student life. We travel with her across France, open to experience and adventure. We see her growing obsession with and attachment to Rodin in Paris. She longed to be more than one of his mistresses, yet her relative solitude, in sparsely furnished rooms, left her free to paint the wonderful portraits and self-portraits that posterity has found to be among the defining images of that period.

Written in the form of a fictional autobiography, Gwen negotiates the conflicting challenges of other people's demands with her own anxieties, of sex, money, artistic integrity. This novel gives us a deep, authentic portrayal of a female artist in her time.'

– Prize-winning novelist Tim Pears, FRSL, author of *In the Place of Fallen Leaves* and the *West Country Trilogy*.

'In *Radical Woman: Gwen John & Rodin*, Maggie Humm embodies Gwen John, bringing her to the centre of a novel that explores the emergence of this Welsh artist from the Slade in London into the vibrant Parisian art world of the early 20th century. Humm's great achievement in this novel is to enable John to emerge from the shadows that she was often cast beneath and to shine a light on her lived experience as a woman and a painter working in Paris with intensity and passion.'

– Anna Falcini, artist and Director of *Chère Julie*, a film about the poetic traces of Gwen John's life.

'A vividly imagined and deeply researched portrait of one of the 20th century's greatest artists. Gwen John springs from the page in all her brilliance and complexity.'

– Annabel Abbs, prize-winning novelist of *The Joyce Girl*, *Frieda* and *The Language of Food*

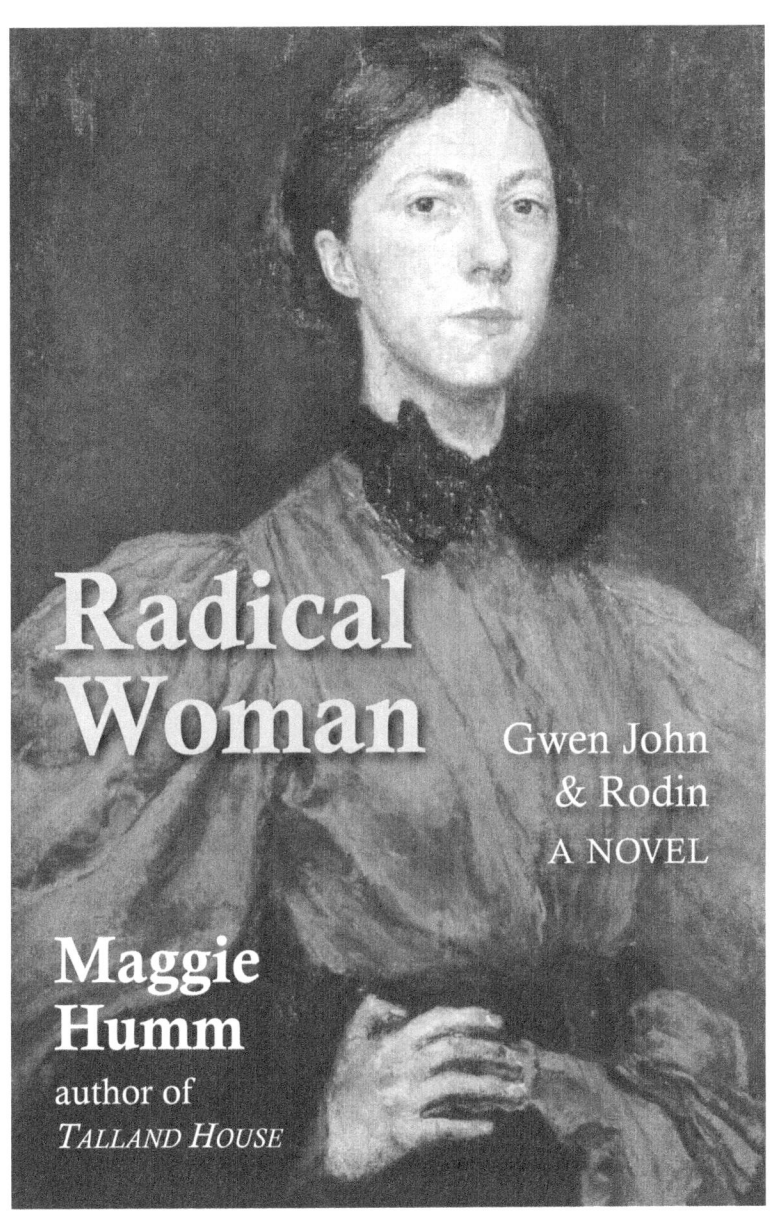

EER FICTION
Edward Everett Root, Publishers, Brighton, 2023

EER FICTION

Edward Everett Root, Publishers, Co. Ltd.,

Atlas Chambers, 33 West Street, Brighton, Sussex, BN1 2RE,

England.

Full details of our overseas agents in America, Australia, Canada, China, Europe, and Japan and how to order our books are given on our website.

EER Books are not available for sale in Belarus or Russia. We stand by Ukraine.

www.eerpublishing.com

edwardeverettroot@yahoo.co.uk

Maggie Humm, *Radical Woman. Gwen John & Rodin.*
A Novel.

ISBN 9781915115027 hardback

ISBN 9781915115034 ebook

First published in England 2023

© Maggie Humm 2023

This edition © Edward Everett Root Publishers Co. Ltd., 2023.

Printed in England by TJ Books Limited, Padstow, Cornwall

Book production by Andrew Chapman, www.preparetopublish.com

'… *being incoherent in relation to desire does not impede the subject's capacity to live on*'
   – Lauren Berlant, *Cruel Optimism*

THE AUTHOR

Maggie Humm's recent novel *Talland House* was shortlisted for the Impress Prize, Fresher Fiction Prize (as *Who Killed Mrs. Ramsay?*), the Retreat West Prize, for the Eyelands Prize and was also longlisted by the Historical Writers Association. *Talland House* was one of the *Washington Independent Review of Books* '51 Favorite Books of 2020'. In 2021 the novel was the Next Generation Indie Book Awards Finalist in Historical Fiction (post 1900s) and in 2021 it was on the Eric Hoffer Award Grand Prize Short List. Maggie Humm is also the author of *Border Traffic, The Dictionary of Feminist Theory* (the first edition of which was named 'outstanding academic book of 1990' by the American journal *Choice*), the bestselling *Modern Feminisms, Feminism and Film; Modernist Women and Visual Cultures: Virginia Woolf, Vanessa Bell, Photography and Cinema; Snapshots of Bloomsbury: the Private Lives of Virginia Woolf and Vanessa Bell,* and editor of *The Edinburgh Companion to Virginia Woolf and the Arts.*

CHAPTER 1

1897, BLOOMSBURY, LONDON

I run all the way from the Slade to my flat, holding tight to my certificate in case it might disappear like distant lampposts in the London fog. It is a chill afternoon, the mist swirling around Bloomsbury, and my bodice sticking to my back as I pass the white stucco houses with their fantailed windows, handsome and solid, distant from the smoke-blackened terraces to the east.

Indoors, a sense of possession comforts me each evening. The mangy tabby cat, which I rescued last week from a pestering schoolboy, nuzzles my boots in congratulation. While I saved her, I was thinking how brave I would appear in my memoir but writing only has power if someone reads the book and who will read mine? But I do feel gleeful and scan the certificate again to check that the whole morning was not make-believe.

Gwendolen Mary John. Year 2. Slade prize for figure drawing. 'Young Woman'

My first prize. I was silent with embarrassment when the tutor presented the award in front of the other students, his normally severe face softening into a smile. The day suddenly seemed to expand as if the doors to the studio had opened all together. For once Augustus joined in the applause, although my brother never lets me forget that, as a year three student and already famous, he is superior. My prize has no distinction of gender – just excellence.

It has felt as if for two years I have been crouching inside myself, holding my breath. Now I can breathe freely, and even my basement flat seems larger with its bare walls and sparse furniture – a moth-eaten chaise longue, a low table next to the narrow bed, a tall wardrobe, my paints and brushes carefully stacked on the bookshelves, bare floorboards foot-smooth. Gus gave me a full umbrella stand to prepare me for London weather, but it ruined the simplicity of my surroundings making me off balance, and I quickly gifted it to my landlady. The space has an odd and vacant readiness like a canvas already primed with gesso.

The certificate would look first-rate above the chaise longue, but the spring sun might fade the gilt lettering eventually. Today the fog hovers over the townhouses so that they seem to merge with the grey sky. The kitchen galley is darker, but steam could damage the card. As I stand hesitating, Gus is through the front door without knocking.

Gus's appearance resembles a caricature of an artist: his thick, unkempt brown hair bunched loosely on either side of his face: a brigand's shirt, a violet and magenta neckerchief, and his goatee and moustache curled at the ends so that he has the effect of a portrait rather than my brother.

'Let me see your prize.' He sweeps off his sombrero onto a hook, and stares at my certificate as if he has never seen my name before. His excited expression reminds me of the dramatic day he jumped off a rock into the sea in Tenby, cracked open his head and sported a vivid red bandana proudly for weeks.

'Were you too timid to name the model? She is Grace, isn't she?' His deep baritone trembles with laughter. 'Hers was the only name you mentioned, until McEvoy appeared.'

'*Young Woman*, was all the portrait needed.'

I will not give him the satisfaction of thinking he knows everything about my feelings. Grace was last year, she flitted from admirer to admirer, sucking sustenance, stinging me in the process. Goodness knows why I was so spellbound. McEvoy has almost taken her place, although Gus calls him dull.

'You are following in my footsteps; I was in year two when I won a prize.'

'How could I forget?' I ease my certificate from his grasp. 'The very next day you wrote, telling me to leave Tenby and Father, and enrol at the Slade.'

At first, I missed the buoyancy of Tenby's spring with its lush floral displays, the hot summers of my childhood, the freedom of swimming. The perennial mornings holding a sense of something growing, expanding. Bloomsbury pavements are hard slabs, echoing. Also, I think that Gus is becoming like Father, telling me what to do, who to see – as Father did, forcing me to eat rice pudding, presiding over our dreadful meals. Gus has an air of ownership wherever he is, like a grand umbrella over places and people, and these days living alone, I am more aware of his aura whenever he is nearby.

If I can stand up to him, perhaps I can be bolder with people in the future; I long to be free yet still cannot seem to make decisions on my own. At least, here in my flat, I have a definite presence – all filled in, full of detail, about to become a recognised artist.

'You are glad you came now?' He leans back on the chaise longue, stroking his beard.

'But in the Life Room what are we women given to draw?' Trying to control the squeak in my voice. 'Models wearing ludicrous bathing drawers.'

'You sound so amusing when you are serious.'

It is sibling chaff not rudeness. Such mockery tends to begin our encounters and we amplify our differences as a way of enhancing our closeness. He would defend me in an instant if anyone else spoke the same words. Painting together in childhood was blissful, and in Tenby he protected me from the cheeky street children. My smile matches his; and the bells in the square's church begin to peel as if for a special service. As they ring it feels like I am part of a great party to which, this time, I do not need an invitation.

'No more surviving on nuts and raisins. We are dining in the Café Royal tonight, with champagne to celebrate. I can invite McEvoy along with the others.' Gus stretches out his long legs, watching my face, waiting.

Will drinking with McEvoy encourage him to say more about his feelings for me? Sometimes McEvoy exudes an air of perfect containment making his face both handsome and distant. The effect causes him to dissolve into the background as if I have not fixed his image properly on my canvas.

'McEvoy has never won anything.' Gus tries to hide his smirk with a silk handkerchief, pretending to blow his nose.

'Perhaps his work is less fashionable than yours.' Will Gus hear the scornful tone?

During my visits to the National Gallery with McEvoy, we became good friends with a hint of more to come. Although his eternal copying of Titian began to pall, I enjoy his explanations of glazing techniques, delighted when he said to call him Ambrose instead of Mr McEvoy, his hand holding mine. It might seem like nothing out of the ordinary, but these moments now shine in the week like beams from the sun. The National Gallery feels like my true home, where I can fall into the paintings, feeling the bones beneath the lavish dresses, seeing how figures stand in relation to each other. Is McEvoy as fond of me as I am of him? Will I find out tonight? I breathe out slowly now so as not to give anything away to Gus.

'Invite those friends of yours too, to match mine,' he says.

'You only wish to see Ida,' pleased that he reddens now. I need the support of all my friends. Throughout the two years of study and self-doubt, trailing behind my dreams every day at the Slade, Ida, Ursula, and Grace were my protectors, like painting layers of varnish over my canvases; although Grace was caustic after she found another admirer.

'Perhaps I will call in at the Slade.' Ignoring my quip and reaching for his sombrero, 'as I round up my merry band, and ask your favourite tutor Legros to join us.'

There is a slight hesitancy in his voice. Gus disliked Legros's criticism of his drawings, Legros's cutting down the size of the genitals and saying, Michelangelo made them small. Gus says he always draws himself. My quick chuckle sounds louder than I intended but there is something about his frown which is so amusing.

'Legros's lack of English is irritating,' he continues, squashing his hat down hard. 'God knows he's been in England long enough.

You would imagine he might have learnt by now. He thinks you are the tops. The rest of us are *pas mal*.'

'Professor Legros would not attend a student affair. He spends many hours with Rodin, they are friends.' It was the most exciting news Legros ever gave to us in class, but I also treasure the way Legros's shrewd eyes scan my paintings, his thinker's face smooth when he approves.

'Then I will only invite students. The Café Royal at nine sharp,' He sticks a cigarette between his lips as he climbs the stairs and leaves. 'Be prompt.'

McEvoy will certainly be there; with his customary black and white clothing, he matches the surroundings. He is so elegant every day at the Slade. Perhaps the champagne will make him amorous. I will be ready.

Through the basement window, the fog has given way to the sun which sinks behind the tall sycamore trees in the square, tinging their tips rosy red and tracing enormous shadows on the walls of the houses. The cries of children ripple through the leaves. The evening sky has a kind of opacity, turning Bloomsbury into an impressionist painting of daubes and impasto. A lamplighter is going about his rounds leaving a lengthening line of orange-coloured lights in his wake. At the end of the street, Ursula and Grace are skipping around the corner and reach my front door just as I open it.

'We met Augustus, and he has invited us to the Café Royal tonight. He has already asked Ida.' Ursula makes the invitation sound like a grand proclamation. For such a bird-like girl her voice is surprisingly resonant, especially when she talks about art. She always speaks with an old-fashioned quality that does not seem part of our up-to-date lives as if she thinks about what to say as scrupulously as she paints. 'Show me your prize. What a wonderful achievement.'

'You will never match Augustus,' Grace adds, 'but well done!'

Grace's every sentence seems to carry barbs. There had been moments when I felt as if I would disappear unless she looked at me, until last year, when her sharp wit became as brittle as spun sugar.

'We will help you choose clothes,' Grace continues, twirling her skirt, scarcely containing her high spirits. 'You have other dresses, do you not, than the dull, brown one you favour?'

I had painted Grace full-length, seated against a plain background to highlight the exquisite lines of her cheekbones. Art should show a feeling for character, but her thoughts escape me, as if she is dreaming, and do I even want to know now what she thinks?

'You must wear a striking outfit. The others must not outclass you tonight.'

'Whatever I wear, Ida will be the focus of attention.'

Ida was such a good friend this year with her sisterly conversations, along with Ursula's interest in my work and support. Gus says Ida will be famous before the rest of us.

'She will be the centre of the men's attention because she dazzles,' Ursula says, 'but I think Grace is more elegant.'

Grace smiles, acknowledging the compliment, and with the three of us chattering, the basement seems as noisy as the Café Royal. Grace grows more excited while she speaks and I have the impression that she might still have an interest in me, until opening my wardrobe, she pulls clothes towards her, seemingly scornful of my meagre collection.

'What about the blue cloak?' Ursula says. 'It is sophisticated.'

'No. She has worn the garment ten times already,' Grace says, 'and it swamps her. I will choose another,' throwing clothes on my bed.

Ursula and Grace are making me seem an actress with dressers, changing me between acts before I emerge for my bow until finally, Grace holds up my red blouse to the light.

'This is the one, the bouffant sleeves are exactly like the Mode de Paris fashion plate we sketched last week.'

'I am not sure I can ever be fashionable, nor do I want to,' taking the blouse into the bedroom. I can control my clothes, they console me.

My life is simple and organised, a life that cannot squander a single moment. It has a kind of integrity gained through my hard work, but now, before the mirror, something has changed. The faint check overlay on the red cloth gives my body a fuller shape, like a comely woman. McEvoy's clothes always hang correctly on his tall body; we will make a good couple tonight. I gaze at my reflection, biting my thin lips to heighten the colour. I am not winsome or attractive, my nose is too short, but I look less disdainful tonight. I cannot allow my ardour and my anger to erupt. The knot of tension between my eyebrows has vanished and the black velvet band with the oval cameo is perfect, decorating my neck. I have worn these clothes so often but tonight, after my prize, they feel special.

CHAPTER 2

1897, CAFÉ ROYAL

The evening is temperate. Outside the Café Royal, Ursula and Grace shuffle behind, propelling me through the rotating glass door. Waiters in long white aprons hold trays of drinks high above their heads. Diners' conversations mix with the clatter of dominoes; and well-separated groups – writers, sporting types, politicians, and artists – are dotted around the room on gilt chairs shining in the electric lights. In spite of my small size in the mirrors, I feel a new power take hold of me and tingle when diners glance as we pass, their smiles mixing with the heat of the room. Gus weaves towards us, between tables, still wearing his sombrero.

'How do you do girls? Ida has arrived. Let me escort you to our table.' But people keep stopping Gus to greet him or ask about his current painting. He is such a great swell and so prolific. He could happily paint two society portraits in one evening if allowed.

'Augustus told me about your certificate,' McEvoy whispers, sidling up to us. 'Many congratulations,' and takes my hand to his lips. 'It is a great achievement.'

His thin face and doleful eyes, made larger by the shadows beneath, give him an ascetic air combined with his smooth, immaculately cut hair.

'For a woman?' I say, too quickly.

McEvoy grimaces slightly and drops my hand, standing

motionless, his long limbs arranged awkwardly. The light falls on him from a different angle and his face is in shadow.

I feel the power of his silence and itch to reach out and touch him, with my words reeled in, but Ursula speaks first. 'Pay no attention. We are all desperate for champagne, and Gwen has not eaten all day.'

'Right. Then let us join everyone,' McEvoy glances uneasily at me. 'I did order champagne with caviar. Augustus booked the grand table over there.' And he points ahead, holding out his arm to me which I accept, gratefully.

'Thank you, Ambrose,' I manage a half-smile before the blush spreads upwards from my neck. 'How kind.' His grey eyes are gazing straight into mine, and I feel almost overcome with emotion. But am I ready? I still have much to learn about painting.

The table has lights directly above, giving the impression that we are in a bright, shiny space like a painting's focal point, with the restaurant customers surrounding us visible, but at a distance murmuring indistinctly in shadow. My life has suddenly become somewhat unknowable. Ida is seated on a red plush banquette, glass in hand, her dark beauty radiating across the table. I slide beside her, delighted that McEvoy sits next to me.

At least six from my class have come to congratulate me; or is it the offer of free champagne, and the possibility of being near Gus at the other end of the table? They are trying to say clever and amusing things about art, but the effect is like an imitation of artists talking, and I turn to Ida. 'I hoped you would be here already,' as Ida raises her flute in salute.

'I am glad you have brought Ursula and Grace too, but let us not chatter to ourselves, shall we? I am never sure what the men will think.'

'Including Augustus?' the buzz around us covering my taunt, but he is deep in conversation with an acolyte.

'We are here to celebrate you, not him, Legros said this morning he is so proud of you. And so am I.'

Delighted, I sink into the murmur of conversations, the tinkling of cutlery, the air full of perfume, feeling McEvoy's thigh against mine. The fact of his body. The clarity of being next to a man, the delicious brutal elements under his cologne. Will he kiss me later?

Gus raises his glass to me. At once his friends raise theirs. As I murmur thanks, everyone's arms sink down as if he has cut their puppet strings. He is so sure of himself, it gives me a peculiar sense of security; in the sway of his confidence, there is a warmth and ease.

'Why is Augustus staring at Ida?' Grace mouths over the table.

There is a second before she smiles, and I want to keep her smiling. 'He is imagining Ida naked, for his next portrait.' How often his eyes are on Ida, how often he speaks to her in the studio.

'Or more,' Grace stares upwards at the ceiling's painted amorous nymphs.

'What will you paint next, Gwen?' Ursula spreads a thin finger of toast with caviar. 'Will you change your palette to blues and greens like the Impressionists?'

'They do not know how to construct form,' Gus interjects, switching his fork for a knife as if about to stab a canvas.

'All the galleries are exhibiting their work,' Grace gives Gus a contemptuous look, 'which sells for high prices.'

There is a silence which amplifies the conversations around us, and Grace's red mouth is showy against the soft lights, the subdued clothing of the other students. I sip my champagne, so bubbly that air fills my mouth.

'I saw a Monet last month in Agnew's Gallery. The landscape seemed to glisten in the air.' Ursula speaks with a modest, easy confidence and shares my views, that art is a kind of knowledge that cannot be known until it is experienced, and Ursula is always attentive to new ideas. Sometimes we women are braver than the men.

'Are you suggesting we give up our models?' Gus says scornfully.

'I prefer to spend my time with Old Masters,' McEvoy nods agreement at Gus, 'even if they fill my mind with a confusion of ideas.' And he takes little sips, removing the glass from his mouth to savour the champagne each time he swallows. No one is listening to him as they focus on Grace and Gus, waiting.

'The secret of painting is colour,' Grace persists, glaring at Gus, 'not closeness to a model.'

No one else matches Grace's audacity.

Gus lights a cheroot without asking.

'I agree,' I say quietly, the second glass of champagne having loosened my tongue. 'It is all about tone. I work very slowly to get the exact blending of colours.'

'Where is all this from?' Gus says, 'not from the Slade.'

'Seeing the exhibitions in Bond Street,' I am unable to stop, 'it feels as if I am in a new world.' I have changed but I am uncertain when, like a canvas with each brush stroke adding colour and light but keeping to the original design.

Another flicker of unease crosses McEvoy's face at the word 'new', but he winks at me and keeps his position.

As the conversation around us continues, Ida squeezes my hand, whispering into my ear, 'McEvoy is very fond of you.'

'Not as fond of me as Augustus is of you,' I squeeze back.

Ida blushes, almost matching her pink silk dress, the tight ruching on her waist shaping her into an hourglass.

Goodness knows my chest could never match hers, but McEvoy glances at me and I clink my flute against his. From his expression, the gesture seems to settle whatever has troubled him, obliterate my ill-judged remark.

The conversations fall silent as a lanky well-dressed man approaches.

'Professor Legros,' Gus stands, as Legros appears. *Should I imitate him and stand to greet Legros?* No one else has, and sandwiched between Ida and McEvoy, it is difficult to move. The slim bushy-bearded professor flicks his wrist as if brushing away an insect.

'*Je dois te féliciter,*' Legros speaks directly to me, ignoring Gus.

'We have all been congratulating Gwen,' Gus says, before I can speak, as if Legros's praise is not particularly special. Perhaps I am the only one to notice Legros' '*te*' not the formal '*vous*'?

'*Demain, je dirai de ton triomphe à mon chèr ami Rodin,*' Legros continues, '*j'aime me vanter de mes étudiants,*' and keeping his eyes on me not on the crowd, bows, replaces his top hat, and strides towards the exit.

As the name Rodin circulates around the table in a Chinese

whisper, the clatter of plates becomes applause, as if the swell and glitter of the whole room is solely for me. In the thick congregation of diners I feel my insecurities ease.

'How exciting! He is telling Rodin about you, and I like his final comment about enjoying acclaiming his students,' Ida says, but McEvoy stands up, calling out, 'A toast to *une artiste extraordinaire* Gwen John, as Professor Legros would say.' McEvoy's accent is dire, but I smile.

'Well done McEvoy,' Gus shouts. 'Let's toast my little sister again.'

Although Gus came to the Slade before me, I am almost two years older than him. For the most part, he sees me, not as others might, eking out a life as an independent woman artist, living alone, but as if attached to him. A kind of puzzlement settles why I am still vulnerable to his thoughts floating over me. Is it a family affinity? That is why I tolerate his sometimes-sarcastic remarks and he always hugs me afterwards. Gus says I am beautiful like Mother, but I was only eight when she died, and I always see her framed with a softness I cannot touch without losing her altogether in my mind. I have made my own way and what matters tonight is that Legros said 'te' and placed me in the same sentence as Rodin.

CHAPTER 3

THE SLADE, LONDON

What a long day in the studio, hot and dusty as usual in spite of the high ceilings. One ribbon at a time, the May sun pushes its way into every corner, making the model glisten with perspiration. Her pose is awkward. As we take up positions in front of our easels, Legros instructs her to stand on one leg placing the other on a low stool to her left. The young woman seems uneasy, off balance. I remember standing on one leg in the tedious ballet lessons Father insisted were good for my posture, but I never knew where to place my hands.

'McEvoy seemed devoted to you last night,' Ursula holds a stick of charcoal vertically in front of her, eyes narrowing at the model on the dais. 'He is old-fashioned artistically speaking, but sweet and gentle. Why not consider him?'

The studios are segregated, so McEvoy is far away and cannot hear, and Professor Legros is engrossed in a painting at the other end of the room, but what should I say? Although the class is sparsely attended today, perhaps others could overhear.

'I do not want a fiancée.' Rubbing out my first line with a stump of bread, but I am uncertain.

'We will probably all end up with a husband.'

'Better to die with a brush or a pencil in one hand, than marry.' My routine never deviates – arriving at every event clutching a sketch book, and sitting in picture houses, pencil in hand, book half-propped up on the seat in front, little time for relationships. 'But I have learnt so much from McEvoy, about how to build up colour,'

Ursula is managing to hide a yawn with her free hand, but I cannot stop. 'He helps me. The others pontificate, but the problem is that McEvoy's technique seems too perfect as if he is not there in the painting at all.'

Ursula gives a knowing look, quickly completing her figure. 'Have you allowed him to kiss you?'

'We kissed.' It was a fleeting moment – in the dark alley behind the National Gallery, the stone wall hard on my back, McEvoy's hands gripping an umbrella shading our heads. The sun had smoothed the soft, pale sky and vanished leaving streaks of pink. He bent over and kissed my forehead, gently as a prayer. I felt the intangible scent of his body next to mine, the warm, fresh smell, his soft lips were enough. And his smile afterwards.

'*Mesdames John et Tyrwhitt, s'il vous plait.*' Legros snorts into his full beard.

'*S'il vous plait, excusez moi,*' Ursula blushes.

'*Moi aussi,*' I add, quickly smudging some charcoal into the background, deepening the shadows. Do I want McEvoy's hands to explore my body? There seems no time, no place because he lives with his parents. There was one visit to their dark house in Bayswater. My parents have artist friends, McEvoy told me proudly, Whistler had visited. It must have been during Whistler's black and grey period; it was impossible to see colour in their dimmed rooms.

As I sketch on throughout the afternoon, the conversations around me, their markings on their canvases, all become hazy like a London fog. On my easel the surface comes alive with emotions, some shapes seem sharp, and others soft, and I can address the figure now that the charcoal seems to absorb the light without constricting the model.

Legros is peering over my shoulder. '*Très bon Mademoiselle John.*'

I had forgotten him entirely, as if the heat of the day is driving my gestures not the teaching. The rest of the class shuffle waiting for Legros's next comment, and he approves Ursula's sketch. She stands erect, her five extra years giving her a veneer of sophistication and strength the rest of us lack.

'Well, McEvoy certainly admires you,' Ursula whispers, as Legros moves away. 'When you talk together in the Fitzroy Tavern it is the one time his face gains a regular colour, rather than pallid white.'

'I care for him more than I thought I would,' especially the way he leans over me when speaking, as if protecting me from the world.

Ursula is not listening anymore, and my fingers are black with charcoal and too dirty to use for smudging shadows. Even my rubbing-out bread is full of dust.

'Work is what is important. I want my paintings to be smooth and glossy. But I have not succeeded yet; and marrying McEvoy would hinder me. I would not have time to paint,' willing my sketch to better reflect the image in my head. Nothing makes sense until an emotion is shaped in a sketch. My brain is a mixture of confused thoughts. Legros seems as tired as me.

'*La leçon est terminée*,' Legros pronounces. The model stretches her legs in relief.

'Perhaps you should stop meeting McEvoy for a spell. Give yourself time to reflect.'

Ursula proffers the best advice. Gus's ideas are centred on him, but Ursula listens before making judgements which are always more relevant than his.

'We could sketch together instead. Maybe in the British Museum? I hear Rodin is obsessed with the Greek sculptures; he once kissed the horses' nostrils.'

'The marbles should really return to Athens, don't you think? It was reprehensible of Lord Elgin to seize them from the Parthenon.' My voice must be louder than normal because Legros descends on us, frowning.

'*Jamais! Je prendrais un fusil!*'

Worried he might actually keep a rifle among the jumble of paints and brushes in his art cupboard in the corner, I desperately try to remember the French for a joke. '*Pardon, pardon Professor Legros.*'

Legros's face is puce. He sweeps an arm imperiously across his chest, indicating the door.

'*Partez immédiatement Mademoiselles John et Tyrwhitt.*'

Breathing deeply and slowly, I step out of the studio alongside Ursula, avoiding the faces of the other students. As we emerge from the colonnaded entrance, we dissolve into laughter. All these months, there has been the pull of the Slade with a twist of joy in scanning the façade every morning. Now the building's windows seem like heavy-lidded eyes, as if the Slade is refusing to see us.

'Will he welcome us back tomorrow?' Ursula giggles. 'I am uncertain whether I have much more to learn from Legros.'

'Well, everyone respects him including me, but I have to admit I have always disliked his portrait of Carlyle.'

'Then we should go to the BM soon; try to see outside the frame. Perhaps forget painting for a while. Study sculpture.'

She was the most sensible of us all, calm, and full of purpose in the long days in year one working together, in our full-length thick overalls as if the Slade must keep us covered up, away from the men in their day clothes. We sketched replica classical busts, but no one took us to study the originals.

One evening last week, sauntering in Bond Street, a small head in a gallery window stopped my breath. The almost silk appearance of the face rising out of a rough black block, gouged by chisels, seemed to hover over the sculptor's marks, and a name was just visible on the base – Auguste Rodin. I looked at the bust first from the street and then moved close to the window; so few people take time to study art, but I felt for the first time that I was seeing what I needed. Painting in the same way as Rodin sculpts, surfaces flowing in colour, with my brush strokes subtly visible, perhaps at the edges, could be a new kind of art.

'Let us walk to the BM now, we have hours before meeting Ida and Grace,' an image of Rodin's sculpture hovering in front. 'And perhaps, after qualifying, escape the country altogether, model in Paris?' The day feels full of promise.

'I had to fight Father for five years,' Ursula moans, 'before I could leave home for the Slade. He will not be too pleased for me to join you in Paris, even though of course, I would never mention modelling.'

RADICAL WOMAN

As we leave the Slade, stepping onto the late afternoon pavement, we are met by friendly faces. London streets never fail to inspire me with the sense that I am in a wider world with people who might share similar thoughts. Part of why I enjoy talking to Ursula is that, last year for the first time, I learnt that other women thought about families in the same way as me. It was reassuring to know that while I had been sitting at home fuming about Father, another woman in another room had an identical feeling. 'Tell him you belong to Art.' I want to add art is immune to temptations but, thinking about McEvoy, is it true?

'Father is a vicar, Gwen,' Ursula laughs instantly. 'He has never considered art to have a place in heaven.'

'Then we will make our own heaven, here on earth, all of us painting together in Paris.'

Glancing at me, Ursula's eyes light up. 'We should persuade Ida and Grace to join us, four can live more cheaply than two.'

'And we could all enrol at different ateliers,' I say, excited, 'share different techniques and approaches.'

The familiar street, its flagstones hot from the late sun, pushes us forward. Although May is a month for tourists, pedestrians are sparse, and Ursula and I are abreast, elated, talking about Paris. Pigeons circle, pecking at the pavement curb. The rear entrance of the British Museum looms ahead, its oblong flat pillars resembling an opening into a Mayan temple.

'Tell your father we are all believers, Ursula.' We rotate through the turnstile. 'Only we have different buildings in which to worship.'

The galleries' chill air and subdued lighting always takes my breath away. A few windows, dotted here and there, display everyday life on the streets outside as a fast-moving silent film, while we step as noiselessly as we can through the Greek rooms. Seated, we each choose a different sculpture to sketch. Ursula is staring at a terracotta head, but I prefer the polish and sleekness of white marble. I want to stroke the surface, but it is amazing how quickly a guard can appear when the sculptures are touched.

A calm envelops my body when sketching. My heartbeat slows.

The heaven of almost completion, the moment between gesture and form, the feeling of inevitability about a drawing which is about to separate itself from me, a thing waiting for its frame. Legros, McEvoy, the Slade, all filter away as if the gallery lighting contains only a few thoughts in the pool from one electric lamp.

'We should visit the BM more often,' Ursula whispers, 'away from the Studio, I think I sketch better here than I do there.'

'I agree. It is such a relief not to worry about Legros, and not to hurry to finish work in time for the next exhibition.'

It would be a dream – to hide away in a corner and stay here, sleep among the sculptures tonight, in the empty galleries. Turning to tell Ursula my madcap idea I see Legros in front of the Elgin frieze at the end of the room. He must have left the Slade just after us. Next to him is a shorter, plumper man with an equally bushy beard, who is pressing his nose so close to the figures he almost touches the sculpture. He resembles Rodin. The men are much of an age, their top hats nodding in tandem. They are murmuring and pointing out details to each other. It *is* Rodin.

As their conversation grows louder, '*la plus belle chose*' comes from Rodin and he turns to gaze at us, removes his hat and makes a half-bow. His brow is steep above a strong, straight nose with delicate nostrils. With my pencil freezing in my hand, I feel like a marble Leda seduced by Zeus, and, for a moment, Rodin and I are alone in the gallery, as if Ursula, Legros and other visitors have slipped away through the walls. I imagine Rodin's profile from inside as if I had physically entered him.

'What are you looking at Gwen?' Ursula turns towards the frieze.

'It is Rodin,' my voice scarcely manages the words. 'You remember, in the Café Royal, Legros said he was seeing Rodin '*demain*'– tomorrow, that is today. And, last month, he told us Rodin always stays at the Thackeray Hotel opposite the BM, so he can see the Greek sculptures as often as possible.' The strength of Rodin's gaze has gone straight through me, then Legros places a hand on Rodin's shoulder and the two men shuffle out.

'It is destiny,' Ursula says, 'we chatter about Paris, and Paris comes to us.'

Perhaps it is kismet. Rodin's face lingers – the thick, pomaded hair cut noticeably short, so it is bristly erect, the beard tinged with grey, his round spectacles giving him a distinguished air. As we leave the BM, the street is empty under a darkening sky, just hansom cabs clip-clopping. Disappointed, I turn to Ursula.

'Remember we are meeting Ida and Grace in the Fitzroy Tavern,' Ursula says. 'Shall we mention Paris to them tonight? Or Rodin?'

'We have over a year to go before graduating, it is too early to speak of the future, although we could hint; and if we mention Rodin the men will think we are simply frivolous fans.' Ursula nods.

By escaping the Studio, the day has made me see everything with a fresh eye. Now I know the good art from the bad, and that Rodin's art is certainly more significant than the Slade's.

CHAPTER 4

BLOOMSBURY, LONDON

The Fitzroy Tavern has a dark, secluded façade, as though wishing to deter visitors. We push through the heavy stained-glass doors and see Ida and Grace directly ahead at a small marble-topped table. Drinkers overlap, move apart, and return like moths fluttering from wall to wall. Groups of students are a patchwork crowd, some still dressed in their paint-splattered clothes like rustics in a romantic painting's foreground. Waiters never fuss over us here, unlike the Café Royal. With the air already thick with smoke at seven in the evening, and the anaglypta ceiling, brown from years of cigarette fumes, the tavern is such an antidote to formal dining. Seven is too early for Gus so we girls have time to ourselves for a while.

Ida and Grace light cigarettes as we join them. The sweet smoke begins to cover the familiar undertow of the tavern's stale beer and fried onions.

'I long for one at the end of the day.' Ida is sophisticated in her red turban. 'Do take one.' She pushes over a black and gold packet.

'I am trying not to be tempted into smoking. Too expensive.'

Ida is so elegant with the pink, oval cigarette between her fingers, but there is little enough to live on each day, even relying on Gus's favourite nuts and raisins instead of meals.

'Augustus asked me to pose for him,' Ida blurts out as if she cannot contain the invitation for an instant longer.

'Be careful,' Grace says. 'He will demand more than a pose. I had to be very unyielding.'

Ida gives a weak smile, and my hand reaches to Ursula hearing her sharp intake of breath. Gus flirted briefly with Ursula, indulging in his usual glances and ardour. He accompanied her home one evening, and she told me that she cannot decide if she wants to love him or not.

'Did you and Augustus draw each other as children?' Ida asks, as if trying to ease the awkward moment.

'Sometimes, but also there were many interesting children on Tenby beach,' remembering a boy about my age, who made animals out of coloured paper to sell for a penny. I can visualise his golden curls and grey velvet suit but what was his name? 'Father let us convert a back attic into a studio where Gus and I would draw and paint our friends. Father never fully approved; but we insisted.'

'We have been sketching in the BM,' Ursula breaks in, glancing at me as if willing me to add more.

'The atmosphere of the BM was less daunting than the Slade, and we saw an intriguing visitor.'

'Have you seen Peter Kropotkin at last,' Grace says, 'from the anarchist club in Tottenham Court Road!'

'No, we saw someone in the BM more exciting than anarchists. Rodin together with Legros examining the Elgin Marbles.'

'By Jove! Did Legros introduce you?' Ida asks, her voice rising with excitement. 'Did you speak?'

'No.' Ursula says, 'the men were at the far end of the gallery, but Rodin stared directly at Gwen.'

So Ursula noticed Rodin's glance too, a tight straight line between us. My heart misses a beat remembering Rodin's gaze, how it felt as though he saw right into me.

'Was Legros still riled?' Grace's eyebrows are raised as if searching for a sarcastic comment. 'We heard about your earlier contra-temps in the studio.'

Suddenly the Museum encounter, or lack of a meeting, must

sound absurd. Two much older men were simply visiting a museum, no more. So why is it of consequence?

'Legros did not look in our direction, and it was merely a moment,' giving a dismissive wave. 'But the sight gave Ursula and I a tremendous idea.' I nudge Ursula, willing her to take up the story.

'Gwen and I want to visit Paris. My father will try to forbid the visit, but he must know that Paris is the centre of the art world.' Bending over, she holds in a chuckle. 'And Gwen suggested if we have no family support we could model for money. Do join us you two, when all our studies here are over.'

Grace gives an artificial gasp, as if she has never had a similar thought. I am sure she would never agree to be nude.

'Gwen.' A heavy, familiar arm suddenly rests on my shoulders. The chatter and clinking of glasses covered Gus and McEvoy's arrival and I am stunned for a moment seeing McEvoy's thick, black glossy hair framing his face like an Elizabethan miniature.

'I noticed you ladies already had drinks so just bought ours.' Gus is always so parsimonious. 'May we push another table alongside to join you?' He is staring hard at Ida, as the men sit.

Paris must not be mentioned in front of Gus and McEvoy. The trip would be a year away at the earliest, and I suspect Gus will try to control the planning, as if his sister is incapable of independence.

'McEvoy and I have exciting news,' he says, before anyone can speak.

McEvoy is smiling too, watching me carefully, as if Gus has an amazing proposition.

'A friend has invited us to stay in his house in Le Puy to paint. It is in the Auvergne. You are all very welcome to join us.' He sweeps a hand around our group but is gazing at Ida.

'Is Le Puy near Paris?' I nudge Ursula under the table again before she can speak. 'I simply wonder if we would be able to see exhibitions on the same trip.' McEvoy's closeness, the scent of his eau de cologne, is already beginning to disperse the image of Rodin.

'Paris is distant from Le Puy, Gwen.' Gus turns to Ida. 'There are the most exquisite hills.' He models the shapes with his hands.

Is it only me who sees Gus sketch the outlines of breasts?

'And valleys tilled by peasants, watered by gentle streams.'

McEvoy is still watching me, rubbing his hands awkwardly together. I picture us swimming together in the streams, then enjoying a local wine in the sun after the physical exertion. We could sit side by side at our easels, me testing one of his glazes, as he approves. The image is intensely attractive. 'A visit would be delightful. When do we leave?'

'Late summer?' Gus says. 'August?'

McEvoy is almost beaming, his hands now on the table, reaching for his beer glass. 'To August.' Holding up his tumbler, he says, 'after our end-of-year exhibitions. We could pose for each other in Le Puy. It will be cheaper than paying the usual shilling each time.'

The Slade models have weathered features and work-worn hands; in Le Puy Father would be far away, so we could be informal, even nude, taking ambitious poses, alive to each other rather than static figures. My breath catches in my throat. For a moment I have an image in my mind of Rodin's full-bearded face with the Elgin Marbles gleaming white behind him, but McEvoy is here and the prospect of mixed bathing parties in Le Puy and painting together every day.

A week later, Bloomsbury is bustling with activity. An organ-grinder at the corner cranks up, his monkey alongside is dancing on the street to the mechanical chords. The square seems to be tapping its feet, with the click-clacking of pedestrians. It is that moment in the day when time changes slowly, unevenly, growing further and further away from breakfast and yet no closer to dinner.

We are in Gus's studio, which seems as roomy as the whole Slade, with Ida sitting in half-profile, her head slightly inclined towards Gus and the rest of us working at our easels. Gus, bold as ever, chose oils for painting Ida so his portrait will take much longer than a sketch, but perhaps this is what he wants – hours alone with her in his studio after we all leave. The portrait has real depth – he has captured Ida's 'character' as he would claim – her calm beauty. My sketch is full of activity – a rough, wilfully simplified version of the room with all of us dotted about: Ida seated with Gus, his paint brush in one hand, Grace near the door as if about to dance outside into Bloomsbury, McEvoy in his usual shiny black and white clothing, an eyebrow firmly gripping a monocle, Ursula elegantly petite. The sketch has a kind of celebratory ease – with the figures loosely interacting, dynamically fluid, our student gang and I am happy. When I was a child, I often cried but now my strength, rather than sadness, surfaces frequently, and visibly in the sketch.

'May I move, Augustus?' Ida stretches her legs.

'Of course. A pause? I need to let the black dry. Shall I prepare tea? Or something stronger?'

Will this be the signal for the two men to drink, pushing us women to the margins of their afternoon? McEvoy turns to me and the gap between us seems filled with sizzling energy, my restlessness. Putting down my charcoal, I rub the dust from my fingers.

'I prefer whisky,' McEvoy says, 'but perhaps the hour is too early? Would the ladies care to join us in China tea?'

'Perfect.'

'I have good news,' Ida raises her voice as if to fill the whole room. 'I won a scholarship to visit Italy.'

'Tell us more. I have always wanted to see Rome,' conscious Gus must have heard, and not wanting to sound too enthusiastic. 'When do you leave?'

'I can choose the date. Perhaps next year – December when Bloomsbury is frozen or drowning in fog.'

'Next year seems a decade away.' Thanking Gus for the tea. He seems more cheerful after I said 'decade'.

'I would rather be in France with you all. We girls work well together. Perhaps a visit to Paris soon?'

Grace and Ursula nod in unison with me. No one will know me in Paris, and I can be whoever I want to be. I look out of a window at the plane trees in the street. It is as if I am seeing the branches for the first time, fixing on one section so as never to forget, taking in all the details: the way the large leaves droop at the edges, the scaling bark, the fluttering flowers, and seeds. Paris suddenly shivers in all its possibilities.

'Le Puy comes first.' McEvoy's face is almost pink as if bottling up excitement. There is a scent of lemon eau de cologne, and he gazes at me.

'Our end-of-year exhibition is first.' Grace's words sound faint, as the same exhilaration washes over me as when McEvoy suggested I call him Ambrose.

'What will you submit Augustus – this painting?' Grace continues, 'and will you be brave enough to title it *Ida Nettleship* or will it be *Girl with a cup of tea*?' gesturing at Ida and winking at me. 'Or you have probably several society portraits stacked in your wardrobe over there.'

Grace's sarcasm is lost on my brother. His eyes are on Ida, he is already painting again.

'None of us can outdo Gus,' I say. 'It takes me all day to even prime a canvas.'

'What do you use?' McEvoy is looking at me, as if I am the most interesting person he has seen all day.

'Chalk and animal skin glue,' glancing down before I blush because, right now, I want to stretch out and touch his lustrous hair. 'From rabbits usually. What brush do you use to prime?'

The conversation resembles our National Gallery talks, apparently commonplace, yet oddly comforting.

'I find wide brushes are best.' McEvoy glances quickly at Gus as if embarrassed to discuss banal technical issues, probably dreading his quick ridicule.

'I'm not sure what to submit to the exhibition,' I say, quickly, 'My glazes take an age to prepare.'

'You're hardly Turner at Varnishing Day.' Gus sneers, stubbing out a cheroot on his palette.

'Gwen creates wonderful tones.' Ursula smiles at me as if I should immediately give a demonstration. 'Subtle and perfectly judged.'

'So, I am not the only one to appreciate your work.' McEvoy is eyeing me again.

'I follow your advice.' A flush is rising up my neck and McEvoy bends over, taking my hand and kisses the back.

'Sadly, I must return home. But we will all meet tomorrow at the Slade to make plans?'

As McEvoy kisses the girls' hands in turn, I can see his gestures with them are more perfunctory and breathe slowly for fear the beat of my heart will echo from the walls.

'Luncheon tomorrow?' McEvoy murmurs to me as he puts on his coat. 'Perhaps we could discuss Le Puy?'

'Of course. In the café, after morning class?'

Gus seems impatient as if wishing us to leave. Ursula and Grace finish washing their brushes in the sink, and I pull on my cloche, but Ida stays seated, and Gus points his paint brush at her again.

The next day, the late afternoon sun sweeps low along the studio's floor. Miss Elder, my least favourite tutor, dampens down our group with her usual, 'A man has greater creative, more imaginative, force, than a woman,' and leaves the room. Ursula is next to me, scowling as we all are. She is the one person in whom I confide. She has a way of searching my face as if scanning a painting to find the significant motif to confirm an artist's signature, alert to my feelings. After a two-hour class, my brain should be as exhausted as my right hand, but something is buzzing inside me like the fly on the wall and I must tell Ursula my news. She removes her baize uniform and strokes her hair back into its neat chignon. Mine is pushed into an untidy bun and stray hairs cluster over my face.

It is difficult to concentrate on ordinary actions after my luncheon with McEvoy. The topic turned from glazes to Le Puy and, as usual, my timidity prevented the important words from being uttered. I have not been to France, I said, I have not been abroad at all and I long to visit. I did not add 'with you'. The phrase seemed too direct. McEvoy beamed. I have an image of McEvoy strolling with me by a river, my arm tucked into his; the golden light of the early evening reflecting in the water; earnestly describing the French countryside. Ursula will understand.

'This must be the hottest room in the whole building.' Ursula stretches out her arms, 'I feel saturated with perspiration.' The studio's tall windows give an ideal light for painting but have been closed for years.

'Let us sit in the courtyard for a moment,' I say, 'before we return to our lodgings.'

The dry earth in front of our bench is cracked into a mosaic as if shoes have been impatiently scuffing the ground for days, but a fresh breeze gusts through the courtyard colonnade and at last I can breathe. 'I must tell you all about my luncheon today.'

'I guessed something happened,' Ursula stares quizzically at my hair. 'You are normally neat as a pin.'

'I was uncertain that I would have anything positive to say about McEvoy and me,' reaching for Ursula's hand in excitement. 'We discussed Le Puy over the meal.' In my excitement, I could not touch the lamb chop McEvoy insisted on ordering, only a few peas and mashed potato. 'It is all settled. He loves me.' Learning to love is like learning to paint. Both have infinite capacities.

'Did he tell you so?'

'Not in so many words, but he will in Le Puy,' remembering his tender glances and soft voice. 'He is already planning walks à deux,' and our hands will slide into a grasp, our fingers intertwined.

'Will Augustus approve?' Ursula gives a quick shake of her head. 'He thinks little of McEvoy's work, or his conversation.'

'Gus does not consider that any of his peers deserve much respect,' wondering why Ursula thinks his views need consideration.

'Except you. Augustus always speaks highly of your paintings. One evening, in the Fitzroy Tavern, Augustus said you 'had a fine sense of character'.

'He was probably drunk, but let us not mention McEvoy to him, or to the others?'

Standing, Ursula puts a finger to her lips and, as we step into Gower Street, a burst of warm air from the traffic heralds summer, tempting me to throw away my hat and gloves. The street is rushing into the evening. Omnibuses vie with each other to reach the bus stops. The usual flower seller at the Slade's gates is packing away her remaining stock, her terrier jumping up at her, seemingly desperate to scamper. Hansom cabs, sleek in black wood, accelerate down the road, oblivious of pedestrians as if their passengers paid for a chariot race not a journey home. There is a sizzle, an excitement in the air. Ursula's omnibus is alongside, and she leaps onto the platform with a swing of her artist's satchel. I can return to my basement alone and dream about McEvoy.

CHAPTER 5
LE PUY, FRANCE

Le Puy glimmers in the distance as the train puffs intermittently, descending into the town. When the smoke clears, the buildings seem to be sitting in water. A river, glinting with sunlight, mirrors the air; I am swirling with excitement. Not a day has passed without me thinking of Le Puy, and of McEvoy there with me, and now here we all are.

It seems as if we were planning the trip for months. The Slade girls scattered for the summer. Ida postponed her trip to Italy, but her mother insisted on a visit to relatives instead; Grace and Ursula returned to their respective families to secure another year's funds for the Slade. Providentially, Father guaranteed the fees for Gus and me. It is just the three of us: Gus, McEvoy, and me. McEvoy is chatting with him, their backs stiff against the hard wooden carriage bench opposite. How does he manage to retain the monocle when his low fringe of hair sweeps from side to side whenever he disagrees with Gus?

Through the window, the landscape is hazy, but when the sun shines, bright patches appear in the fields like little scenes in a crystal ball. As Le Puy looms larger, how will the trip end? A future with McEvoy? Not marriage. That would be too much of a constraint, and, in any case, I could not bear more of his parents. Lovers living together in bliss creating wonderful art? He described how the French countryside is drenched in beauty and light, as he touched my cheek with a hand in farewell after class one day. He must love me.

'Daydreaming again, Gwen?' Gus says. 'We have arrived. Can you reach down your valise, or should we assist?'

Determinedly, I heave my suitcase through the carriage door into a chatter of children and the clean scent of pine trees. A month with McEvoy here, and I smile up at him, as he offers to carry the case.

'We will need to rent a donkey and cart to carry all our canvases and trunks.' Gus counts coins into a porter's hand who collected everything from the luggage carriage.

'*Certainement Monsieur.*' The porter touches the peak of his cap and points ahead at a group of gypsies lined up, their wagons embellished with roses and trailing vines.

Gus beams at the sight of his favourite people, and rushes over, mouthing a few words of Romany, leaving me with McEvoy to guard the valises. Will the month be full of days like this? Hours alone with McEvoy while Gus dashes about with the gypsies?

As we clamber onto a cart, Le Puy rolls up a hillside, its medieval cottages struggling to rise above the mist, crickets chirping everywhere. Above, a giant statue of the Virgin hovers. Father is an avid churchman, but he would detest the image. He always read Anglican Sunday school books to us and would be aghast at devotion to the Virgin, but the statue seems to float over me, as if it might descend and wrap me in its veil. On the cart, McEvoy's body feels warm next to mine; it takes immense strength not to reach out and grasp his hand, but he must make the first move, especially in front of Gus. Behind, the town is lit up, a mixture of sunlight and water reflections on the cottages, almost pulsing with feelings.

The donkey turns through a ramshackle garden gate and Gus, excited, points up to the first-floor apartment. 'All ours for four weeks, and the garden too.'

'I enjoy cooking,' McEvoy says at the chickens clucking around a peasant girl. 'A simple dish of eggs with onions and bread tonight?'

'And local wine,' Gus adds. 'I asked the landlord to provide us with flasks.'

That evening after supper, as Gus impatiently starts on a canvas, McEvoy and I trek higher up the cliff along a narrow path overlooking the town, a balmy breeze enveloping us. We peer over a wall, still warm from the afternoon sun, and stare down at the town's black expanse dotted with streetlamps. As I stare, the black becomes almost flat planes of dark colours overlapping, held together by stars.

'Have you planned what to paint?' I ask. In profile his handsome Roman nose peeks above the old-fashioned high collar.

'I will paint the landscape,' McEvoy gently places his hand over mine on the wall. 'But only seen through windows perhaps like da Vinci.'

'Why not just paint what is directly in front? Capture the light and colour rather than imitation.'

It is too bold, and McEvoy removes his hand. The word 'imitation' sprang out before I had time to think; it must have been the wine with dinner and, seeing his pained expression, the usual flush spreads up my neck.

'I did not wish to criticise. I paint small works so they will not be hopelessly out of place in small houses,' attempting a quip.

McEvoy is not laughing but he does lean towards me, kissing me on both cheeks as if practising a French greeting or a goodbye. His mouth is soft, almost wet and my heart thumps. Can I step forwards into his arms? He is beaming in delight as if he has finished a major painting. 'How the night sky is bejewelled. You never see such skies in London,' sliding his arm around my waist.

Light-headed I lean against him, as he offers his cigarette case. 'I do not dislike women smoking, even in public,' while shaking my head, in case he should jump to the wrong conclusion. 'But I have never acquired the habit.'

'Perhaps I could teach you tomorrow, among other things. But we should return to Augustus. It is extremely late.' Around us the night darkens and settles, and we return to the apartment.

I have never felt so content.

∼

The next day the sky is cloudless as if encouraging us to paint out of doors. Gus is staying at the apartment, grumpy because the peasant girl refused his initial salvo, but he never gives up.

'I am setting up an easel in the garden to watch her,' he murmurs in my ear. 'I will bide my time.'

McEvoy and I climb to a vantage point, and I remove my boots wanting to feel the grass between my toes, the last of the morning dew. McEvoy glances at my feet uneasily. I can feel the beginning of another flush so dip my head, hoping McEvoy will not see. By the time we reach the brow of a hill, he refuses to go further.

'Such a day is made for reflection, not for walking.' He stretches out his lanky legs from a small painting stool.

He seems regretful for a moment as if a thought carries him away to a gap in the scene.

'Augustus said that there is a natural pool in the woods,' I point ahead, 'a mile in that direction,' but McEvoy is scrutinising his first line of paint.

'Perhaps we could swim later today when the heat has dissipated?' I imagine our naked bodies together at the lakeside. 'I swam often at Tenby. Once I sat at the edge of a rock to see what would happen, and a great wave rolled me out to sea. It was terrifying – but I was washed up again.'

'I have never swum,' McEvoy clears his throat, running a cautious hand over his curls. 'I prefer to remain on terra firma.'

'Have you not wanted to learn?' beginning to feel disillusioned with his negativity.

'Swimming is for Serpentine boys, not for artists.'

A surge of disappointment sweeps over me as strong as the sea wave. McEvoy seems more withdrawn than last night, but the touch of his hand can start my heart throbbing so easily. Do I need a man to make me feel fulfilled; surely art is as important as love? Gathering my thoughts, I focus on the canvas. My painting will be modern not realistic; like an iridescent wave pinned to the canvas without scaffolding, just areas of light and dark. The cross-hatching at the edges of the canvas, the thin black lines seem to work. Sometimes my paintings decide to be sweet-tempered and cooperative, at other times they are cross and inflexible, but I know I must keep working and the image will eventually come right. This painting will soon be my friend.

A couple of hours later, we stop painting at the same moment.

'Shall we eat?' McEvoy lays out bread, cheese, and fruit under a leafy oak as if to prevent any more conversations about swimming. 'I brought wine too,' pulling the cork from the bottle with his teeth in a well-practiced gesture.

The wine eases my dissatisfaction with McEvoy's inhibitions, and after eating, I stretch out prone on wild lavender. McEvoy's face is pink although whether this is from the heat of the sun or his love for me is not clear. If only he would hold me around the waist again, as he did last night, but he seems intent on finishing the wine.

'Augustus will admire your drinking ability,' irritated because McEvoy has not taken advantage of my splayed-out body on the ground. 'You are easily up to his speed and volume.'

McEvoy is silent for a minute, distracted. My directness must have soured his mood again.

'Apologies. You do not see me at my best. Perhaps tonight we could share some entertainment – visit a café in the town's main square. I will ask Augustus to join us,' as if an evening alone with me would be a terrible prospect.

All the way back to the apartment, my feet squashed into my boots, it feels as if I am shrinking. When we reach the garden gate, McEvoy holds my face with one hand and pushes his mouth towards mine; but then turns away, holding open the gate for me. Is it the drink making him want to kiss me? Hard to tell. The scent of his cologne is as exciting as the shape of his lips and perhaps I should be bolder; put my arm around him for a change? How would he react? It is too late. McEvoy's floppy hair falls over his eyes as we return indoors.

∽

The terrace of the town's central café is full of locals clutching tall slim glasses of milky-white pastis. Gus and McEvoy seem determined to match them drink for drink. With only one glass of wine, I am detached from the thunderous conversations, underscored by the strains of an accordion. In the square below there is an interesting group of figures, and the relationship between one head and another has a certain symmetry. Occasionally an appealing face or a gesture stands out. It all belongs to such a different world than the Slade.

McEvoy and Gus loll back on narrow, basket-weave café chairs which seem too fragile to support their drunkenness. How much does McEvoy drink in one day? I have only now recovered from luncheon. I chatted to him as we all strolled through the town to the café, secure my words could not be overheard by Gus among the hubbub, hoping we two might share something personal, but McEvoy seemed oblivious of the nearness of my body. Surely the drink will eventually loosen the rigidity he seems to depend on like a stout wooden cane.

'Are you painting *en plein air* again tomorrow, Gwen?' Gus leans towards me. He can work anywhere, even on a pad on his knees as now; sketching with one hand, swigging pastis with the other, hopefully the sketch will be of me and McEvoy to treasure from the holiday.

'I was thinking the self-same thing,' McEvoy nods. 'Perhaps we could all paint together in the garden.'

Pausing before replying, I struggle to control my feelings. Why does McEvoy always want a threesome? Why is he so dependent on Gus's opinion?

'I need landscape to free up my designs.'

This is not true of any of my paintings as they must know, but I want McEvoy alone with me. He appears surprised and I start to speak again but stop. Whatever I say always seems to sound inappropriate. The dream is to amble through the French countryside, hand in hand with McEvoy; the sun will pick out buttercups, and the warm Auvergne air will encourage us to undress in the privacy of a wood. We can lie together, and McEvoy's hands will explore my body at last.

'More daydreams Gwen or should I say evening dreams?' and Gus beckons to the waiter. 'You need another glass. We all do,' clapping McEvoy on the back.

Earlier, the soft evening darkness seemed to insinuate a closeness between McEvoy and me, but now I stare alone at the night sky. The town, and its river, are stretching away from me, in the direction of Paris where I should be, with modern art. Rodin is suddenly in front of me, the intensity of his gaze. McEvoy and Gus have ruined the evening, and I want nothing more than for it to end.

'I am tired,' loudly in case the alcohol has deadened their hearing. 'Let us return to the apartment.'

~

Sipping morning coffee in the garden, the heat of the sun on my back relaxes my tight shoulder muscles as I wait for McEvoy to rise. Last night, the café terrace was busy, too full of quaint townsfolk who had obviously taken Gus's eye, especially the young women with their tight-fitting peasant bodices. We all walked back in silence and parted with swift kisses cheek to cheek. McEvoy was too drunk to do more.

What McEvoy and I need today is a space in the woods, a grassy hollow flecked by sunlight, swifts flitting between branches, bird chirrups the sole sound. A place where we can sit and talk, and embrace, hidden from Gus, from the town. McEvoy will stop talking about glazes, about his love for the Old Masters, but instead of his desire for me; say he has come to Le Puy to be with me, not Gus. We will speak of the future, of our lives after the Slade. We will agree to live together, staying in Bloomsbury to be near our friends but not too close, perhaps on the margins, the other side of Tottenham Court Road. We will share our expenditure; and, flushed after a night of lovemaking, help each other to paint the next day. Exhibiting together, my carefully toned pictures will contrast with his classical manner, and I will seem modern, even avant-garde in juxtaposition. There will be prizes.

'Oh, here you are Gwen, shall we take our sketchbooks out into the countryside?'

McEvoy's footsteps were silent behind me. My throat is dry, but the coffee is stone-cold.

'I am ready,' trying to subdue the rising excitement.

We walk for ten minutes then McEvoy points to a green pasture sloping down to the river.

'This is a beautiful spot; shall we stay here to sketch?'

With his long, gangly legs, McEvoy does not enjoy walking. I imagined a strenuous hike, so we could rest together, breathless with desire as much as with tiredness. Yet sitting by the river is appropriate. McEvoy was strictly raised, he told me, and always seems to see happiness as if on the far bank of a river. On this bank is the McEvoy I love, and there across the water, deep and unreachable, is a mirage of our future.

Sketching side by side, the customary whiteness of his face has green tints as if he has been ill in the night. Hardly surprising since he has been drunk most days. I toss a pebble into the water; the flat stone sends rings of ripples outward on the surface. Perhaps McEvoy will reach out to me when he starts talking about anything other than drink or painting techniques?

On my sketchpad, I have ignored the landscape, the twisting path alongside the river, the water reflections sharing the sun. Instead my pencil has sketched two lovers, kissing, their bodies intertwined like the ivy and branches on the pear tree ahead. The figures seem to be moving one to another like waves, curved shapes in the light, with no clear outlines. Perfect. Everything I have done this last year has a flawlessness and I know it now.

'Drawing is quite impossible,' McEvoy looks abashed, pushing away his sketchbook.

'What is it, Ambrose? Are you feeling unwell?'

'I am in mental bewilderment not physical illness.' His hands tremble on his lap. 'I have been very remiss.'

'Remiss in what way?' What could it be? McEvoy is so punctilious. His every gesture is planned, nothing forgotten until the past few days of drinking. Today his clothes seem weighted down with stones. 'Has your work been less good than you hoped?' reaching for his hands to steady the tremors.

McEvoy pulls away as if my hand is tainted and his eyes gaze into the distance, not at me. 'I must tell you now. This is all so unfitting.'

A darkness shades the bright dream I carry.

'What is unseemly, Ambrose?' What will he say? It must be about the way I always seem to reply sarcastically without meaning to. Or my dedication to art. The sun is fiery, and birds above are wheeling and criss-crossing the bright sky, becoming trails of paint flung across a white canvas. How to capture the movements of the birds' wings, the texture of the air as if the air is full of ridges and ripples? McEvoy is still staring ahead. Has my intensity discouraged him? Or worse, is he disenchanted with me? My hands begin to tremble as much as his.

McEvoy takes out a handkerchief as if to blow his nose but is immobile.

'I am engaged to another; for three years now.'

He sits inert, seemingly exhausted by the revelation. I cannot look at him. He is smaller, diminished in scale like his pathetic, derivative paintings whose colours will fade like the Renaissance frescoes he so adores. I stand up, shaking, tears trickling down my face, as McEvoy weakly offers me his handkerchief.

'What is her name? Where did you meet?'

'She is Mary Edwards. We met in the National Gallery.'

Where else of course; he feels safe there. Her name is familiar. When I arrived at the Slade and read the rollcall of past students in the entrance, running my fingers over the embossed gold lettering, wondering if I could ever match them, become an artist, I focussed on students who shared my first name – Mary.

'Great heavens, McEvoy. She was at the Slade too; she is older than us by years.'

'Nine years older,' his voice as feeble as his appearance. 'You are upset Gwen – quite rightly. I do care for you.' He is grasping my arm.

'Whatever we have is finished,' wrenching my wrist from his grip. The grass around us has whitened, the river dried up.

My heartbeat fills my ears as I run back to the apartment, racing along the river path, ducking under the vine trailing over the garden gate, willing my feet to go faster across the lawn, averting my face from the peasant girl hanging out washing. In my room I lie silent on the bed, heaving with humiliation, with anger. Lust has made a fool of me. It is lust not love. Stupidity covers my body like a shroud, and there is an emptiness in the air all around. I will tell Gus that I need to return to England immediately because my work is not progressing. He knows how obsessive I am about art, and I know what can fill the abyss, what I must do, where I will go. As soon as I return to England, I will make plans to travel to Paris – with the girls.

CHAPTER 6

KENSINGTON, LONDON

Through the window of the hansom cab from Victoria, London is a series of tiny moving scenes. The city seems diminished since Le Puy. How many at the Slade imagine McEvoy and I are engaged now? My future will be ridicule in their eyes, shamefaced in the Fitzroy Tavern, avoiding direct gazes.

The hansom driver deciphered Gus's scribbled address – Number 11 Pembroke Cottages, Kensington. He will be there, he said, having rushed ahead of me to see Ida. For once it will be good to share, enjoying his brotherly support; glad he arranged free lodgings borrowed from Rothenstein. Is Rothenstein one of Gus's drinking companions? There are too many to recall. A 'delectable cottage' apparently, although how long the place will remain delightful with his drinking and mess is another question.

My anxiety eases immediately at the sight of him standing in the hall ready to envelop me in his arms, his gypsy earrings, and hair as wild as his beard. I want to be held like something small and treasured.

'I will take care of you; the sitting room can be your studio; I will commandeer the back room.' He makes busy with a few coals in the grate. 'Rothenstein is allowing us free rooms for three months. We can use the spirit stove in turn, there is only one. Tea?'

'Thank you. I crave something warm.' There will be months

ahead to watch pity in the eyes of acquaintances, so before humiliation can sweep over me, I unpack my sketchbook; my sketches will be talismans for a future without McEvoy, without any men.

'McEvoy returned to family in the country.' Gus hands me a teacup. 'You will not be troubled.'

I draw a black line firmly down the page to replace the last sight of McEvoy's white, thin-lipped face.

'Ida has invited us to a supper party at her parents; the Rothensteins will be attending. You must come; I will not have you hiding away from people. I insist.'

Despite the firm tone, he smiles. Meeting Ida's parents. He has travelled much further on his journey of conquest than seemed possible months ago.

'I am longing to see Ida again,' If she knows about McEvoy, she will be sympathetic. I try to be calm. 'You need not worry; we are miles from Fitzrovia here. Life will be a serene sea, without big waves.'

'Your life, perhaps. Ida is turning mine into Dante's proverbial inferno rings. We agree one minute and then I am pitch-forked into despair when she is unavailable to meet.'

'You are in love at last then? I never thought you could stay true to one lover.'

'Love, lust, plus whatever else adds up to nine circles of hell.' He pulls on a dinner jacket. 'Come to Ida's parents after you unpack.'

Through the window, as I gaze at the white glossy facades of Kensington, it is my favourite hour – a warning of dusk before the visible signs of darkness. In Le Puy, the evening light gave a warmth and generosity to figures and objects alike – a pinkish, radiant tinge. Now this evening needs to be unexceptional, just like any other English evening, everything placid with no foreign memories.

∼

Ida's Wigmore Street home is imposing. Three stories stretch up to the sky, so high it is impossible to see the servants' attics in addition. Or perhaps the servants live, like me, in basements. As I enter the drawing room, Ida's mother seems about to clasp me to her over-endowed bosom, but hands me a wineglass instead. Ida's father has clearly drunk several glasses, and his handshake is loose, but he seems friendly.

'Gwen, I must introduce you to our guest,' Ida says. 'Augustus is already a friend. Do you know William Rothenstein?'

A short man, in horn-rimmed glasses, shakes my hand. He has a more self-important air than Gus's usual drinking companions.

'I am delighted to see you again Miss John. We met at a New English Art Club exhibition last year.'

I vaguely remember his glasses but cannot for a moment think of any of his paintings. Was he at the Slade?

'I am hopeful you will temper Augustus's more extreme excesses. I trust you are both comfortable at Pembroke Cottages?'

Gus breaks in before I can answer. 'Nothing stops me. I do not live calmly like you and the rest of the world.'

As children we shared a passion for nature, seeking out wild beaches miles from Tenby so we could swim naked far out to sea. I was once as untamed as my brother. Rothenstein smiles uneasily and looks at me rather than Gus.

'I am so grateful for your generous hospitality, the cottage is ideal,' although it is already blemished by Gus stubbing out his black cheroots on the floorboards.

'Augustus tells me you have won another prize, this time for figure composition. I must congratulate you.'

'Thank you. Augustus, of course, won three prizes this year. There is no keeping up with him.'

'So what are you painting?'

Is that a hint of scorn? His eyes are hidden behind thick lenses. Miss Elder's words, as we left the Slade, were hardly encouraging. Most Slade women become expert book illustrators she said. Ursula and I groaned.

'I have decided to paint the cleaning woman, Mrs Atkinson. She has an intelligent face.'

Rothenstein frowns, as if intelligence and cleaning have no association. So I will not tell him I usually greet Mrs Atkinson with a kiss on each cheek.

'I will paint her with the usual props,' trying to ease his obvious disdain. He has lent me free accommodation after all. 'Dressing up clothes, perhaps a skull for memento mori?'

Rothenstein seems less uncomfortable. Out of the corner of my eye, Gus and Ida are embracing in the hall. Obviously, he is not hiding his desire for Ida from company anymore.

'What are you painting?' before Rothenstein turns in the same direction.

'I am attempting the brighter colours which I saw in Paris. I met every artist who matters – Rodin, Picasso, Degas.'

Despite his bumptious tone, Rothenstein's enthusiasm is contagious. Paris – the very name radiates. The ateliers, the Louvre, artists' studios – a world of free spirits. 'And which of the three is most impressive?'

'Undoubtedly Rodin. He invited me to his home in Meudon, near Paris, to make drawings and lithographs of him. His head is extraordinary. The hair grows as thick as the crest on a Greek helmet.'

'Wonderful.' I am hoping not to flush. Rodin's face is before me, his hair bristly erect. Thank goodness Gus and Ida are alongside; I cannot make a coherent reply.

'Ida's parents have agreed,' Gus seems downcast. 'Ida is to visit Paris with Gwen Salmond from your Slade year – to study.'

'We made the arrangements when you were in Le Puy,' Ida takes my hand. 'You must join us. I so want to share the city with you. Ursula had to return to her family and Grace has formed a curious attachment to a businessman with whom she seems to have chummed, which is why I invited Gwen Salmond; so it would be the three of us – me, you and the other Gwen.'

Ursula would have made the perfect foursome. The other Gwen always seems to walk on the margins of Fitzrovia, never at the centre of student groups, but she is an excellent draughtswoman. We can work together, see exhibitions, see Rodin's sculptures, see Rodin himself perhaps?

'Paris would be a delight.' I turn to Gus. 'But will Father agree?'

'He will not approve, and I am not pleased any of you are going. But I will support you – I always do.'

'Ah, Paris is la nouvelle Athènes. I studied at the Académie Julien.' Rothenstein's outline stiffens into a Victorian caricature.

'We will choose our own academies.' The words came out of my mouth stark, and Rothenstein looks a little startled but Gus grins. 'I will write to Father tomorrow for you.'

∽

While waiting for Father's reply, I can finish Mrs Atkinson's portrait. Although the picture is not showing what Legros calls the 'meaning of life' (how can one painting show all of that?) I placed her on a chair with her back to a wall in a new kind of pictorial space. New for me and new for anyone else at the Slade, I would imagine. I decided to create an abstract unity of mass, colour, and form. Mrs Atkinson prefers sitting down to cleaning but asking her was an awkward moment.

'I would very much like you to model for me,' I said. I must have turned quite pink. The request came out in a rush.

'I'm not sure what you mean, madam.' Her face was unsmiling and with a hint of disapproval.

'Well it is straightforward. You have an interesting face.'

Mrs Atkinson was frozen to the spot, a hand reaching for her face, then dropping to her side.

'But models, ma'am,' the disapproving tone now in her voice, 'they're ….' She paused. 'I am not a lady, but I am not one of those …'

'We Slade girls' model for each other,' before my face could turn puce. 'And none of us are naked. There would be no question of nakedness.'

Mrs Atkinson gazed down at her clothes, and then at my artist's stand for several seconds as if the scene is growing in front of her.

'In that case ma'am, I will.'

The portrait must be completed more quickly than usual in case Mrs Atkinson might change her mind. Despite the speed, her face is natural, alive. I reduced the details to essential components. There is a special thrill in reproducing a mood. I am always learning, moving forward; one day someone will agree. The chill vanishes, and a kind of fever takes over. At the end of each day Mrs Atkinson leaves with a glance at the cold grate choked with cinders and Gus's dirty boots piled by the door. There are a couple of used plates in the sink, but, apart from nuts and raisins, when was my last meal? It feels as if I am hollowed out, emptying my old self ready for Paris.

Father agreed 'with difficulty' Gus said. Ida and Gwen Salmond are already in Paris. Ida's mother read me Ida's latest letter headed 'Gwen John is coming. Hurrah!' I hope Gwen will be content being called the other Gwen. Instead of reading Shakespeare this evening, it will be a Baedeker guide to Paris, Gus's little gift, its green cover stained already with my fingerprints, the margins dotted with exclamation points. Is chapter twelve, 'Concerts and Exhibitions of Pictures' up to date? Ida will be an excellent guide. Pronouncing the names Louvre and l'Opera under my breath to practice, a tingle runs through me. My dark blue travelling dress is hanging ready, and my others packed. The wardrobe is almost empty, I have so few clothes. I put the boat-train ticket next to my bed for safe keeping. Tomorrow first thing I will bake a marmalade cake as my gift to the girls. When I wake next morning, I am clutching the Baedeker.

∼

At Pembroke cottage there is a moment of awkwardness, as in any parting, when Gus hugs me. We both know it will be a matter of months before I return to London. In my mind is the list I lay awake last night composing, itemising things to do in Paris: galleries to visit, ateliers to join as a student; Rodin's sculptures are on the list, although does the Louvre own one? His own studio will be inaccessible I imagine. There are too many items and the list ends in ellipses as if Paris will spring up and suck me in for ever and ever.

'Take care, little sister.' Are his eyes moist or is it the bright morning sun?

'Ida will look after us.' But unable to visit Paris due to a commission, Gus seems dejected at the mention of Ida's name, like the trees dropping their leaves on the other side of the square.

It has been a dry month; the grass in the gardens is more brown than green and a small boy in plus fours rolls his hoop with difficulty across the rough lawns.

Through the hansom cab back window, Gus is locked into a fixed wave, but I am impossibly exhilarated, as the trees slice through my view of the square and frame him in shadow.

CHAPTER 7

PARIS

It feels as if the boat is carrying believers, except I am holding my sketchbook for good luck not a crucifix. Perhaps when I reach Paris I will go directly to the Louvre, although the guards might not appreciate the sight of a marmalade cake. No, I must see Ida first. As the wind blows me away from Dover, I am part of a crowd, revelling in the mêlée of passengers, in the thick of it en route to Paris.

It is already early afternoon when we disembark, and then two hours by train to the Gare du Nord. The station's tall windows, as grand as Notre-Dame's, according to my Baedeker, have an almost violet tinge and I want the colour to seep through me.

'*Un fiacre, monsieur,*' summoning up my meagre French for a porter, wondering if a yellow *fiacre* is more expensive than a London cab, '*vers Montparnasse.*'

'*Bien sur, Madame.*' He seems relieved by my two small valises which he carries in one hand as if auditioning as a strongman for a circus.

I wore Mother's diamonds at the Slade graduation ball in her honour because she never had the chance to train there, and today, I am enacting her dream – studying in Paris. Once outside the station, everything is instantly Paris. The cabby sings to himself, flicking the reins. In London, a singing cabby would attract the police but here the sound underscores a splendid picture. The tables on the pavements look distinctive with red-checked tablecloths, and waiters flitting from one to another. There seem to be hundreds of waiters to one person whereas in London there is one waiter to a hundred customers. Every sound – the tolling of bells, police whistles, every face – is foreign, especially the tang in the air from cheeses in fromageries; and women walking in public without hats are especially foreign. It is so delightfully free. I fold my old life into my purse as I feel for the cabbie's fee. McEvoy fades from a bright portrait as do Tenby and Father. My feeling of pretence dims too. I tried to be a different kind of woman in London – a modest student but here there is so much more – galleries, exhibitions, painting all day.

The horse is panting up Montparnasse's hill and seems grateful to rest when the cabbie takes out my valises. Immediately after ringing the doorbell, a maid appears. She looks astonished at the marmalade cake placed in her hands before I hug Ida and the other Gwen.

'Thank you. What a beautiful cake. There is no marmalade in France,' Ida laughs, 'no kettles either for tea. Do not concern yourself Marthe,' reassuring the maid. 'Marmalade cakes are splendid.'

'It is made with something like orange potage, Marthe,' I say. 'But I am sure your meals are even more delicious.'

Her face, in repose, is tranquil. She would make the perfect model. The lamplit and bare rooms are clean with wooden floorboards, and mine has a narrow bed, a plain wicker chair and a chest of drawers. It is perfect and I feel dizzy with exhilaration. Through the window lies a cemetery, the rows of marble tombstones shining white in the moonlight.

'The room is quiet.' The other Gwen laughs, catching my glance. 'No rackety neighbours.'

'I adore the sight of marble.'

'Are you hungry?' Ida asks.

Last month as I waded through my self-pity over McEvoy, my body was like a weak shadow, refusing to eat anything substantial, demanding little of me. Now I am as eager to eat as a grown man. 'Surprisingly so.'

'We usually subsist on grapes, bread and beer, but tonight,

because Marthe's from Alsace, she has prepared sauerkraut with sausages in your honour.'

As the maid disappears into the kitchen, Ida whispers, 'Oh, I must warn you. The WC is old-fashioned. We throw water down. There is no flush.'

Gus would approve; his gypsy caravan does not even have a WC, Ida delights in hearing about Gus, but I am almost squirming with pleasure that I can forget him for a while. First, I must take possession of the room in a quick sketch. The room is as bare as in Kensington, but the view of the cemetery threatens to dominate as well as the elaborate wooden picture rail. I crumple the sketch and resolve to seek tuition.

～

Next morning, the rooftops are covered with a haze, a misty veneer like a glaze which is still wet, but above, traces of the sun are about to break through. The other Gwen is reading *King Lear* propped up on a cafetière; food stains on the cover match the worn spine.

'What a difficult read for an early morning.' I take the proffered croissant and cup of coffee.

'I am reminding myself, of the tyranny of fathers and of what we have escaped.'

'My father promises to visit, so I need to enrol at an atelier as soon as possible otherwise he may not continue to pay me an allowance.'

'You should attend Whistler's Académie Carmen,' Ida says, entering the kitchen, 'I have visited his studio twice, as has Gwen.'

Gus met Whistler, so he will probably be pleased and tell Father, but there is something lurking at the back of my mind, which Legros had mentioned. 'I heard that Rodin admires Whistler, but is Whistler very exacting?'

'What teacher is not? Remember Tonks at the Slade? But Whistler is endearing, he is quite elderly now.'

'What are his fees?' Will Father support me for several weeks of classes? Gus was not specific about the details of Father's agreement, but the girls know my circumstances, so surely, they would not suggest an expensive atelier.

'Cheaper than the Slade, and our living expenses are less – the market food is cheap. Gwen, do tell her about our discussion.'

'My family is very generous. I would like to fund you. Ida and I talked about this yesterday. We want to help, and we three girls must stick together.'

The relief is instant; worry lines are smoothing on my forehead. *King Lear* slumps to one side with our excited hugs. It feels as if I have been in Gus's eddies for too long, as their waves swept over me. Now I can swim alone.

∼

In the morning, it is a brisk walk to the Académie Carmen. The atelier is in our quartier, Ida said, so there is the possibility of working longer days with shorter journeys, and I am tense with excitement. Along the narrow streets, café dwellers are sipping breakfast coffee, fortunate in having time to spare. The street from Montparnasse runs straight downhill. The view of the rest of Paris, from this height, seems like a ten-foot history painting with me in the middle. The veiled shapes of buildings below, with their odd angles and sunlit roofs, carry a sense of life as something exciting, fresh. Smoke trickles from hundreds of chimneys; voices float up, merging with the drone of traffic, all reaching me in a general murmur like a strange vast herd of cattle. Watching the crowds, everything seems more enjoyable for being an outsider. Places where I am unknown give me a sense of freedom. I can be modern, change into whatever I want to become.

On the staircase up to Whistler's atelier, there are portraits of women all along the walls. Are these his models? Fifteen or so students are scattered across the studio, focussing on their paintings but also chatting in pairs – men and women together, not like the uneasy segregated rooms at the Slade. There is a relaxed atmosphere; with the walls of simple blocks of stone, holding shelves lined with art books. The room mixes the intensity of a library with the conviviality of the Fitzroy Tavern. I am at home.

A jaunty little man, with a single white lock in his otherwise jet-black hair and wearing a monocle, comes towards me. It is Whistler. Repressing a moment of disbelief that I am meeting such a famous artist, I smile. None of his clothes betray a smidgen of colour. McEvoy has clearly been imitating Whistler with the clothing and the monocle.

'Miss John?' and shakes my hand. 'Gwen Salmond has spoken highly of you. Welcome. Let me see your sketchbook.' As he flicks through the pages, his nods and his 'ahs' make me bold.

'Do I pass muster, Mr Whistler?' watching one prickly eyebrow grip his glass.

'You have a fine sense of tone, Miss John, finer than your brother,' smiling as he leads me to a spare easel.

All afternoon he mixes incisive comments with wild gestures. His hands are never at rest, as he gesticulates outlines. I have never seen anyone quite as feverishly alive as this little elderly man with bright, withered cheeks; but nothing is as intoxicating as his comment 'finer than your brother.' Now he is alongside.

'I prefer students to mix colours on their palettes first, Miss John,' Whistler whispers, 'before making a mark on a canvas.'

None of the students seem to have overheard. His words are a simple instruction rather than a rebuke. There is none of the awkwardness, none of the panic Legros induced. Whistler is less attractive than Rodin, and I would have preferred learning with Rodin, but he only teaches sculpture, Legros mentioned one day. In the Académie Carmen I have found my artistic niche. I will write to Father tomorrow and tell him I have no intention of returning to Tenby. Ever.

The sky is dark through the skylights, and Whistler claps his hands.

'We meet again in the morning, ladies and gentlemen, but think ahead to the weekend. As promised, next Saturday I am holding a ball. I expect nothing less than a galaxy of plumages.'

At first Paris drifted past me in segments: the cab journey, the streets, cafes, the girls' flat, but now Paris feels all of a piece.

∽

'We have Portuguese oysters for supper,' Ida greets me with a hug. 'They are cheaper than meat. How was Whistler?'

'He is the perfect tutor, but a quite different teaching style from the Slade and we must use grey tints for painting nudes. It feels like I am modelling clay.'

'His ideas are beautiful and absolutely right,' the other Gwen says. 'He seems to see right into my brain when I am working.'

'Mine too,' drawing my chair up to the table, 'but somehow I do not worry about what he will find.'

Ida laughs, holding out a letter. 'From Augustus. He is determined to see me, to see all of us and Whistler. The letter is not private. You may read it if you wish.'

The letter is brief – just a cursory desire to visit Paris, but it ends in a kiss. Ida's hands move distractedly to her hair as if already preparing herself for Gus's arrival. 'Thank goodness, the oyster smell drowns out the interminable smell of pommes frites in the street.'

'You are changing the subject. We both know you love Augustus. You can talk about him.'

'We have an understanding,' Ida smiles and buries her nose in a jar of Venetian glass heavy with the scent of tuberose flowers, decorating the table.

I am not envious. Gus and Ida are well-matched, and I will have another sister.

'Did you know Augustus is a friend of Whistler's?' I suck an oyster. 'When Augustus arrives, perhaps he could take us all to Whistler's private studio. We can see the latest work.'

'But first it is Whistler's ball,' the other Gwen says. 'You mentioned next Saturday? What shall we wear?'

'My mother is a theatrical costumier,' and Ida opens her sketchbook. 'She made Ellen Terry's costume for Lady Macbeth, so I have learnt useful sewing skills. And I adore dressing up.'

'Especially for Augustus,' immediately wishing I had held back, but Ida seems oblivious.

'We will wear long dresses,' the other Gwen is emphatic, 'with our hair down.' Aesthetic style or Rational dress?'

'Why not full sleeves like Rembrandt's women? and high-waisted. I want to be artistic but not a-la-mode.'

'Not everything has to resemble a painting, Gwen,' Ida laughs. 'In any case, the dresses will have to be simple. No fripperies. My funds are decreasing.'

'I am going to write to Father; telling him I need more money because Paris is to be my home.' Smiling, I raise my glass to the other Gwen. 'And then I will repay your generosity.'

'Pater can afford to subsidise us.'

'We should dress in a modern style,' as Ida sketches, 'not like Rembrandt, perhaps resembling Manet's women?'

'But their décolleté?' The other Gwen seems troubled. 'Manet's women wear very low-cut gowns. And one wore nothing at all in a painting!'

'I will wear whatever you decide.' My voice is surprisingly firm. Father was always so restrictive about my appearance. Even more reason to be progressive.

'So tight-fitting Impressionist dresses for us all.' Ida sketches three outlines. 'We will be the belles of the ball.'

∽

Next week I start a new portrait, remembering Whistler's approving nod as we entered the ball, as if appreciating our style. The moment reinforced my belief in myself. The word modern goes right through us like a sea-side stick of rock: our appearance, our living arrangements. Most of all in our art. I am a modern painter shaping life with colours, not firm outlines, I want to shout out of the open window. Although Father's money is essential, his ideas are not. I can channel my feelings into paint and sketches and forget McEvoy. My tones are finer than my brother's, Whistler said.

∽

Two months later I walk along the river to meet Father at Tuileries Metro station. Gus remained in London, but Ida was consoled by another loving letter. Will Father approve of Paris? You cannot compare the Seine and the Thames. The Seine is a river of sunlight; the Thames a river of twilight, lost in fogs. The Seine has miles of bookstalls stretching between its bridges, whereas the Thames flows between roads devoid of interest.

At least Father will approve of the books. As we shake hands at the station, he is unchanged. A hard bowler pushes down tight on his head to his ears, and a luxuriant moustache grows into his sideburns, although both are now grey. His plaid box suit is tighter fitting than before, a middle-aged spread bursting open his waistcoat bottom button.

'We have a hill walk to the apartment Father, but that will not concern you. Remember our long countryside walks when I was little?'

'At first, you needed persuading; but you took to the exercise.'

'You would always pause to pick my favourite flowers.' I smile up at him.

'Primroses.' Wistful for a moment, he offers an arm as we cross a boulevard.

He has held me in his mind, remembering my childhood as brightly as I do. Or perhaps his memory is triggered by the sight ahead. Mothers are sitting with their needlework among the flowers in the Tuileries Garden and their little charges flit like butterflies around and between. They are paying more attention to their dogs than to the children.

'You will see when we dine out.' I point to the display. 'Restaurants reserve dishes of pâté for dogs.'

He frowns, and then I remember he dislikes dogs. Our home in Tenby was empty of animals.

As I remove my cape in the hall, he stares, scanning my clothes, his face flushed.

'What is it Father? Was the walk too warm? Shall I prepare a drink?'

'Tea would be good, but it is not warmth which worries me. I am shocked. Indeed, horrified would not be too extreme.'

'At what, Father?' Glancing quickly at the easels, worried one of us has left out a revealing sketch or two.

'It is the dress. You resemble a prostitute.'

The word takes me aback. In Tenby, he spoke in such a circumspect, unemotional way.

'I copied the design from a painting.' Wanting to push him out and slam the door behind him. 'From Manet's *A Bar at the Folies-Bergère*.'

'That is as may be, but a lady should never wear such garments.' He is glancing around the room, still frowning, as if our artwork is equally to his distaste. He probably prefers wallpaper.

A metallic taste is in my mouth which no amount of tea will dispel. I fill the teapot wondering what we have in common apart from our name. The next hour seems a day, silently listening to Father's slurps and ramblings about Tenby and the church.

'I will make my own way to the hotel now.' Father puts down his cup. 'I had hoped to see your companions, but they must be absent today. It is best if I leave.'

What more can I say? As he disappears down the street, I watch carefree families strolling together, enjoying the warm weather, parents' arm in arm, and return inside.

Ida's steps are on the stairs.

'I greeted an elderly gentleman. I assume he is your father?'

'He is impossible. He will never give me more money. He called me a prostitute.'

'A prostitute?' Ida sits abruptly on the chaise longue.

'He hated my dress.' I am exhausted with the whole tension of Father's visit. 'I am not the daughter he wants; in any case the family has had its day. Do you not agree? We don't go to Heaven in families now, but one by one.'

'Some people do say modelling is akin to prostitution. You have no end of pluck. Shall we treat ourselves to an outrageous drink in the corner brasserie? Absinthe?'

The little café is tucked between a junk shop and a store selling artists' materials – a haven from all the vehicles rumbling through the narrow streets. The evening is pale grey, turning pedestrians into black pencils against the fading light as Ida twirls her drink round and round the glass, staring into the ripples.

'I must tell you immediately, Augustus has proposed.'

I am not surprised by the news, but marriage is such a disconcerting word. 'Do you love him? Do you want to marry?'

'I am uncertain. His overture was not particularly romantic. He said he was tired of his wild lifestyle, and I was the one to keep him out of trouble.'

'No one can control Augustus,' remembering that sea-dive at Tenby.

'He is everything that is most delightful, and I do care for him. I am uncertain about love, so I must return to London and see him before deciding.'

How has Ida's relationship developed so quickly? How is it Ida and Gus will probably marry? How is it I, who work so hard, fail so spectacularly in love? The touch of McEvoy's hands is faint. Life here without Ida will be dull; Father will not support me in Paris for long after today and I cannot ask the other Gwen for more money. Without funds how will I paint? In London I can exhibit, sell work. It is an unequal battle – reason versus emotion – but for once my passion for Paris needs dousing although it has only been three months. 'We will return together.' I watch the gas streetlamps reflecting on the Seine as the evening bustle parades along the street.

CHAPTER 8

BLOOMSBURY

Ida travelled direct to her parents from the boat-train, leaving me wondering if my new rooms will seem empty without friends. The basement is even dimmer than my first, despite the kindness of the decorator from the shop above, who lightened the walls with pale grey. The window faces a brick wall sooty and dank. At least the coal fire keeps the temperature high. There are plants which cannot flourish in the cold and I, like my house plants, thrive better with heat.

As I stare at a canvas, it seems that in some ways my painting resembles Father. My horizontal and vertical brushstrokes are as exact and conscientious as Father's fastidious use of a clothes brush. Unconsciously, families leave their mark. The new Persian kitten who shares my life, looks up at me as if in agreement; she may be scrawny with rough fur, but she already knows my mind. After I arrived, low-spirited at leaving Paris, she lay on my lap; perhaps doubts have a special scent.

A rat-a-tat-tat of the knocker pushes Father's stiff portrait out of my mind, and I rush to the door. Gus proffers a bottle of champagne.

'Welcome home, little sister.' I imagine he will drink most of the bottle but smile anyway.

'Thank you. I was uncertain about returning; there was little time to properly explore Paris. Open the champagne, and you can report all the London news.'

He perches on the edge of the chaise longue as if ready to spring into action.

'The most important news is from the Carfax Gallery. I am promised space for over forty of my paintings and I want you to share my exhibition.'

'Oh dear.' Everything I have heard about the Carfax is intimidating – the crowded preview night for critics, with wine glasses held perilously close to canvases, the hothouse atmosphere of the London art scene – although being exhibited alongside Gus will bring me attention; and dealers might buy. It is a generous offer, yet I can only imagine how impossible it will be to make myself heard at the private view, as Gus spouts his usual grandiloquent speeches. Am I brave enough?

'What can be the matter? It is the perfect opportunity. I am happy for you to choose your own spaces at the Carfax. You are the other rare blossom from the most delicate of trees.'

I want to hug him but guess he will prefer finishing the champagne.

'It is truly kind, but you know that I am a devil of a slow painter. I only have these completed canvases.' I am indicating the far wall. Although we are below ground level, the deep red of my blouse in the self-portrait, flushes the cheap rug underneath deep pink. The painting is splendid, but my modernist style is quite distinct from his.

Gus delicately removes the self-portrait from its hooks, holding it up to the meagre light trickling through the basement window.

'Remember when you wore this bodice? The evening at the Café Royal celebrating your first Slade prize. Legros said he would speak to Rodin about your *'triomphe'*. I wonder if he ever did?'

How could I forget Rodin's powerful stare in the British Museum, the day after my prize? I want to see his work; I want to see him. He must visit London often, perhaps even private views? 'Do other artists attend your openings?'

'Yes, and I can introduce you. I will only choose eligible bachelors.'

'I never want to marry.' I am surprised at my vehemence.

He looks at me with sympathy. 'Let me inspect another canvas.'

The painting is *Portrait of Mrs Atkinson*.

Gus stares too long. 'It is experimental.' Experimental is not an approving term he uses. He dislikes contemporary art and there will be the inevitable derision.

'You have captured her soul. Few people think cleaning ladies have inner lives.' His response is a pleasant surprise. 'It is brave and splendid. Both paintings deserve to be hung.'

'Well, painting is physically strenuous. I have always thought it resembles housework.'

Laughing, he throws the empty champagne bottle into the fireplace, miraculously intact, practiced in these flamboyant gestures.

'I will need the paintings by the end of the week.' He replaces his Fedora. 'Ida and I are taking the air in Regent's Park tomorrow. Why not meet us in the Rose Garden around eleven in the morning? Better than this dismal flat?'

'Eleven it is,' but he should know by now that solitude is the essence of my being. I did enjoy living with the girls in Paris, but I must be alone to properly work, and this basement now feels like a version of myself – secluded, plain, bare of embellishments. There is no romance in it, yet something not quite analysable – a kind of perfect simplicity. Is it the effect of the small size? I am a little surprised by how happy the sense of being unobserved makes me. Gus breezily assumes that a morning with him and Ida counts as much as my work. My plan is to practice the techniques I learnt from Whistler once I prepare the canvas with gesso, to use thin colours increasing in depth and intensity beginning with grey, and then intensifying the background. Painting will take long hours, so I will have to prime until late tonight to feel comfortably free tomorrow.

∼

Traffic hums around Regent's Park, invisible through the foliage. The lawns ahead unravel in front of us like a length of green fabric, underneath a sky cloth of blue and white. After last night's hours of priming, I am sleepy, but made secure by my achievement, to enjoy the day. Ida's face seems rosier than in Paris, glowing with happiness. She is allowing Gus to hold her hand in public, and he grasps it as if otherwise she will disappear into the shrubbery.

'Augustus said you agreed to exhibit your paintings alongside his, I am so glad for you. Think of the attention!'

The image of hundreds of critics shaking their heads at *Mrs Atkinson* and my self-portrait is alarming.

'I *am* grateful, but I do hope you will attend the opening night, Ida. I depend on your support.'

'Of course, Augustus will never speak to me again if I miss one of his exhibitions.'

'Soon I will be able to speak to you every day.' He winks at Ida, tightening his grasp.

'We must tell Gwen.' Ida is blushing. 'Even though we have sworn not to make the news public.'

I guess what is to come. They have been broadcasting their happiness for the past hour.

'We are marrying,' Gus says, 'but it will be a small wedding – a handful of guests. Nothing grand. We are keeping the event secret until the date is fixed.'

I never desired to attend a wedding, including my own, and feel a sudden sense of inadequacy at my inability to act like other women, to require the same things. Will Ida wear white? What do people do at weddings apart from say I do? I stare ahead at the shrubbery as if the answer to life is hidden among the bushes. My fear of conforming must be etched across my face.

'We are all unconventional.' Ida places her free hand on my arm, 'There will be no bridesmaids, no dressing up. You must attend.'

'I spy a familiar figure over there,' Gus interrupts, squinting into the distance. 'I am certain I know him. Do you, Gwen?'

I follow his gaze and catch a glimpse of a short, stout man, sniffing roses in the next bed, seemingly about to dive in. The shape, his gesture is familiar. Has he taught at the Slade? As he notices our little group, his eyes stare straight into mine. It is Rodin. What earthly explanation can there be for Rodin's presence here in Regent's Park? Is it truly him? 'I think it is Rodin.'

'Monsieur Rodin,' Gus calls out, doffing his bowler. '*Le Maître de sculpture.*'

Ida seems about to curtsey, but Rodin is staring at me. The rose scent is like a wave flowing over me as if it will sweep me to the great man.

'*Mesdames, monsieur, merci et enchantée,*' Rodin tips his top hat before he ambles slowly away towards the park gates.

'How extraordinary,' Ida says, 'I always wondered what he would look like in the flesh.'

Despite his short height, Rodin has a bull-like body, and his hands are large and well-shaped. I take a deep breath to steady myself.

'The very image of a Napoleonic guardsman,' Gus pronounces, 'as dominating in person as he is a defender of true art.'

'*Enchantée*' carries me all the way back to my basement. I hear nothing else – not the squealing of trams, the horns of omnibuses and hansoms, or the organ-grinders and newspaper sellers – nothing but his '*enchantée*' again and again.

∼

The wedding is a month later. A fog casts a yellow sulphurous mist over St Pancras registry office and the wedding party is as small as Gus predicted. Father will not be attending, Gus said, though he wrote a letter of congratulations. After Father's visit to Paris, I am relieved not to see him for a while. Ida's parents, unsure about Gus's disreputable reputation and number of previous lovers, declined to attend as well. With the fog, my basement is almost too dark to see my clothes this morning. I must not wear white, it will clash with Ida, Gus said, and I hold up my blue empire-line dress. The vivid colour is perfect. I add my black velvet necktie complete with its cameo, feeling it can buoy my head through what promises to be a demanding day. Gus invited his friends Evans and McEvoy. How will I greet McEvoy? He is bound to be drunk. At least he is attending without his fiancée; and the larger party afterwards in

Pembroke Cottages promises to be full of ex-Slade students. I can hide in the throng.

'The fog will conceal you if you decide to run away,' I whisper to Ida, as we walk through the building to the registrar's desk.

'I am sure Augustus would never forgive me. I am so glad that you are giving me away. You are a much better companion than Father.'

Ida's matching white jacket and tulle gown give her an innocent air; her face is sweet as ever. Gus does not know how lucky he is. Seeing McEvoy standing alongside Gus as best man, I realise with relief I feel absolutely nothing for him. He appears weak, unmanly in a strange kind of way as if his long legs had shortened in the past months. His usual white face is a blank canvas, and all my past anger has quite drained away. I have absolutely no desire to touch him, stroke his hair. It is finished. He nods sheepishly as we listen to the music. Watching Ida and Gus kiss after their vows, the day should feel romantic, but I feel intensely averse to their conventional gestures and would rather be at work, solitary.

'You are all invited to Pembroke Cottages,' Gus sweeps us out of the registry office with a wave of his arm. 'The Rothensteins are hosting a party.'

He booked one hansom to take us to Kensington, so, we are crushed with McEvoy, Evans, and me, facing the happy couple. I keep my eyes on Ida for the whole journey. McEvoy stares out of the window.

The cottage's rooms are restored to the cleanliness which greeted Gus and I when we first arrived, and which we failed to maintain.

Rothenstein welcomes us as we enter, 'We had the walls whitewashed.' As if noticing my glance. 'A perfect backdrop for Ida.'

He has invited half the Slade it seems as we crowd into the tiny rooms. I am glad that the other Gwen is here, returned from Paris, as well as Alice, Rothenstein's wife. We were friends at the Slade, in my first year away from home. A little of the old affection lingers and we are all smiling. The fog lifts and the sun, glinting through the window, picks out Ida's new wedding ring. By early afternoon everyone is a little drunk, the hors-d'oeuvres disappeared quickly. After the toasts, 'Charades,' Ida calls out, drunkenly, 'let's play charades.'

This morning Gus seemed nervous, but now quickly impersonates with aplomb his favourite tutors – Tonks and Steers. I imagine no one could mimic Legros after several glasses of wine. His French is too difficult. McEvoy is slumped on a sofa, seemingly asleep with drink. I am happy not to hear his monotonous voice again and mingle with other students for the rest of the afternoon. What a long day. Ida's parents decided to attend the party but are clearly tired and putting on their coats, shaking hands with the remaining guests. The afternoon's camaraderie seems to have infected them. The party is ending. It feels as if Pembroke cottage is a doll's house emptying of little figures. As Gus and Ida climb into a brougham, dressed with white ribbons, for their first official night together, all I want is my basement, my kitten, and the pleasure of painting in silence, alone.

∼

The other Gwen demanded that I attend a party. She has made friends with other art students, she said. I have been indoors for a week, painting, and repainting, wondering if I will ever finish the glazes with the right tones. Gus's exhibition garnered excellent reviews, but my work was not mentioned. Rothenstein bought my self-portrait but having acquaintances buy your work does not signify. Should I simply paint for myself, selling privately, not for exhibit? Mixing the exact quantities of paint on my palette, as Whistler dictated, is becoming a torment and feelings of inadequacy threaten to overtake me before I start on a canvas. I have fed the cat but not myself and feel weak. The other Gwen is right, I would enjoy a little recreation.

'It is a student party, a different crowd – from the Westminster School not the Slade. You will meet new faces.'

She also insists on collecting me, probably to prevent any last-minute hesitancy as well as to check my clothes. There is a knock at the door.

'You appear well.' She scans me up and down, 'Though you

are thinner than when I last saw you, and the dull brown attire gives you a sallow air.'

'I have been working extremely hard, so I am glad you suggested a change, although I am unsure about parties.'

'It will be entertaining. Try to be merry.'

A young man with a handlebar moustache opens the front door of a narrow Bloomsbury terrace house. The floorboards are bare, and the meagre furniture is pushed into corners as if we are all expected to dance. Music spills out of a phonograph cylinder being turned by a clean-shaven young man swaying in time. Students mill around, seemingly deep in conversation. My hands feel clammy, and I wonder how to insert myself into their closed circles.

'Let us repair to the back room,' the other Gwen reassures. 'There is always wine available. We can fortify ourselves and then take air in the garden.'

A relief to be taken in charge. As I step into the room, a striking woman with a pale complexion, younger than me by a few years I guess, smiles across. She is wearing a simple, slender blue dinner dress, tied with a darker blue sash, and her black hair is smooth, her lips a hint of carmen and above her mouth lies a delicate black shadow. I imagine kissing and feeling a slight bristle, and find myself blushing, embarrassed by the thought. I wish I had worn a more colourful dress, but when our eyes meet, I have a certain, but elusive, sense we will be friends.

'This is Dorelia,' the other Gwen says. 'Dorelia this is Gwen John. Gwen's full name is Gwendolen Mary John, but she prefers Gwen rather than Mary, although having two Gwens in the same group leads to all sorts of misunderstandings.'

'Well, I was not named Dorelia,' and she gazes at me. 'I am Dorothy McNeill, but Dorelia sounds more artistic, and I am learning to be an artist.

'Dorelia is a beautiful name,' I cannot take my eyes off her. 'Do you prefer painting or sculpting?'

'I paint, but I also love sketching in charcoal, the speed of drawing.'

Her gaze is steady, and she has an enigmatic authority giving depth to her beauty. I have never seen a woman like her, with her head resembling one of those Greek figures in the BM on a slender neck. She shares Ida's calm demeanour but seems uneasy with the kind of small-talk parties demand, as she slowly answers the other Gwen's chatter. My mouth is dry, and I cannot think what to say, yet meeting Dorelia I am centred in the room. Something shifts like a painting settling into its frame.

'I would appreciate showing you my work.' Thinking about her smooth skin, 'And you must meet my brother Augustus.' Gus is so famous now all art students want to meet him; anything to bring Dorelia into my life.

Dorelia hesitates as if surprised by my sudden invitation. I have surprised myself.

'I would be honoured to see your paintings, and to meet Augustus. I have heard a great deal about the two of you.' We smile at each other.

∼

When Dorelia arrives at my basement door, I am waiting for her in the hall, full of anticipation. She is as handsome as the other evening and everything seems unexpectedly easy, although we have only a few minutes before Gus and Ida will join us. He promised to bring his latest work, and Ida is already learning not to allow Gus to see attractive young women on his own. It will be an intimate afternoon; perhaps Dorelia will find my little family circle engaging and be intrigued by the unconventionality of our lives – the bare rooms and the lack of servants. No one in London opens their own front doors to visitors themselves or sits in rooms without wallpaper and stuffed animals. Most of all, she will admire my work, admire me.

Dorelia follows me into my studio and, chatting gaily together, the air fills with her as if her body creates a heat that pervades the small space. Then Gus appears in the doorway, Ida in tow, holding up two framed sketches for inspection. Dorelia jerks away from me, as if shocked at the sight of Gus, but I am unworried. She made her feelings for me clear at the party. Her pink flush and long handshake as she said farewell was sufficient.

'I brought drawings rather than oils.' Gus places his work against a wall next to mine. 'I must not outshine my little sister.'

Ida nudges me, mouthing 'pay no attention'. I never do. Gus is always his own best audience.

As Dorelia stares hard at the work, she has a kind of radiance, and the basement seems brighter, larger.

'Well, how do the two Johns match up?' and Gus admires his own work.

Dorelia motionless, gently nods at the paintings. Her high cheekbones and slanted eyes are exquisite. Gus is eying her, fascinated, as if itching to grasp a sketchpad and begin another portrait.

'You are very different kinds of painters,' Dorelia smiles at us both. 'Like Jack Spratt and his wife, one using black outlines, the other full of suggestive space and delicate tones.'

Her reply seems mysterious rather than banal. Gus is still staring at her.

'You must model for me; you would be a perfect gypsy. I picture you in long dresses and tight bodices.'

Ida flinches at the word 'tight' and I place an arm round her shoulders. We all seem bemused by Dorelia's serene sensuality. I must not lose her.

'All in good time, Augustus. Dorelia has promised to sit to me.'

I intended to ask her at the party but inviting her into my studio seemed a more pressing matter. Will she give me away?

'Touché, Gwen,' Gus bows as if removing an invisible sombrero, his eyes on Dorelia. There is a tension in his face but also a kind of enchantment. Ida moves towards him but seems reluctant to lose the security of my arm.

'We have an early supper invitation, Augustus. We must not be late.' Ida turns to Dorelia. 'A joy to meet you.'

'Of course.' Gus holds out his hand to Dorelia. 'Promise you will be my gypsy very soon.' He guides Ida up the stairs while managing to smile back at Dorelia. 'I will collect my drawings tomorrow, Gwen.'

'Is he always so direct?' A flush is speeding up Dorelia's swan-like neck. 'I am pleased you said you had asked me to model.'

The relief is instantaneous. She wants to model and for me.

'Oh, he has hundreds of women. I worry about Ida. But let us not discuss Augustus.'

For the next hour or so we exchange tiny details of our lives, switching from topic to topic as if in rhythm. Our sentences overlap, flowing together as I hope our lives will.

'May I tell you my secret wish?' she suddenly says. 'I have never told anyone.'

Nodding eagerly, it feels as if I am connected to her life, could share her desires.

'I have always wanted to visit Rome to see the Old Masters.'

'We will journey together.' Ignoring the 'Old Masters' and clasping her hand. 'We can ship to Bordeaux and walk to Rome.'

What on earth gave me such an impulsive idea? And how will I manage this madcap scheme? The vision takes shape immediately as Dorelia smiles.

'We will carry blank canvases and paints, and only a few lightweight clothes because it is August. We can sketch people we meet for funds.'

'It will be so exhilarating. I have never travelled abroad.'

I cannot mention Le Puy. 'The journey will be our pilgrimage to art, like devotees walking to Rome for their beliefs.'

Dorelia's hand is in mine, a warm shape refusing to cool, as she agrees.

CHAPTER 9

TO ROME

The boat to Bordeaux is an immense hulk after cross-channel ferries. A wide, white stream follows with seagulls screaming at the waves' froth, like an angry crowd hating a performance. Dorelia and I remain on deck for the whole two days, dozing on long chairs, carried through the darkness by the muffled rhythm of the engine.

'We have little money.' I am reminding Dorelia of our plans. 'So we must earn our keep by drawing people for francs in different villages as we walk.'

'The hardship is part of the pleasure.' She smiles. 'We will be united against conventions.'

Her faith in me is touching as if I am an older sister, and I am excited by her phrase with its hint of the possibility of an unconventional liaison. In the mornings, the sun is warm on the backs of our hands as we clutch each other, wondering who will be first to admit to seasickness. I hoped we might kiss for the first time, but the occasional vomiting put paid to intimacy and when we speak our voices float away in the sea breeze until the ship docks.

We are clear of Bordeaux in a couple of hours and are striding up the valley of the Garonne, pulling a small cart containing our blank canvases and valises. We agreed to walk to Rome, but I am weary already. Resting for a moment above the city, Dorelia hands me a water flask.

'Thank you. I am relieved that the seasickness is ended.'

'I feel well too. Now we are abroad, I have decided not to contact my family in case they insist I return. I envy you and Augustus and Ida. You are a complete family without the necessity of parents' demands.'

'Is this why you changed your name? To draw a line between yourself and home?'

'My father has no sympathy for art. He works in an office and requires me to work in an office. Art is my evening passion.'

'Are you missing the teaching at Westminster?'

Dorelia's eyes catch mine, 'Not anymore.'

It is difficult to know what she really thinks of me. Her body projects a sort of sultriness enclosing us, but nothing revealing has been said yet.

'Dorelia' is a Greek name, it means gift. I have not mentioned to Father my new name. He already thinks me too fanciful.'

'Dorelia.' I smile.

'You like it?'

'I do. You are a gift to me.'

Dorelia laughs. 'We are both reinventing ourselves.'

Our talk is easy, and intimate. Is she seeing me as a sister, or will she become more, fill the void of McEvoy?

'Such a joy to be free of Augustus for a while. He tends to be dictatorial.'

'You are an independent woman. You do not need to follow his ideas.' she is unpinning her hair, loose and jet black against the violet of the evening.

The anxieties I carry with me, like something heavy, deep in my pocket, fall away. Gus's protection keeps me safe in London but here, in the dark with Dorelia, the air tastes different as if something has changed already. We travel on side by side. The night is calm, cooler for walking and in any case, we need to ration our money, save it for necessities rather than accommodation.

After a few hours, I am so tired I lie down on flat stones slanting towards the river and go straight to sleep despite the cold. My sleep becomes a waking nightmare – a mixture of Legros, Father and McEvoy – and Dorelia awakes too. We lie beside each other for warmth and cover our bodies with our portfolios, but the stones underneath are blocks of ice. The night feels long. We are intimate but not in the way I wish. When day comes, we doze in the sunlight on the side of the road before walking on.

Poplar trees line the river giving us a perspective towards the village ahead, like a landscape painting. The sun has risen, and the day is windless. Dorelia is pulling the cart and I march ahead but as we approach the village outskirts, an old man leading a flock of sheep shouts out that we must not take the dangerous bridge ahead and instead follow him down a side path. 'Are you alone?' His speech is peculiar, a patois too difficult to fully understand and his espadrilles seem about to fall apart, but his voice is strong as if he is used to controlling people as much as sheep. My body stiffens with incoherent fear, and I tell myself to be calm, that he may simply need our company, but his face resembles a gargoyle.

'Let us walk very fast so we will leave his sheep in our rear, and he will be forced to remain with them.' Dorelia nods, but whenever the sheep bunch far behind, he whistles, and they canter to join us. The man is closer, intimidating.

'Why are two young ladies here alone?' Women do not walk unchaperoned without an escort, and I cannot reply that we care little for conventional society without seeming even more vulnerable than we already are. My hands are trembling, but I must seem confident for Dorelia's sake.

The path runs alongside a wood whose shadows darken the day, partially obscuring the man's face until he draws even nearer. When he speaks, his few remaining stained teeth could scarcely chew anything. Our cart encumbers us, and we are tired; I feel unable to move away at speed and fear his next question. He seems determined to march alongside, spitting at intervals onto the dust. Dorelia seems even more anxious than me. We must break free somehow; I pluck up courage.

'*Merci, Monsieur,*' my voice is firm, and I hold out my hand. '*Nous restons ici. Au revoir.*'

His hand around mine lacks a little finger and two other fingers are bent; and I dread what will follow, until he loosens his grip and begins to marshal his sheep. Dorelia clutches my skirt as we watch the sheep disappearing with him into the distance.

'I was frightened. I have been threatened by men before.'

She seems reluctant to say more. If I had a cloak, I would throw it around her, or in front of her feet for every puddle.

'We will be mindful in future. Trust me.'

She releases my skirt, but her eyes remain fixedly on me. Do I intrigue her? I could only leave home when Gus arranged my enrolment at the Slade, and he watched over me through the first difficult year and since. And I am not a beauty; I always pull my hair tight back into a plain bun resting on my neck. 'Severe' is Gus's description.

'You resemble a Dutch girl,' Dorelia says, 'in a painting by Rembrandt. As if your life is about to begin.'

It is. 'I will begin painting your portrait today.' The sunlight casts her left side into shadow. My portrait could capture the whole woman.

'I have not modelled a great deal, but I am eager to learn.'

'I will happily show you some techniques but first we can sketch the village people and sell the drawings. We need funds.'

Outside the village inn stretches a long deal table ready laid, as if to accommodate the entire village. The street is tranquil, lined with horse chestnuts and ancient cottages, and we sit, sketchbooks in hand, as workers from nearby fields arrive in huddles for the midday meal, and we sing to catch their attention. A few sketches later we have enough francs for food and a room for the night.

For the rest of the week, we go immediately to a village bar in each village, and draw all comers for two francs a sketch, or sing songs for one franc. Our food is simple: bread and cheese, almost ripe grapes stolen from vineyards alongside the roads, and beer while we sketch; but even simple food like bread dipped in red wine – *une trempête* the French say – has a festive quality. Washing side by side in the Garonne, Dorelia undresses first. She removes her heavy walking boots, rolls down her thick woollen stockings, and scans the riverbank for strangers. Her dress is off in a moment, and finally the chemise with its laced underskirt. I am dazzled by the smoothness of her skin, its white, unmarked surface which catches the sunlight like the light sources in a painting by Whistler. I would like to run my finger down the lines of light but feel entirely content to stare, as we sunbathe naked in fields of wheat ringed by sunflowers, slowly rotating their heads as if checking on unwelcome visitors. My breasts are small compared to Dorelia's creamy bust and I am tempted to stroke hers, but what would I say if she refused?

'Dorelia, should we live here for ever? We could undress every morning in the wheatfield and survive on peasant food.' The light is expanding around us.

'We must reach Toulouse first.' She laughs but seems pleased by the suggestion.

Dressing, we continue walking and talking. Sometimes we earn enough money on the journey to share cassoulet and wine as well as a room. Tonight, is one of those nights. As I carefully tie my black velvet band with its cameo around my neck, Dorelia laughs again.

'You dress for dinner as if we are in Kensington.'

'I need rituals, to cope with the day's uncertainties.'

My dependence on order underscores everything, although there is a heady sense of frivolity with Dorelia. Away from Gus, away from Bloomsbury, away from England, I can be a different person, but I need the certainty of a frame, a grid over the day to contain all its little squares of excitement.

At Réole, the next village, I ask for water from the innkeeper's wife, young with an intensely interesting face, and give her my name and occupation, so she will know we are more than mere tramps. To my surprise, she hands me a letter from Augustus.

'What does he say?' Dorelia asks.

Why is she so interested? Would she sleep with Augustus? She has met him only two or three times, but he has such charisma. Her expression is impossible to read; she is entire like a glass of wine filled to the brim.

'He is bullying me to produce more work. He wants me to enter London exhibitions, but I cannot finish your portrait on the road.'

'Then we should travel quickly to Toulouse. We could remain there long enough to complete several paintings.'

'Oh, and here's a five-pound note for you. Augustus worries you will lose weight unless he assists with food purchases. Here, read for yourself.' I toss the letter into her lap; angry Gus seems more concerned about Dorelia than me.

Dorelia places the letter crumpled on the table without reading, a wave of irritation across her face. 'He must think he can buy me.' She gives a dismissive sweep of her hand. 'He reminds me forcibly of a sculptor who treated me in a similar fashion.'

'Augustus likes to control everyone. I have suffered for years.'

The thought is unfair. Flamboyant, self-centred maybe, but most people agree he is basically good hearted. In any case, I will soon be an independent professional. The time is coming.

'I will sketch our landlady for funds, then we can eat well tonight.'

After the meal, as we sketch on with the aid of extra candles, a young man, roughly our age, stands at one side watching. He has a head of luxurious thick curly hair and an inquisitive expression, as if curious to see us in such a remote inn. He gazes more at Dorelia than at our paintings. There is a light blush on her slim neck as if she senses his interest without glancing directly at him.

'Apologies, ladies.' He has a gentle voice. 'The landlady told me of two English artists residing in the inn. I am also a painter, from Belgium but currently living in Paris. Leonard Broucke at your service.' He makes a slight bow.

Instantly Dorelia holds out her hand, smiling up at him, as if Leonard is an annunciating angel without the halo. 'I am Dorelia McNeill, and this is Gwen John.'

'Pleased to make your acquaintance.' He hands her a card. 'If you ever visit Paris, I would dearly love to paint your portrait.'

'Thank you, but we are travelling to Toulouse.' I feel surprisingly forceful.

'Yes Gwen, but a Paris address could be useful for the future could it not?' She smiles again at Leonard as they gossip about the inn.

Is she trying to inveigle me into a scheme to be with Leonard? I told her my stories about Rodin, of my desire to return to Paris, my sense that only Paris can satisfy my ambitions. I want to agree but she is gazing at Leonard not me, and I desire Dorelia more than an uncertain Parisian future. A flutter in my stomach is like the pages of my sketchbook flicking loose in the evening breeze. Am I being unreasonable? Yet Dorelia seems as easily attracted to strangers as she was with me in Bloomsbury. She might leave me. McEvoy did. We should travel quickly to Toulouse.

'Do you want to stay with him in Paris?' I ask as we climb the stairs.

'I was merely being friendly, and I am enjoying our journey together. Are you jealous? Let us not think about Paris yet.'

'I cannot imagine what is in your head sometimes. You must have noticed when visiting my basement, assessing my pictures, how much you interested me.'

'This is a great deal too much for one night; let us pack for Toulouse in the morning.'

A relationship with Leonard will take her away from me, away from Bloomsbury. I worry I appeal to the carefree Dorelia, and there is another, more conformist woman buried deeper, one who wants a marriage. I can never be a modernist painter if I am a slave to social conventions. The candle splutters, about to expire.

∽

Toulouse seems a capital city after the villages of the Garonne. Romanesque buildings stand in tree-lined squares with medieval streets of mellow brick. As the sun descends, the sky becomes lurid and everywhere turns pink in a sublime glowing frieze. Our cheap room is sparse – a bed, two chairs and a table – but with plenty of space for our easels, although the squat landlady with a black kerchief on her head has a strange expression. I worry she might guess my intentions for Dorelia and push a chair under the door knob each night. The first time I pulled Dorelia close, all I sensed was the sweet smell of her body, her dark hair falling over my breasts. My heart swayed as if she was clutching it in one hand. I want this so much she said. My relief was instantaneous, and every morning I wake with Dorelia's arm across my stomach, while light pushes its way into the corners of the room. The weeks speed by.

The first portrait of Dorelia allowed me to stare at her for hours at a time. As the second reaches its final glaze, there is a restlessness in the room and in each other. In the painting Dorelia appears to be moving out of the frame in a new kind of portraiture, as if about to fly out of the window like the dove who briefly pecks at our offerings on the windowsill each morning. Now, when I gaze at her face, all I think about are shapes and colours, not the person in front of me, not the whole of Dorelia. My new brush technique with quick dabs makes the painting surface shimmer like a mosaic. I care for Dorelia, but my love is less intense. She is fading, tucked away behind the glazes and I am happy for her to remain there. The portraits are new and good. That is what matters.

One day together in the square below, Dorelia bites her nails in between puffs of her cigarette. 'We should journey to Paris.' She extinguishes the cigarette. 'I adore being surrounded by artists.'

'To see Leonard?' Our lovemaking is less passionate, and our feelings for each other are cooling, but I do want her close to me.

'Not necessarily, although he could provide us with accommodation at first. You always say Paris is your idea of heaven.'

It is true. 'We could model to earn enough money.' Excitement inside me like a slow burning fire.

A breeze blows, and a few leaves drop onto the manicured gardens. The air smells dank. Dorelia stares into the far distance, not at me. Part of me knows our relationship will inevitably end at some point. My others did. But it saddens me to think Dorelia might want a complete separation. I do dream about Paris though I no longer know if my memory is still accurate, and I need to find out. Not all roads lead to Rome; ours leads to Paris. Our plan is changed.

CHAPTER 10

PARIS

We are independent of Leonard. He met us at Paris Austerlitz station a week ago, holding up Dorelia's letter like a talisman and giving lodging suggestions, including his own apartment.

'We will make our own way,' Dorelia said, 'but we are grateful for your assistance.'

Dorelia does not wish to stay with Leonard. I felt relief.

'Do write with your new address. We artists should support each other. I would be happy to give you introductions.'

'We will.' Dorelia rested her gloved hand on his arm, for a moment too long?

'Thank you,' I said. 'We will live in Montparnasse I hope, where I resided before.'

Since that meeting at the station, we found a modest apartment and then filled the days with sketching and writing letters. Dorelia posted our address to Leonard whose reply was reassuring; Leonard is returning to Brussels, and Dorelia folds the page swiftly. We can enjoy painting together without distractions, I reply, and Dorelia seems content. Boulevard Edgar Quinet is in the next street from my previous flat with Ida and the other Gwen, so I felt at home as soon as I saw the old cemetery flanked by tall poplars. Some marble headstones are now covered with moss and

I long to scrub them to a pristine white, remembering Rodin's marble, its exquisite surface.

Our Hôtel Mont Blanc's furnished rooms also give us a view of Notre-Dame, but there is little time for sightseeing. In any case you can scarcely see the façade of the cathedral from the street, for the bicycles and trams rumbling in front. I found a stray tortoiseshell cat sleeping on our step and called her Edgar Quinet, after the name of our street, so she can find her way home amid the street artists painting portraits. The whole quartier is full of artists' studios.

It is spring already, but the morning is almost too cold to be walking the streets, with paving stones flecked with ice, but we need work. Today we will knock on concierges' doors together, hoping one of us will find some modelling. An artist Miss Hart, in the room next to ours, told us of a nearby building where almost every room is a studio. Its front door is imposing – solid wood gates mounted with brass fittings. After my gingerly knock, a square window in the door opens and a mouth asks, 'What do you want?'

'We are seeking work,' I say.

'We are models,' Dorelia adds, quickly.

'Enter,' the concierge points to a wide, curving staircase running upwards through the entire house. 'There are several artists at home today.'

I knock on a first-floor door, clearing my throat.

'Who's there?'

'Two models.' A short bald man in a dirty smock beckons us inside. He asks us to undress, but I can hear rats scuffling and there are dirty plates stacked on the floor. Fear flickers through me, like a spider scuttling across the dust, as I glance at Dorelia who is shaking her head.

'No, thank you, *monsieur*.' I am quickly grasping Dorelia's hand. 'We will have to undress,' I add, safely outside on the landing, 'Nudity is to be expected.'

'I disliked the smell,' Dorelia says, 'and the flat was squalid.'

'There are other studios.' Climbing up to the next floor and knocking on what seems the cleanest door.

'Who's there?' again.

'Models,' and the door opens swiftly.

The man in the doorway is tall with an imposing head and a mouth full of shiny teeth. As we step inside, the studio walls are covered in landscapes, with only one portrait. Expecting a quick no thank you, I frown at Dorelia, but he stands, eyeing us up and down and puts a hand on my breast.

'But you are a landscape painter?' I point at the walls, while moving away backwards.

'Yes, but I need to see if you're *dévélopée*.' He grins.

Dorelia reaches the entrance before me, throwing the door wide open and we leave arm in arm.

'Today is becoming impossible, what next?' We climb further.

'We will try one more door, and then treat ourselves in a brasserie.'

My stomach is grumbling with anger as much as hunger. Ahead, a recently painted door carries an enamelled miniature of a cat. The artwork is a good omen; someone who likes cats must be agreeable.

Before the echo of my knock dies away, a tall, fair-headed woman stands in the entrance. 'You are models I assume? Surely not prostitutes at this early hour.' She smiles.

The accent is marked. Scandinavian? Small sculptures and unfinished maquettes stand at three workstations. There is scarcely room for the bed pushed tight against a sink, and a stove gives out little heat.

'Hilda Flodin. Apologies for not shaking hands,' glancing down at her dusty, clay-spotted hands.

'Gwen John and this is Dorelia McNeill.' She looks us up and down.

'The best models apply personally like you. I like the shape of your heads.'

'We are happy to undress too.' Dorelia adds. 'We know this is expected.'

'Unnecessary because I will focus on your heads, at least for a time. You may attend on alternate days.'

As we clamber down, Dorelia is frowning. 'I am not certain

that I wish to model for this sculptress. She seemed disappointed we are not prostitutes.'

'We have no choice.' Tucking my arm in hers.

∼

'Did you find work?' Miss Hart asks, later that evening.

'We are modelling for Hilda Flodin, and she has promised to pass on our names to other clients. We have decided to model only for lady artists.'

Miss Hart's leathery face cracks into a smile. Perhaps she hopes we will only love women. She revealed her predilections one night over her whisky. Luckily, she made no attempt at physical contact. Like me, she dreads returning home before finding fame if not a fortune. We had another whisky for good luck.

'Hilda's a force of nature. She models for Rodin, so she can copy his techniques. When she is not sleeping with him, that is.'

Closer to Rodin. The enamelled cat augured well.

∼

Hilda is as good as her word. There are invitations to several women artists. Dorelia is reluctant to travel too far, so a yellow tram, trundling down the leafy boulevards, sometimes carries me alone through one arrondissment after another to German, Swiss and English painters. The tram's anonymity is almost arousing. In the dimly lit interior, clicking through the crowded streets, I can drop away from the circling whirls of sound, and think about my paintings, and about Rodin. Will I ever see him again? Will he remember me? It was two years ago when he spoke to me in Regent's Park. The tram reaches the seventh arrondissment and my first artist of the day. After greetings, I am free to dream once I adopt the requested position; keep my hopes alive.

Gus was furious when Dorelia wrote about her modelling. In his reply I can almost hear him snorting. Why are you sitting nude for devilish foreign people, he wrote, when you refused to sit naked for me? Dorelia threw his letter into the waste bin and modelled naked next morning for Hilda. For me, the set pattern of each day is sufficient. The mornings devoted to modelling, afternoons for painting, evenings for sewing and sketching. You can embrace life if it has a clear order, but Dorelia seems despondent. She talks guardedly, and when she does, she mainly complains about the artists' demands.

After one morning's modelling, when I return to Hôtel Mont Blanc and Dorelia, the boulevard seems different. Today it is like seeing the houses for the first time before the shapes have fully taken hold of you, as if my time with Dorelia will also become less fixed. Holding onto shapes and colours is all I can manage some days, and house have a strange way of resembling people with their windows as eyes into my feelings. My body sometimes senses events before my mind can create a scene. A bag lies near Dorelia's easel.

'Dorelia.'

She sits in our kitchenette, holding a glass of water in one hand, smoothing out a letter on the table with the other. 'Augustus has written again. He wishes to see the exhibition at the Pavillon de Marsan and take me back to London with him. He wants me to live with Ida and him. Permanently.'

Gus had visited Dorelia a few times at Westminster School of Art in the evenings when she studied. Have they done more than meet? I quickly scan the letter. His visit is next week; the letter must have been delayed. My mouth feels dry, and I pour myself a glass of water too. 'Why are you packing now if he is not arriving for a few days.'

I already know the answer. She does not want me anymore. For a moment, all I sense is the cold glass against my lips.

'I cannot commit to Augustus. There is Ida and their children. I have to leave.'

'Why? I will miss you a good deal. Where are you going?'

Another letter is on the table. It must have been tucked under Gus's. I recognise the handwriting.

'A letter from Leonard? You are travelling to Brussels to live with Leonard.'

'Not Brussels. He has moved to Bruges.'

My mind is blocked, congested with memories — mostly of Dorelia naked in bed with me and I cannot speak.

'I do care for you. I will write often and visit.'

I wished we had never visited Toulouse, never met Leonard.

'I think I loved Leonard from the first moment in the inn as we sketched while he watched. But I am very fond of you Gwen. I want to remain your friend. I will post my address.'

After she leaves the walls seem further away and the room grows wider, longer. Echoes of my cries reverberate. It is as if the house will expand and expand without me having a space within. I do not care if Miss Hart can hear me on the other side of the wall. Every dream I have of spending my life with an artist collapses; every act of love turns sour as if filling me with acid. First Ambrose and now Dorelia. I am naive. I thought a woman would stay truer to me than a man, become an extension of my body, my mind, my feelings.

～

I told Gus not to visit because Dorelia is with Leonard, and the next weeks are a frenzy of letter writing to him, Leonard, Ida and Dorelia. Leonard replies that he and Dorelia are content together, that he has no intention of losing her to Augustus, and that happiness is not just a tasse of coffee after a meal. My letters to Dorelia at the poste restante in Bruges produce a surprising reply. Dorelia has married Leonard; I write to Gus. So Gus will remain now with Ida, my friend. The feelings I can share with Ida are more important than responding to Gus's imperious demands, although that is easier to write than to say aloud to my brother.

Gus writes that he is posting his poems to Dorelia. After a month he travels to Belgium to bring her back to London, Ida has agreed apparently. The poems must be accomplished but I worry about Ida. At least when I visit London, I will see all the people I care for in one glance. One midday I return to the apartment, aching from a difficult pose, to find a postcard from Dorelia on the mat.

'*I have yielded and am with Gus. How is the cat?*'

Will I recover? Can I find love again? Life is speeding like a carousel. This month I am sublimating my feelings into letters instead of into paint, such a strange kind of art. Words are an impure medium, and it is far better to paint; but letters are a form of creativity I had never fully explored until now, and there is a kind of relief when I place another into an envelope. But my future must be about art not about describing relationships. I will create a plan for each day and return to my original love – painting. My life must be my art.

CHAPTER 11
RODIN, PARIS

My daily routine is restored. Mornings I model for women painters and sculptors, all connected to one another in a web of eccentricity. Each artist has a different story to tell. Isobel is the sister-in-law of an English symbolist poet Arthur Symons, and she regales me with his complicated affairs. He desires men as much as his wife, apparently. Ottilie wears men's clothes with a man's watch and chain in her waistcoat. Afternoons I stand in front of my canvas painting, remembering to mix paint on my palette first as Whistler told me. I miss Dorelia less and less with each brush stroke.

A few days later, Hilda glances back and forth between me and a block of marble, chisel in one hand, hammer in the other. Her studio floor is so dusty, slivers from the marble land silently. My pose is awkward, legs akimbo, hand on hip, bent over. The right leg is stiff, and I am desperate to stretch but this will annoy Hilda. Out of the atelier window, the sky has a misty quality with fog rolling in from the Seine.

'Thank you, Gwen. I am managing to capture the shape of your muscles. You do have a lithe body.'

We both know Hilda's underlying meaning, but the growing familiarity between us has not developed into anything more intimate. She is happy to simply stare at me without touching. I feel embraced by her stare rather than being an object. Hilda is tall, but with an uneasy awkwardness, not helped by her dowdy clothes. I am about to ask if I can adjust my legs for a moment, when the door opens without a knock and a short, top-hatted man stands in the entrance. In the mirror I can see him gazing at my buttocks and somehow his look excites me. My dress and underwear are on a chair and only my coat is near.

'Excuse me *Mademoiselle*.' And he removes his hat, glancing quickly at Hilda. His face is instantly recognisable. Shocked, I sit down on the platform, sharply bringing both thighs together while throwing my coat around my shoulders.

'Auguste, you are most welcome, but I have said before – always knock first. We could be engaged in any number of activities.' She is winking at me.

It *is* Rodin. The moment before anyone speaks lasts for ever.

'Permit me to introduce *Mademoiselle* Gwen John, Auguste Rodin.'

My blush must be extending over my whole body. It is difficult to keep the coat stretched over my breasts with my hands trembling and I focus on keeping my legs together as if adopting a new pose before glancing up. He examines me, his gaze taking in my whole body with appreciation, and I cannot think of anything to say. I want to mention those casual encounters – in the British Museum and two years later in Regent's Park – wishing I were my younger self with smoother skin.

'Tea Auguste? We have finished for the morning.'

She is very casual with him; is she sleeping with Rodin?

'Thank you, but I have to meet a client. I admire your new marble.' He is stroking his hand over Hilda's sculpture and giving me a side-long glance.

'Marble is such a difficult material. Perhaps I should try maquettes first as you do.'

'You have caught Miss John's elegant shape.' He smiles.

Before Hilda can answer, Rodin is standing directly in front of me. 'I would be honoured if you would be my model, you have an exquisite physique.'

His hair now has streaks of grey, but his body, underneath his frockcoat, is muscular, solid and seems to tower over me. My heart is fluttering, and my face must be colouring. Hilda frowns, but nods at me as if giving me permission to agree. Perhaps her affair with Rodin has petered out; I heard she acts as one of his secretaries now from time to time.

'Certainly, *Monsieur*. I would be delighted.'

His hand reaches for mine and his skin has hot clay in its cracks as we shake.

'Tomorrow.' He replaces his hat.

∽

As I travel home, the lightening is nearer than this morning. There are silver zig-zag flashes over the houses to the south-east. Thunder growls over the Eiffel Tower, and it is hard to breathe with the air solidly damp and warm. The oil lamp shines on my hand – the hand Rodin shook – as if he imprinted an image of himself in my palm. The day becomes like one of those dreams which, when you wake, it is as if you are living simultaneously in two worlds – still in the dream but also alive to the light and objects in the space around you. Unwilling to sleep I gaze out of the window waiting for the next sliver of lightening. My hands tremble, my body aches, with longing and with uncertainty, as if the moment in Hilda's studio will disappear with the dark sky when the clock hands reach five and dawn breaks. As I stand with my forehead pressed against a windowpane, a flash of light shows my easel, my books, my few dresses all tidily arranged. The room resembles a nun's cell, pristine and almost empty. I breathe slowly several times, feeling my body relax and lie down, staring up at the other attics through the window. There is a swell of promise in the sky, a pink line on the horizon.

∽

Next day, my usual yellow tram crosses over the line to rue de l'Université and Rodin's studio. As I rush from one tram to another, the Seine is visible down a sombre street – dark blue, smooth, and empty of boats and the air is crisp for autumn. Will I be seeing this sight every day, the other passengers, sleep still lingering on their faces while I feel alive, in the present? The tram rockets through the September morning and uncertainty returns: will he respond to my body in the same way as he did in Hilda's studio? Or will full daylight reveal my age? I straighten my empire dress, check my hair is still tight in a neat bun, and stare up at the studio's façade. Stout iron balconies jut out over tall open wooden doors and young men in workmen's overalls, their shoes covered in dust, weave in and out. A mixture of excitement and extreme nervousness is making it hard to swallow and I stand silent, unable to move. One of the workmen, his smock spattered with red clay, tips his cap at me, eyes me up and down.

'Are you a new model? I have not seen you before.'

His eyes are friendly, and I nod.

'The main studio is through the courtyard.'

Handing the workman my card for Rodin, I follow across the rough cobblestones into an enormous space buzzing with men in identical smocks scurrying around or standing on metal frames. The high-ceilinged room has walls stacked high with shelves full of metal sections, pieces of plaster bodies – hands and feet – and lumps covered with cloths patterned with sunlight. A few men perch on tall ladders chipping at the heads of marble statues. Chips fly in every direction showering the stone floor. The area seems as substantial as a quarry, designed solely for work, and everything is in a state of growth.

A striking sculpture ahead contains an endless variety of figures whose features seem to be listening to their inner depths and most are massive, impressive, giving the studio a sense of an art gallery preparing for a private view, although a smell of glue and the dankness of wet clay pervades the air. Ahead is a platform draped in cloth, surrounded by screens; so, wondering if Rodin is behind, I peek around. A young woman, about twenty, stands with one leg raised on a chair. Her pubic hair is as bushy as the hair on her head. Stepping backwards, I rearrange my skirt, keeping my eyes on its folds and manage a gentle cough.

Rodin emerges from another room, wipes his hands down his blue workman's overall and takes my card from his assistant. 'Welcome Miss John,' he says quickly shaking my hand.

As he speaks the room hushes. Workers stop their chatter, and there are only the chimes of chisels meeting marble and the wet slapping of clay on clay. My hands are trembling at my sides. What will he do next? Will he ask me to model now?

'Please sit for a while by the stove to warm yourself.' He is smiling and dusting down an old wicker chair. 'It is a chilly day, and you are shivering.'

I smile in return, hoping he will release the model. My hands rest on the chair arms he cleaned, and I want to touch everything he has held in the studio. Rodin whispers in the model's ear and she dresses, frowning, bustling through the layers, missing a button on her ankle-length boots. Throughout, Rodin stares at me, his eyes widening, as if full of anticipation.

After a few minutes he says, 'Are you rested *Mademoiselle*?'

'Perfectly *Monsieur*,' wondering if *Monsieur* is sufficient. Augustus called him *Maître* and, as I entered, I overheard workers using the same title. Everything must be correct. Modelling for Rodin means more to me than completing a new painting. Can I become his only model, preparing the clay, handing him the usual bowl of water to keep the maquettes moist? Last night his face was continually in my mind but now he is so close his eyes seem even more azure and intense. 'Or should I call you Master?'

'*Monsieur* Rodin is sufficient. Undress.' He indicates the empty platform.

With my sweaty fingers, undoing the boot laces takes forever. Rodin stares at me throughout the whole process and the strength of his gaze seems to enter my body as I remove my dress. He has an aura of amazing precision about him which makes the rest of the studio blur.

'You can place your clothes on the chair,' his voice is gentle, warm.

I dare not look into his eyes in case he sees my desire and I remove my chemise as slowly as possible, prolonging the delicious moment.

'You have good legs, and a graceful neck.'

The heat from the stove seems to intensify and I must be flushing. What can I reply?

'*Merci, monsieur*,' and after a moment, 'shall I pose for you today?'

'Certainly. I need athletic poses. Can you manage one?'

'I am very able bodied,' immediately I am resting one foot on the chair and touching my toes with both hands.

'The pose I have in mind needs less dexterity.' He laughs. 'I have been commissioned to create a memorial to Whistler. I am calling it the Muse. You will be my muse. Please place one foot on the old piece of marble, your head slightly bowed, and mouth partially open.'

I will be his model and a muse – more than I could have imagined for my life; and dedicated to Whistler, an artist I admire almost as much as Rodin. I will be as graceful as possible. I breathe slowly, at last able to meet his glance, and although stooped, my pose feels strong, not submissive.

'Perfect,' and he picks up a pair of iron compasses.

Measuring sections of my body, his face almost touches mine. His breath is moist and, as he moves down my body, my skin tingles. Hairs are upright on my legs as if I have suffered an electric shock and in an odd way I have. The first sight of Rodin in the British Museum felt like a jolt, and today my chest is tight making it hard to breathe, but I am longing for him to touch me. Such a thought never came into my mind with Ambrose or Dorelia at such a speed. Yet, with Rodin, my desire is instant and completely intertwined with admiration for his art, with a sense my whole life has led me to rue de l'Université. Before he turns to the clay, he gently runs a finger slowly from one ankle to my thigh and smiles, then replaces the compasses on the sculpture table with his other tools.

An ache settles in my stomach, wanting his finger to explore higher but he starts moulding lumps of clay. His blunt fingers push and squeeze, like the cook making bread each morning at home, but much more delicate, darting in and out, building a skeleton figure. I am desperate to see a resemblance to me, but he is too quick, changing the form every minute, spitting at each ball of clay to keep it soft, and he is so close a light spray lands on my foot.

'*Pardon, Mademoiselle,*' and continues to sculpt without waiting for me to reply.

There is no embarrassment in my nudity before this man, even when his assistants peer around the screens from time to time, asking his advice. It is as if my soul is naked too and Rodin can see right into me. My previous sightings of him were too fleeting, and I delight in his shape. His body is like a workman with a powerful build, large head and wide hands – the antithesis of Ambrose.

Someone once told me – was it Ursula? – we love men resembling our fathers, but Rodin's dirty clothing and passionate glances would cause a sensation in Tenby. He would be an untamed mastiff in Father's neatly organised study. Watching him as he stares at me, there is a wire joining us together. My body feels his every gesture, every flick of his fingers. I struggle to stay calm, not to move an inch from my pose, but I can feel him pulsating with energy. The next hours are exquisite, and happiness dampens down any tiredness or strain. The clock of Sacré-Coeur rings its deep bass, audible above the traffic outside and the assistant who showed me into the studio is alongside Rodin.

'It is five o'clock, *Maître*, may we leave?'

Rodin nods and gazes, tenderly, up and down my body.

'Miss John will be tired too. Bring in the candles.'

Is he expecting me to resume posing in candlelight? I stretch my legs, rubbing them to reduce the cramp. Time has stood still since he first started sculpting and I am surprised to see a darkening sky through the studio windows.

'Come, my dear,' and Rodin hands me a soft Indian shawl. Taking the candles, and dismissing his assistant, he places several on the studio shelves. The evening transforms from the flat brightness of gas lights to a softer, mellow radiance. The studio darkens, the ceiling no longer visible, the cloth at the edge of the platform a solid green rather than patterned. He washes his hands in a sink against the wall. What should I do, dress now or remain naked under the shawl?

'Before you dress, my dear, may I kiss you?'

I want to say this is what I desired all day, desired since I first met him, but will he think me too easy-going, like the prostitute Mrs Atkinson thought she would become by modelling? Before I can reply, his hands hold my head, and his lips are firmly on mine. A wave of pleasure sweeps through, and I lean into his beard, into him. Like two statues conjoined, we stand without moving until Rodin releases my face and strokes my hair.

'*Merci, Mademoiselle* John,' picking up my card. 'So, your full name is Gwendolen Mary John? May I call you Marie like Mary? Maria was my dead sister's name.'

'I would be honoured.'

'Well then Marie, please attend again in one week from today. We will properly begin my Muse. I have a maquette to finish first with the other model you saw but I will be thinking about you all week.'

These are the most thrilling words I have ever heard. As he changes into his frockcoat, I dress dreamily, smiling up at him as I place one garment over another. Finally, he blows out the candles and, taking my arm, escorts me to the tram stop. The tram grinds to a halt far too soon.

'To next week, *Mademoiselle*.' He is making a slight bow and kissing my hand.

'Marie,' I blush.

CHAPTER 12

RODIN'S STUDIO

Sunday night is interminably long. The clock of Sacré-Coeur chimes the hour four times before I drift into sleep. I dream I am sailing with Rodin on the ocean. All I see, in every direction, are tumultuous waves. I scan Rodin's face and he seems untroubled by the threat of drowning. I am overcome with anxiety and the possibility of being swept away, losing sight of Rodin for ever. Sunlight is filtering through the shutters, and the time on my watch is seven o'clock. I am late. My stomach is already tense for the day ahead. The dream waves linger.

The water jug is warm from the sunshine so I can wash and dress quickly. I have a few minutes for coffee and a slice of bread with confiture before travelling to Rodin. In the mirror, the maroon dress shapes my figure into an hourglass, lifting and rounding my breasts. They feel firm to the touch, and I imagine Rodin's hands smoothing over each and then travelling down my body. Edgar nibbles the crust I discard in excitement.

Only one of the great gates leading to the studio is open today. Perhaps Rodin's assistants will arrive later, and I slide through the opening, holding tight the delicious thought Rodin and I will be alone. Sadly, a few men are busy readying the studio. One, sweeping the floor, glances up and beams, the same assistant who first took me to the Master, and it seems as if together we began creating my new life as Rodin's muse.

'You know where to model? The Master is waiting.' Giving me a knowing glance.

Has he heard Rodin kissed me? Surely Rodin would not gossip. Last time there was a turbulence within me, desire swirling together with anxiety. This morning will be easier because I know how to pose for the Master.

'Good morning my dear.' Rodin emerges from behind a screen, smiling broadly.

Smiling in return and discarding my clothes, I settle into the Muse pose with every line of my body like a seasoned ballet dancer with the Paris Opera Ballet. Rodin's face seems alive with pleasure. His eyes are soft, and he scrutinises all of me while removing scraps of cloth from the statuette. My breasts are hard, swollen, under his gaze, aching more than my muscles. It is a new sensation. The residue of last night's dream reminds me of the rough sea at home and running from the tide into a cave with one of Gus's friends. What was his name? All I remember is his perfunctory kiss and attempt to do more, but I felt nothing and pushed him away. Now my body is tingling. I grasp my toes and raise my left elbow to keep my balance, yet it is difficult to maintain tranquillity with Rodin so near, the sweet scent of his beard. He examines the contours of my body, running his left hand along the line of my thighs, checking the positioning of the joints, while his right hand shapes the clay.

Throughout the day he allows me to rest every half hour, carrying a chair himself to the stove for me, covering the dirty seat with a throw. I ease the tension in my thighs with gentle pats and his eyes remain focussed on me.

'The first sight of your body, was like the sun breaking through the clouds.' Such a beautiful sentence but what does he expect me to reply? I glance around the studio to verify that we are alone, expecting a cough or a snigger from an assistant.

'Do not concern yourself my dear, I asked the assistants to finish early today. You will not be embarrassed by the men's stares.'

'I am untroubled by my nakedness.'

Will the hint be enough? Am I too eager? It is only the second day of modelling, but already I imagine our bodies intertwined like Greek statues, beautiful from every angle.

At last he removes his rounded tortoiseshell spectacles, dangling them from one hand while he gestures with the other at cushions on the platform.

'Please rest. We have completed our work for today.'

The cushions are silk, smooth against my nude body, and I position myself in what I hope is an erotic pose. He pulls the screens together, hiding the platform from the rest of the studio. Taking candles from his cupboard of art materials, he places them on the shelves, lighting each slowly in turn as if we are sharing a ceremony, a religious service, as his assistant did the other evening. His wash at the sink, after removing his dusty smock, all seems part of the same ritual. How many women have seen the candles? Are candles always a prelude to intimate relations? As I stretch my limbs, he watches me and my heart beats fast.

The bell of Sacré-Coeur rings out five times. Five o'clock – the end of the working day. As if waiting for the sound, Rodin walks slowly towards me, undoing his jacket buttons and clasps me, holding me tight. With my face on his chest, the beating of his heart matches mine.

'Miss John.'

'Marie,' my voice is soft, almost inaudible.

'Marie. May I?'

He undresses quickly, his body hair golden in the candlelight. It occurs to me that, except for one boy on Tenby beach when I was a child, I have never seen a man fully naked. The Greek statues in the British Museum lack Rodin's details – his dark hairy chest, his arms flecked with raised muscles, his pink member thrusting erect, against thighs hairier than his chest. More than this: when McEvoy kissed me, I felt no exhilaration as I do with Rodin. His lips brush my lips, and my heart is beating loudly. Rodin is kissing me; I say to myself. I realise that I could never feel this happiness today if I had not experienced the unhappiness with McEvoy and Dorelia in the way I did. Rodin's member is huge, erect. I place his hand on a breast so he can sense my elation, and, with his other, his fingers play back and forth on my body. I am hot, aching with voluptuous sensations. I imagined this moment for so long everything almost seems unreal until I gasp as he enters me.

'Are you in pain?' He kisses my ear.

'No my Master,' my voice thickening with desire.

He is inside and part of my body, bringing a kind of an intense pleasure, lifting me on a wave, making it hard to breathe, even after he withdraws. He is releasing me from a life which contained me too tightly, launching me into one which will free me from time, from certainty. I touch his hairy chest while we lie together, silent, until the church bell rings out again, and he reaches for his clothes. What is he thinking? It is hard to read his calm expression. He stands and dresses, watching the movements of my arms as I slip undergarments over my head and pull on my dress.

'What a beautiful dress. Maroon is very becoming on you Marie. Women should always be well dressed.'

Why is he mentioning my dress and not my body? His eyes are on me continually as I finish. I want to stay here with him because my life is changed, I am now his, but, after dressing, he escorts me to the street and kisses my hand in farewell, asking me to keep our affair a secret. He is right, keeping secrets encloses us in a bubble of two and he will be continually interested in me. Instead of going home, I will go straight to the Bon Marché store with my fee from Rodin and buy materials for a new dress because he said he loves clothes. Hilda and any other models will appear dowdy by comparison.

The clouds which hung over the city this morning have disappeared, and the evening sun turns the sky orange with pink stripes. Walking to the store, on a hill overlooking the city, sounds reach me from below. Traffic buzzes, murmurs of conversations, the smells of Paris – pommes frites mixed with sweet scents from cherry trees – all crowd in, as if I am the single central figure in a busy landscape. I think of Rodin along the streets. Today I am a true woman, loved and wanted by Rodin the great artist.

The store straddles the corner of rue de Babylone, stretching right down the street. Mannequins glisten in large plate-glass windows, wearing the latest fashions. What would Rodin like? Presumably not a dress which draws too much attention to me; he will want me all for himself. He asked me to undertake fewer modelling jobs to be fresh and beautiful for him. Black suited shop assistants scurry about and the wide staircase to the room of dress stuffs is ahead. Ascending, thinking of Rodin's touch, passing through rooms piled with handbags, shoes, gloves, all the different scents mingle, almost overpowering. On a table is the same kind of cloth which Dorelia wore the night we met Leonard, presumably part of her attraction but I will never wear anything to remind me of her. Among all the bolts of silks, one stands out, a light green shot through with silver. Holding it up against my body in a mirror, I am more attractive than when I was with her because now, I am Rodin's lover.

Exhausted by posing all day and shopping, the tea room beckons. A few ladies, wearing furs, are dotted about and their gestures, touching each other's arms as they speak, form interesting shapes, quickly into my sketchbook on the table. The subdued early evening light perfectly captures the detail of their bell-shaped hats resplendent with tulle and feathers. I cannot transfer them to paint because they would dominate my canvases, but sketches expand my sense of line, help me develop. While drinking my tea, focussing, a man with a handlebar moustache, touches his hat to me and I look away. Shuffling my papers over the table surface, I make it impossible for him to find any space.

'May I join such a beautiful woman?' without bothering to remove his hat, twisting the ends of his moustache.

I fix him with a stare.

'Confound you,' without any of my usual hesitancy. 'Bon Marché has a tea room for men, so ladies can be alone in peace in theirs.'

Rodin has given me a new kind of strength, and he will inspire my art. Tonight, I will begin sewing a stylish dress.

As I enter Hôtel Mont Blanc, for the first time the concierge willingly engages me in conversation. What a pleasure to see her open face rather than the habitual frown. It is my new appearance she must be reflecting because my body tingles all over with joy, spilling out into the lobby, touching anyone nearby, even the concierge. She hands me a letter with an English stamp. Gwen Salmond and Ursula are visiting Paris. My changed appearance will surprise them; what you wear matches what you feel. Shall I confide the reason for the change? Ursula I can trust, the other

Gwen might divulge the news and Rodin asked me to keep our affair secret; I can make clear, as soon as they arrive, that I have modelling hours, and they should amuse themselves at times, but I will be silent about my relationship with Rodin. Nothing I can talk about to the girls.

CHAPTER 13
RODIN'S STUDIO (2)

The next day I am early again. The assistants are still drinking coffee in the courtyard, and alone, I undress behind a screen in the empty studio. Rodin must have heard my footsteps because he rushes into the room and, climbing onto the platform, places his hands on my naked buttocks. 'I must enter you.'

The request is so amazingly sudden, and he is coming into me from behind, his cock sliding back and forth, hot against me, his fingers moving simultaneously on my quim. He wants me so passionately and I quiver with excitement. My back arches against his stomach, and he grunts several times as if gratified. Wet spunk trickles down my thighs. If it dries on my skin, I will be able to smell him tonight when alone in my room, but he seizes a cloth from a sculpture and brusquely wipes himself and me.

The moment is over so quickly, but I am half-swooning with an intensity more satisfying than anything I have ever experienced; being loved so ardently by such a great man. I begin to think of myself as living only in the present, forgetting my past, feeling giddy with the irresponsibility of it all.

'Thank you, Marie. Please take up your Muse pose.'

He thanks me as if someone handed him a tasse of coffee, but he gave himself to me with such a fervent passion, words are irrelevant. Although the stove is unlit and my breath hangs misty on the chill air, I am throbbing inside as if Rodin's soul is igniting my body. My muscles tense to the ends of my fingertips and toes as I sweep into position, and I hold my body taut in an easy grace.

'Beautiful Marie.' He moulds the clay as vigorously as he entered me, as if the statue and my body share one spirit.

'I wrote you a letter last night Master, signing it, Marie. You brought so many ravishing ideas into my head, and I had to capture them.' I sat at my desk, filling sheet after sheet, discarding several until dawn broke out.

'Do not move,' he silences me.

Breathing slowly, keeping my head fixed as before, I can hold poses far longer than other models. He seems content, but we will need more than good poses and sex to bind us.

'I have been told you are an avid reader, what books shall I read to my Master while you work? We could converse.'

'*Pamela* is my favourite novel,' without looking up. 'It is English so you will find it undemanding. Your French is poor.' Smoothing down the statue he continues, 'Before you leave tonight, I will give you other titles. Right now, we must think about art not literature. Silence.'

For the rest of the day I pose, and wonder how to improve my French, perhaps I could talk more to the concierge now she seems friendlier. When I am fatigued, Rodin suggests I stand down from the platform and warm myself by the stove, to rub tension from my legs and back. Glancing at the statue as I pass, it is much the same. The clay has been worked over and over, but the statue lacks a head and arms. Good. There will be weeks, months perhaps, of modelling, with Rodin absorbed in my figurine and perhaps my flesh.

The sky through the studio windows is turning dark and the assistants are cleaning their tools in the sink. One in a corner still taps away.

'*Terminé*,' Rodin pronounces, loudly. I wonder if the instruction includes me.

As the workmen stroll out of the studio, chattering in pairs, Rodin is washing his hands and turns to watch me. I pick up my thin silk chemise and stretching up my arms slide it over my head.

'Perfect,' and he moves closer, breathing heavily.

Reaching for the garment's hem as if to remove it, instead his hands slide up my thigh. 'Leave on the garment. I wish to ravish you partially dressed, as if taking you unawares.'

The thought of Rodin seizing me abruptly before I have time to notice is the most electrifying thing anyone could ever say.

'Lean over the chair, my dear.' He undoes his trouser buttons. As his erect member slides out, the tip is bright red, engorged. He wipes it lightly across my buttocks, gripping my chemise and then plunging into me. I moan uncontrollably and contract, to pleasure him and myself, as his cock slides in and out. This time he leaves my thighs wet and, as I dress, the hot stickiness momentarily glues my legs together until I can stand to recover my breath.

Rodin slumps in the chair.

'My dear, I am so much older than you. You tire me; we must restrain ourselves. I need all my strength for sculpture.'

'I will behave more like the Muse I am becoming,' touched by Rodin's vulnerability which is as exciting as his manliness. 'We can confine ourselves to kisses.'

'I find myself unable to resist.' He smiles, stroking his trouser buttons.

My fingers are on my body in imitation. The subdued Bloomsbury girl has completely vanished. I am an entirely new person, more alive, caressed by pleasure.

'Stop, not three times!' Laughing up at me.

It is all I can do not to climax again; but he stands, putting on his frockcoat and his face is stern, his eyes are not on me, but on his bookshelves. Taking a cigarette from a pocket, he smokes, concentrating, as if I am suddenly absent.

'Those names you wanted. There is Baudelaire and Mallarmé of course but classical Greece is my passion.' And reaching up, hands me a slim volume from a shelf.

He has remembered my earlier request.

'I will read the stories tonight; all I wish is to amuse you.'

'You must never cease drawing.'

So he appreciates me as a fellow artist as well as a model.

'Bring me a sketch of the cat you mentioned,' turning his back on me and working on another maquette, absorbed, distant, his back a square of black at the rear of the studio as I leave, clutching the book and my fee.

∼

The Seine is illuminated with lanterns, and yellow squares shining from windows, as the tram clicks up to Montparnasse. My Hôtel Mont Blanc always has a poverty-stricken appearance but tonight it shines like the dense white glazes of a Sargent painting. Reaching my room, I am too excited to eat. Rodin's book is full of stories, a few familiar, like the death of Procris because *Landscape with the Death of Procris* one of my favourite paintings in the National Gallery. Others, like Iphigenia, are new. I will have to research all of them to fascinate Rodin with my knowledge, so our minds and bodies align – an extension of Rodin, an artist too. Nibbling a sugar biscuit, marking up passages to learn by heart, imagining extraordinary poses like the Greeks, the scenes seem to flash around the walls.

The air tonight is humid, heavy, even with a window flung wide open and my chest is tight, suffocating like an asthmatic, so I will sleep out of doors. The concierge would be horrified if she knew, perhaps ask me to vacate my room, so I slip silently past her office. Concierges can be so conventional. The sky is dark blue, with dense clouds threatening to block out the moon but no hint of rain, and the streets are empty of passers-by. In the Luxembourg Gardens, the paths are shaded by trees and a copse ahead promises cooler air among the bushes so I can drift asleep on top of my shawl. I do want Rodin to see me in moonlight. Gus said I was more beautiful at night and my master must see me in all kinds of illumination, as well as the usual candles and studio lamps. The only time I saw him out of doors was the moment in Regent's Park.

Abruptly I wake.

'Are you willing?' A silhouetted outline of a tall man is standing on the path to my right. Half asleep it takes me a moment to translate. I listen for sounds of others nearby who could assist, but the gardens are empty – merely a breeze rustling leaves. Trembling, I shake my dress free of dropped leaves while backing away. His cane is sweeping the grass between us, its silver top catching the moonlight, moving nearer.

'Leave me alone,' I shout, 'my fiancée is over there,' and rush panting to the park gates, listening for footsteps. Is he on the path now behind me? A muttering noise flies towards me, then silence. Glancing back, a dark shape disappears deep into the bushes.

The walk up to Montparnasse is exhausting, my heart is still pounding. I must sleep for the rest of the night to be strong enough to hold my pose for my Master tomorrow but before I do, I will write down my adventure, make the stranger truly threatening. A seductive scene will arouse Rodin. Stories will substitute for my poor conversation where I am limited in French vocabulary. With stories like Scheherazade, I can bewitch Rodin.

CHAPTER 14

URSULA AND THE OTHER GWEN

Next day, carrying my notebook into the studio, I undress quickly, excited to read aloud. Ahead, an unfinished sculpture is full of movement. It is something about the lines, the overlapping contours like the way I sometimes try to capture my figures in mid-movement.

'My Master,' tensing my muscles ready for the pose, 'shall I read a story?'

'Leave the notebook on the table. Your French is too poor for literature.'

It is true but painful and he barely glances at me as he works. He seems absorbed, far away. He measures my legs again with the compasses but is not touching me, not caressing my breasts although all I want is for him to arouse me. When Rodin gives all his attention to a statue and loses himself in the work, I wonder if he will ever emerge.

When Sacré-Coeur chimes five will we make love? I stretch out my legs, bend into the pose, hoping the lines of my body will flow into his brain, connect us in love.

'I have clients to see later, and I must cancel our sessions for a few days.'

Tears pool but I must not ask who he is seeing. It will seem intrusive, too questioning and I cannot interfere in his affairs. Has he slept with others? If only he would stroke me, kiss me, even just place his face for a moment next to mine.

'I will give you extra money, to cover the cancelled hours.'

Money is not what I want but him, his touch, the sight of his eyes turning dark when he enters me; being held so tight we fuse together. Am I only a piece to work on and then discard?

'Please do not mention money. Please do not try to buy me. I am your lover and an artist too.'

I feel like a hot water bottle turned upside down. I must stop; he will hate my lack of control and I hate myself.

'I have no time for unnecessary emotion,' washing out the clay from his fingernails in the sink. 'Get dressed. Ask my assistant for the money,' gesturing to a man who puts his head around the screen.

As he stalks out of the studio, tears obscure the francs the man counts into my palm. Rodin's words sting more than his actions. I finish dressing, uncaring that the assistant is happily staring at my breasts until my bodice is fully buttoned. I push down my anguish and follow the assistant to the front door. He tips his cap at me, and desolate, I stand alone waiting for the tram home.

Ursula and the other Gwen arrive today. The train should bring them to me by evening. My love for Rodin will be my secret. Would either of them understand how a soul can be caught up in such bodily pleasure and such despair at its absence? My friends are not prudes, but Ursula's father is a minister, and the other Gwen is devoted to her conservative family.

The hot day seeps into the evening. Tree leaves are browning in the park and the pungent smell of horses is overpowering. A heatwave has enveloped Paris all week, blanching the grass in the Luxembourg Gardens and melting tar between the cobblestones, flecking the wheels of cabs, making streets seem to expand. Changing in Hôtel Mont Blanc, ready to greet the girls, sweat trickles from my armpits. The weekly bath in the bathhouse at the end of the street was three days ago and it is probably closed at this hour, with no time before they arrive, so a soapy cloth will have to do. I can wear the maroon dress that Rodin praised.

The writing pad is open on the table with an imprint of my story for Rodin visible on the surface. Each word was so painstaking, I must have pressed hard down with the pen, determined to make each character full of feeling. Perhaps he will read the story tonight. Despite my bad French, he must see my love and passion for him are greater than the glitter of easy compliments from other models.

A knock heralds the girls.

'*Chère* Gwen! *Je suis ravi de te voir*. How is my pronunciation?'

'Good,' holding back tears which threaten again. At least Ursula's French is more limited than mine. And I have been ravished by Rodin.

Hugging them fiercely, their warm bodies are a comfort, like the cuddles of my nurse in Tenby whenever Gus pulled hard on my plaits.

'How are you both? And Ida, Augustus, Dorelia and the children?'

'All well. Together with Dorelia's baby, they have four children to care for.' And the other Gwen carries their valises into the bedroom.

'And by the time you return,' I say, 'Ida will be with child again. She gives birth to babies more often than to paintings.'

Ursula glances at the other Gwen, and they busy themselves unpacking. Have I been cruel? We all love Ida and Dorelia, but why do women create children? My trusty rubber sponge will keep me safe from pregnancy, but my anger which I managed to control this afternoon, rises again. 'Monuments are erected to celebrate great art. There are no statues for giving birth.'

'Well, none of us is gestating.' The other Gwen laughs. 'And we are painting. What are your latest works?'

What can I say? My art is preparing for Rodin, making ready my body and mind.

'Oh, a few sketches. I am not submitting paintings to exhibitions at the moment, because I model a good deal.'

There is nothing else to add. They could never understand the wild sensation of being loved by a great master. Sitting together at the table, they resemble two Victorian women in a domestic interior about to begin knitting.

'You were the best in our Slade year, we all thought fame and fortune would be yours before anyone.'

Why is Ursula talking about the Slade as if those years are the only significant times?

'That is in the past. My future is here.'

Ursula glances again at the other Gwen. 'At least, you are blossoming.'

'What should we see in Paris?' the other Gwen says, 'What is new since my last visit?'

'Not a good deal, and I may need to model as well as paint while you are here.'

They seem puzzled, but I want to be available in case Rodin might suddenly ask for me. 'You must be hungry. I will start cooking.'

With my tiny stove, I can manage simple spinach and eggs, although the sliced salami with the dish smells greasy and is clearly too hard. Ursula and the other Gwen are delicately discarding remnants on the side of their plates.

'What about the Louvre tomorrow?' the other Gwen asks.

'Certainly. We will visit in the morning.'

Rodin is refusing to see me for a few days but how many are 'a few'? I will write to him again tonight.

With Ursula and the other Gwen sleeping safely in their room along the corridor, I can open the writing pad. I draw a tiny cameo of the cat as a heading to a letter, to reassure Rodin I am working, sketches are my children I tell him, thinking about this evening's conversation about Ida and Dorelia. The candle burns down, and another. So many words – my feelings of passion, descriptions of Rodin's lovemaking – are not in the dictionary. When he touches me, it is like a succession of small waves followed by an enormous cresting seventh wave. A thin yellow seeps into the grey light before I finish, and finally sleep.

Next morning, over coffee, we plan our route through the museum.

'I have a letter which I must deliver first; it is important.'

'What can be more important than the Louvre?' the other Gwen says, 'We cannot return from Paris without seeing the Mona Lisa.'

'Who is the letter to?' Ursula asks. 'If it is to Augustus, it will be quicker for us to deliver it when we return, rather than posting.'

'It is not to Augustus, and I must deliver by hand.'

'Is it to Rodin himself?' the other Gwen stares at the envelope. 'You know Rodin?

'How wonderful,' Ursula adds. 'You are modelling for Rodin. Could we meet him?'

'It might be difficult. He is absent from Paris for a few days, so I am free,' my throat tightening. What else will they ask? In any case I cannot take more young ladies to him. He is attracted to English women; he might want them to model. Or more. I must save him for myself.

'But if Rodin is away why deliver by hand now?' the other Gwen says. 'We could post the letter en route to the Louvre?'

How can I explain? Our passion must be kept secret. He said so the first time we made love. The other models, the people surrounding him, might see the envelope.

'I am to give letters to the concierge, he told me,' My eyes liquid. 'It is safer by hand.'

'My dear,' Ursula places a hand on my arm. 'No need to say more. We can guess.'

Tears are falling now.

'If being a model means being a mistress you must be careful.' Ursula hugs me.

'I am his muse; he has turned me into a true woman.'

The girls stare at each other. The other Gwen seems about to speak but Ursula frowns and takes my hands in hers. 'We are concerned about you. We discussed this last night for a while after you went to bed. You have changed. You were only passionate about painting. *Nothing else matters* you told me once and I was quite hurt by the implication.'

'I apologise. Your friendships do mean a great deal to me, but Rodin is my Master, and he inspires my work.'

'Perhaps I should not say this,' the other Gwen is frowning, 'but you are in danger of becoming a fool. Everyone knows Rodin has many mistresses. He is not married. If you mean so much to him, surely he will propose?'

'I cannot explain, but he is everything that is beautiful in my life.' I will not describe his lovemaking. The girls might be shocked and think me even lower than a mistress.

Gwen sighs, and Ursula shrugs her shoulders.

'Please do not say anything about this to Augustus.'

'By all means.' Ursula puts her arm around my shoulders. 'He has mistresses and gives them babies. Men escape society's judgements.'

'I apologise for my abruptness,' the other Gwen gives a sympathetic glance. 'Is Rodin's studio near the Louvre? We will hand in the letter to his concierge together.'

'And, after the museum, visit a brasserie,' Ursula adds, smiling. 'Enjoy our day together. Just us girls.'

CHAPTER 15

PARIS AND THE GIRLS

Two days later, Ursula, the other Gwen, and I are strolling through Bon Marché in search of fabric for me, and gifts for their families. No word from Rodin at least means I am at liberty to sightsee. Following the hours in museums, shopping is a respite after the hard mental work of staring at art, comparing colours, shapes and gestures. Light pours through the shop's stained-glass windows turning everything multi-coloured like fireworks after a party; perfumes mingle with polish; the air is heady and claustrophobic. I want to be home alone to dream about Rodin, but the girls are leaving tomorrow. When she was last in Paris, the other Gwen supported me to study with Whistler, and I must give her my time and attention. Ursula was my rock at the Slade, my steadfast friend. Friendships are significant relationships, more important than families. Also Ursula admires Rodin's sculptures, she said, making me treasure her even more.

'I must see those necklaces,' Ursula says, as we are about to leave the store. 'I lack a present for Mother.'

A shop assistant starts fussing over the jewellery.

'I apologise for taking your time, but I cannot decide what Mother would wear.' Replacing a glass necklace on the counter with one of paste diamonds.

'Choose the cheapest?' the other Gwen has a bored expression, pulling on her gloves. 'No one will guess the price.'

Reflections from the stones are blending into the window-lights and the shining glass of the counter, dazzling. Suddenly I am overcome. Even squeezing my eyes shut and opening them again, everything is distorted. Hot and weak, I clutch the countertop and Ursula holds my arm. 'We must take you home.' She is staring closely at my face.

'I am out of sorts and need to rest.'

'It is Rodin is it not?' Her arm now around my waist supporting me, as we leave the store. 'Your relationship exhausts you.'

'Why not forget Rodin for a time? Take a brief holiday – return to England?' the other Gwen says. 'You could stay with Augustus, Ida and Dorelia. You must miss them?'

'I do, but working in Paris is my life now.' I am putting a hand over my eyes to block out the sunshine.

'Do think about visiting,' the other Gwen gives an exasperated sigh.

Perhaps Rodin will miss me more if I travel and am not so available. 'You are right. I will think about returning in a few weeks.'

'Augustus resides in the country, but I promise we will attend to you, if you can visit London, we will see exhibitions.' On the street outside, Ursula waves down a *fiacre*. 'Please do.'

Back at the apartment, loaded with parcels, there is a note from Rodin waiting on the mat.

'Is it a love letter?' the other Gwen asks.

'Do read aloud,' Ursula says, 'if the message not too private.'

'It is not private at all,' I say, scanning the two lines, and read slowly. '*Model for me on 26th August. Votre ami, Rodin.*' Two days' time.

My imaginary conversations with him accompanied the girls around Paris. They put down their packages, staring at each other.

'Well, at least he wants to see you again.' Ursula unwraps her parcels.

'Were you expecting a more loving signature,' the other Gwen says, 'like *chère*?'

'Not at all.' I keep my voice as calm as possible. 'He is a busy man. The studio is full of assistants working on his commissions. His notes to everyone are very brief, the assistants told me.'

A lie, but I cannot say more. There will be no repetition of the fainting, tomorrow the girls will be gone, and then it is only one more day to wait before his body is close to mine. I can use the hours to sew a new dress to wear with the Bon Marché stockings, picturing his face as I slowly roll the stockings down my legs, opening my thighs.

'You are often withdrawn, far away, as now. Last night, after Gwen and I retired, I heard you talking to yourself.'

'I am simply composing in my mind, nothing more.'

It is my letters to Rodin. Saying each aloud as I write helps me capture the perfect tone.

'You used to talk, when you painted at the Slade, and when you were drawing in those notebooks, eccentrically staring at us as if we were new acquaintances, lost in your work. But never as excitedly as you do now, late at night.'

'I have been living alone far too long.' I try to laugh. 'The cat and I have extraordinary conversations.'

Both girls have disbelieving expressions, but I will see Rodin the day after tomorrow.

∼

Rodin's smock is hanging on the door of the empty studio. Naked, I slip my arms into the sleeves, relishing the smell of clay and the sweet scent of Rodin's body and cuddle myself. The smock warms me, as if he is holding me tight, protecting me, and I only just manage to return it to the hook, when he returns from talking to an assistant in the next room. Walking over swiftly, Rodin seems impatient for me to assume my pose. Before pulling the screens around us both, he kisses me full on the lips. In front of an assistant. It is the first time our love is public, broadcast to the world. Will his other models hear about our moment? Excited, I move quickly into position.

'Please extend a little further. You are pleasing in the pose.'

Stretching again, happy we are exploring my body together. As usual, he switches between me and the statuette, tracing a detail of my body with his thumb and then modelling the line in clay. I am tingling with excitement, wanting his fingers to do so much more than smooth my skin. The lemon of his eau de cologne fills my nostrils, and more – the scent of a man, sweaty but not acrid – with the aroma covering my body.

'*Mon Maître*,' trying not to move. 'Promise me that if you kiss other models, I will never hear about the moment.'

The thought is always there beneath the surface, every time the women I model for talk about Rodin. If Rodin confirms their stories, then the unpleasant image of him with another will be in my dreams, not memories of our own lovemaking.

'We are together today, *ma chère*. It is what matters. Keep stationary.'

I try to breathe evenly but with a frisson of anticipation thinking of his lovemaking tonight. 'As long as we make love often.'

'You can love me best, by taking care of yourself and not being uneasy. Anxiety will spoil your appearance, and you are already thinner.'

Surely passion must have improved my appearance. The rapture with Rodin brings my body alive, but my waist has shrunk, and the new dress is slimmer. It is so hard to eat when I am intoxicated with desire?

'I have been hard at work, making my room beautiful. It can be a sanctuary for us, away from prying eyes.'

Rodin looks up and smiles. He will appreciate my discretion, my sensitivity to his wish for secrecy.

'Good,' coming closer and kissing my forehead. 'I will visit once a week, in the morning when you are not modelling here. You keep me young.' He laughs.

His phrase might sound banal to another but not to me. I am his muse, although one hidden from public view. All afternoon I pose, content, and make a list of necessities for his visit to my room. First, I will sweep the shelves and floor, place fresh sheets on the bed, and tidy the kitchenette each morning. Flowers must be on the windowsill and in the centre of the mantlepiece. His books, *Pamela* and the Greek myths, will be prominently displayed. Reading them helps me understand his conversations, his views about art. I must also remember my appearance – iron my skirt, clean my belt and boots, brush my hair a hundred times, and pinch my cheeks pink before greeting him.

I have been dreaming all afternoon and the light is darkening. Will he make love to me tonight? I glance over, trying not to let any anxiety show in my face.

'You can rest now.'

I wanted to shift positions all day, and I open my legs as seductively as I can. Rodin once described an oil painting, he admired, depicting a woman in such a position, nothing visible above her waist, her white thighs splayed wide in the foreground, her bush thick, jet black. Erotic was the term he used.

'Get dressed, *ma petite*. I am needed in Meudon this evening.'

Closing my legs together, I try not to cry as a wave of disappointment floods through me.

'Come walk with me to the station.' He is glancing at me.

My face must be more revealing than I think. At least he wants to continue our talk as long as he can.

There is a housekeeper in his Meudon home. Hilda told me her name – Rose; but she is sixty, and it is understandable that Rodin needs an everyday assistant. There is no competition – I am his lover. Will we walk arm in arm to the station? In public? The memory will fill the forthcoming evening.

With my new tea-party hat at an angle, he gazes at me with his eyes lit up, and the hurt of not making love drains away. Earlier today, he did murmur in my ear that I am beautiful which suffices until the next time. All the way to the station my steps are slower and slower, hoping to prolong the length of the day before the moment he disappears. Once the studio is behind us, out of sight, he takes my arm with a firm grasp. We are a couple out for a stroll. Everyone will see our closeness, our normality; and I nod at other couples passing by. At the station, Rodin takes my hand, raising it to his lips in farewell. The kiss will remain all night; and Rodin has promised to make love to me in my room at Hôtel Mont Blanc.

CHAPTER 16

RODIN VISITS

Over a week now, not the expected few days, since my Master said he would visit, and I must remain in my room each morning in case he arrives, because mornings are the only possible time of day for him. He sculpts in the afternoons and returns to Rose in the evenings. So I write to him about my love, together with stories and anecdotes. The letters are my new art form. Although I spend less time on each letter than on a painting, every word is checked in the dictionary, and only the most faultless phrases and interesting anecdotes will do.

Once, I told him about the baby bird who flew into my room. The window and wardrobe were both open, and a finch flew in right onto a skirt. I held Edgar tight while the mother bird called from the windowsill. Turning the event into a mini drama, I imitate Edgar's meows and the bird's 'pi-pi' tweets. Another day I tell him about posing naked for Miss Hart next door, refusing to chatter in case I missed Rodin's step on the stairs. Everything flows into my letters, with a special emphasis on my breasts. The tone is the most difficult – how to attract him without sounding a cheap coquette.

As I start another letter, wondering if I should date and time each so he will know my constant devotion, a footstep sounds outside my door, followed by a knock. The noises of everyone in my building below are so distinct and Miss Hart left early this morning, so the knock must be Rodin's.

'Wait, wait,' and I push the letter into a drawer.

My body shivers and I rush to the sink to bathe my face.

'Wait a little,' pinching my cheeks, biting my lips red.

Delay makes me more excited, prolongs the pleasure, and I cannot seem too keen.

'One moment,' loosening my hair around my shoulders, and brushing it again.

The door handle turns, and he stands next to me, removing his hat, gazing at me with parted lips.

When he touches me, will I climax immediately with excitement? Taking deep breaths, I smooth my skirt and notice, out of the corner of an eye, Edgar has left a gnawed bone on the bed.

'Filthy!' Rodin exclaims, and flushed, I rush the bone into the kitchen. Please, please dear God above, do not let Edgar disgust him, in case I seem repugnant by association. I have waited for my Master all week. I need him more than he can possibly know.

Back in the bedroom, he is already half undressed, his cock engorged, pointing upwards at me.

'*Ma petite*,' and he unbuttons my bodice, squeezing my breasts.

He pushes his body and mine onto the bed, as I struggle to pull off my clothes. The weight almost squashes me breathless. I throw my arms wide apart so he can take me while I remain motionless. Rodin is Tarquin and I am Lucretia, although my body is not as white nor my face as luminous as hers in Tintoretto's painting, and I am much thinner. Rolling me over, he comes into me from behind, one hand pushing me down onto the pillow. I can barely breathe, but the luxurious sensation is exquisite. I inhale his eau de cologne, as he wipes himself on the counterpane. It is over so quickly, but I have reached the pinnacle and shudder. On his back, he stretches over to his coat, and pulls a cheroot from a case, offering one to me and lighting mine from his – a sign of love, and so modern. After we smoke, the ache is melting into wetness, and I kiss his hairy stomach.

'No more! You exhaust me. I will have a migraine.'

'I will rest too,' sliding into his arms, but my passion is heating my body and I lick the thick hair around his balls, loving the contrast between the softness of his skin and the bristles roughing my lips.

'Stop, I have little time today. I travel to Chartres on Sunday and need to leave now to prepare. I will be there a week, perhaps two. It is for commissions, not for pleasure.'

'Are you travelling alone or taking Rose?'

There, I said her name. What will he reply? Avoid the question?

'I am uncertain. But she means nothing. She travels with me because she is my housekeeper. I love you.'

The golden phrase hangs in the air above us. Spoken out loud, not murmured in my ear when he enters me. It is solid, meaningful and stops my breath. My smile must be enormous.

Placing his cheroot stub in a saucer, he dresses as if about to rush to Chartres immediately. 'I will write soon.' He leaves.

He is taking Rose. There was no denial. She is in Meudon every day for him, and in Chartres she will be there every night when he returns from meeting clients. Hilda told me Rodin never introduces her to anyone; and she wears the same dowdy clothes for weeks at a time, but it is her very presence which troubles. He and I are not full-time lovers. A vinegary taste is in my mouth as if my stomach is full of acid. Perhaps I should plead with God, pray tonight for Rodin to think of me while he travels, and my prayers could be like writing a new kind of letter. Rodin has swept me up into his world as if I am a maquette stuck on one of his workstations; as if he has all his models dotted around his studio so he can walk from one to another – the Rodin gallery. I need to escape for a few days to find myself, and gain strength for my art.

∽

The ferry puts out to sea and Boulogne slips back, hidden by the morning mist as if France is already becoming a hazy memory. The last visible buildings resemble Whistler's etchings of the London docks, houses in shadow, in deep perspective outlined by light on the river. How long ago my studies with Whistler seem. A time before Rodin. It was good of Ida to invite me. The other

Gwen was right – I need a little idleness with Gus and his family. I have only a few free days, I replied to Ida, but not divulging the reasons why. Chartres may not attract Rodin for as long as he said. He could return at any time, and I need to be in my room, cleaning every surface, making myself pretty in a new dress, ready for a visit.

Miss Hart reluctantly agreed to look after Edgar, and I can be calm. The salt air coats my face, and the fog is covering the boat with a white blanket. The low sky stretches out like a person's palm lined with clouds. For once, I am not talking to Rodin in my mind; I will not think about him while I am in England; I will not think about his hands caressing me and his statues, nor about his cigarette smoke perfuming the bedroom air after we make love, his coat hanging ready on the hook. Gus and Ida will ask about my painting, especially Gus, and I can tell them about my new self-portraits without divulging their inspiration. I glance over the passengers, assembling them into a tableau, studying hair, body shapes and gestures. It is too damp to sketch but I am energised, renewed by the sight of their expressions, anxious figures clutched together as if in a Renaissance tondo. Even if Rodin's love is vital, my painting will never cease. After a couple of hours, the waves are calmer, the sun's heat is dispersing the fog, and ahead the white cliffs of Dover shine out.

What kind of family life are Gus, Ida and Dorelia sharing? With four children between them will both women be pregnant again? At least Gus has relinquished his caravan. You will have your own room, Ida promised. At the edge of the wooden viewing deck, the breeze lifts my skirt as I join the passengers assembling to disembark. A tall, well-dressed man raises his bowler at me, smiling, as we shuffle down the gangway. Every day I will practice not thinking about Rodin, and certainly not about Rose.

CHAPTER 17

ELM HOUSE, MATCHING GREEN, ENGLAND

The hansom from the station drives past ponds, streams, woods and a romantic village – the kind of pastoral landscape the Royal Academy would label 'picture of the year' in its Summer Exhibition. Bobster is the first to greet me, barking all the way up the drive from the house to the main road, closely followed by Gus. Elm House faces southwest so he will probably have a studio at the rear. He desires to paint in northern light every day, though, knowing Gus, he will probably spend more time in the Chequers pub next door. The house's long, brick exterior is solid with regular sash windows as if the whole façade is painted with a wide brush. Ida will be pleased not to be living in a caravan anymore, especially with all the children.

'The nursemaid has resigned on moral grounds,' Gus kisses me. 'Welcome to Elm House.'

Is this why Ida invited me? She should know I am never good with children, often I feel like one myself.

As Gus hangs up my cape in the hall, Ida stands there smiling, and tries to hug me with one arm, while holding baby Robin, swaddled with a shawl.

'I'm dreadfully off babies,' she murmurs, and we chuckle, while Bobster jumps up, barking, almost touching Gus's shoulder, so thank goodness he could not overhear Ida. He can be so irritable.

'But Dorelia is patient, cheerful as always; she is beautiful to look upon and ready to laugh at everything and nothing. So, we survive.'

There she is, radiant in the doorway of the kitchen, flushed, wiping flour-covered hands on her apron, with Ida's boys, David and Caspar clutching her skirt on either side.

'You are unchanged.' I flush in turn. 'All of you are.'

It is the first time I have seen Dorelia since she left me, but all the love, all the tension, feeling as if I was walking on eggshells in case she became annoyed, all has disappeared. There is no physical attraction, none of those sudden little twists in my stomach when I see her, just a sense of the way her forehead catches the light ready for a portrait like Dürer's devoted women. I may seem the same on the outside. My face unadorned with rouge, my hair pulled back into a bun, a demure travelling dress topped by a neat pique collar. The passion for Rodin is restrained by my dress buttons.

'Augustus is still a lazy wretch in the house,' Dorelia says, 'painting is all to him.'

A smile lights up her face, but her dress is dowdy, dishevelled. She is no longer the vibrant young woman who walked with me to Toulouse, and it is a relief. Rodin supplies me with enough emotion.

'My dear Dorelia, you know my life is dedicated to art.'

'As were ours once,' Ida replies, curtly.

'Are there no recent paintings?' Glad the discussion is ignoring me. I have no children.

'If I do find time to paint, 'Ida says, 'I am certain to tear my dress and have to mend it. My life is all domestic.'

'Or I spill a box of pins,' Dorelia adds, 'and have to gather them up before the children suffer stigmata on their hands and mouths.'

Ida dumps Robin on Gus's lap and takes me to my room.

'Augustus is incorrigible,' as we climb the stairs, 'but my happiness stems from his.'

'We are sisters.' I am itching to say more, reveal my life with Rodin, but Ida nods as if taking the phrase at face value.

Downstairs, the baby is howling, and another child sounds as if he is banging his head on a coal scuttle. Ida is exhausted.

'Come and eat as soon as you unpack.' She squeezes my hand. 'We miss your sanity, your calm.'

She will never guess. How could she? The past months have been the most turbulent, the most exciting, the most erotic of my life.

'Your eyes are shining; I wish mine were as beautiful.'

So it is true. Someone once said the eyes are the gateway to the soul and my soul is Rodin's. I promised myself not to, but I am thinking of his body, imagining his stomach, and the curly swirls of hair around his navel. He is plump, without evident muscles, but I adore everything about him – his solidity, his firm fingers, his magnificent head.

An hour later, Dorelia has miraculously managed to put the children to bed, and candles in the middle of the long table turn the dishes of potato, ham, and cabbage into a Dutch still-life. Gus is waiting, seated at the head. 'Wine, Gwen,' and holds out a glass, 'we will toast your return.'

I hold up my glass in salute, avoiding his eyes.

'Describe your new paintings; are you doing your interminable glazes? You must submit to the New English Art Club's next exhibition.'

'I work so slowly Gus, you know me.'

He leans forward, fixing me with a stare.

'Titles, Gwen, and medium. Oils, watercolours, charcoal? What's your preference now?'

'Augustus you are sounding like Legros,' Ida says, 'or as demanding as Tonks. Gwen arrived barely an hour ago.'

'Allow her time to rest,' Dorelia adds. 'She had a long journey.'

'Gwen's been travelling on trains and the boat – both very comfortable, and we are scarcely twenty miles from London, but I will stop interrogating my little sister.'

'You escape so often to the capital,' Ida sticks a fork firmly into a potato.

Women are beginning to rebut Gus. I would never think such a thing possible. Perhaps I enjoy Paris not just because of Rodin but because it is a sanctuary from Gus's demands.

After the meal, Ida shows me round the grounds. In a large orchard sits a block of ancient stables, empty of horses and caravans, and full of old easels and discarded canvases.

'I rarely use a canvas now, just quick sketches on paper,' following my glance. 'I am made horribly irritable and depressed by caring and cleaning; Augustus is such a beast at times.'

'He has always been domineering,' I say and place a hand on her arm, 'you can flee to Paris and me.'

I hope she refuses my invitation because my time with Rodin is so precious, but she is my friend.

'I might, but the children need me.'

The moon floats above and the air is cool. Indoors, Gus starts playing his concertina, singing vociferously.

'Nothing is subtle with Augustus,' she says. I give Ida a cuddle.

'I live the life of a slave, but I would not change because of Augustus – he is a man to die for.'

So is Rodin. Am I becoming his slave? But Rodin inspires my art, my desire to be a great painter, and my style is developing.

'You are very isolated here; without telephone and electricity, you must feel abandoned sometimes. I understand.'

'I am surrounded by cows and vulgarity.' Ida laughs as we return indoors.

The days fill with the usual chatter, and the older boys David and Caspar throwing their toys at each other. On the third day, I pack hurriedly in the early morning, itching to return to the station, to Paris. Waiting for the adults to rise, the children play, ignoring me, saying silly things to each other, and running up and down the stairs, so I escape for a moment.

Outside is sunny and warm, the closed door behind blocking out the children's screams and fist fights. Ida is right. A herd of cows are in the field alongside, chorusing the dawn under a spreading horse chestnut, but the church at the end of the path might be cool and inviting. Inside, it is unadorned with no special features, plain and musty, any frescoes long ago painted over and smelling dank but somehow full of its past. The tall statue placed centrally is familiar. My boots echo on the gravestones as I near the altar. St Mary the Virgin, a plaque at the base announces. I am no virgin, but David and Caspar persuade me never to have children, delightful though the boys are with their big smiles. Father's Sunday bible class dissuaded me from his version of religion, but this statue is serene, so I pick up a matchbox and candle and it flickers into flame; closing my eyes I can make a wish.

'I will become a great painter,' astonishing myself with the certainty of the phrase. There is a feeling behind the ordinary aspect of religious things, candles and matches, which brings out hidden desires, promises so much. The Virgin looks on benignly as if inviting me into her quiet, contemplative life. It would be pleasant to follow. Perhaps a second candle might bring that kind of peace. The sun is shining through the few stained-glass windows and the colours are lustrous like enamelled miniatures.

Saying goodbyes, Gus insists on a family photograph. The boys are too active to pose, scurrying in and out of the room with their teddy bears pretending to pursue a mouse. So, there are just the four of us – Gus, Ida holding baby Robin, and me.

'Dorelia is amazingly competent; she handles a camera like Julia Margaret Cameron herself.' Ida adopts a fixed smile.

'Then the photograph will probably be out of focus.' Gus sarcastic as ever. 'But at least quicker than waiting for one of your portraits, Gwen.'

Gus is positioning us as we were in the first photograph we had taken in a studio. Then Ida was clutching David in swaddling clothes. How many babies will she endure? Dorelia bends over the Frena without replying. As we stand breathing in to hold our positions, what will I think of the photograph in years to come? Gus staring hard at Dorelia behind the camera, thumb in jacket pocket, a leg confidently sticking forward; Ida cradling the baby, leaning against Gus, as if tired before the day has begun; me apart from them both, shoulders pushed back as if disassociating myself from the family tableau? Eccentric again, I am not wearing a hat. None of us smile.

∼

Waves slap the sides of the ferry as it pulls away from Dover heading for Boulogne. Every so often one wave dwarfs the others.

In Tenby the seventh wave was always the tallest, cresting over me as I flung myself under and the waves shaped the shoreline too, with snakes of water engraving lines on the sand. Ahead in the mist, Rodin's fingers will soon carve my statue and the thought makes me content. The vision hovers gleaming until the sun breaks through the clouds. I will be home soon.

CHAPTER 18

RILKE, PARIS

Rodin's studio is even dustier than usual, but I barely notice with the excitement of being there again.

'Euripides resembles you, my master; he believed everything has beauty.' To anyone else that would sound pretentious, but Rodin is so knowledgeable and appreciates well-read people. I want him to know I am intelligent, and so the Greek stories I read for him, tumble out. Rodin twitches. Is he irritated with the way the clay is refusing to adhere to the frame? Or with me? Perhaps the Muse will take longer than he imagines, a happy thought for today. I continue to proclaim a speech I translated as if I am alongside the heroes in ancient Greece, but Rodin is scowling.

'Stop talking; your French has not improved. I have a headache; and you are becoming too thin for the statue. You must eat more.'

'If I were Rose, sharing your bowl of morning milk, I would fatten up.'

'You know this is impossible.'

A dull pain envelops my body. He works for nine hours at a time on the Muse. We share ten-minute pauses. There is little time for food, and I am too exhausted to eat much in the evenings. Rodin is so absorbed in his work. Today, he stares at me as a vivisector would, measuring the structure of my body and displaying no emotion, while I am full of emotions welling up. The continual distress reduces my flesh, and my cheeks are hollower every time I look in a mirror. I read myself to sleep with his volume of Greek myths, learning a story to intrigue him today but it seems all in vain.

'You must understand, carving is delicate. I need to focus completely. I do care for you.'

The word 'care' is enough, and my head is now firmly in position, strength rushing back. In the silence, thick between us, it feels like the smallest movement will ruin our reconnection and I stay completely still. All afternoon, Rodin is working so close, he will hear my heart, the way the rhythm changes every time he glances up from the statue directly at me.

'My new secretary arrives in an hour. We are making sense of my paperwork together.'

'So, we will not make love tonight?' She will be beautiful, intelligent. He said I have become thin, so he will want a more rounded body to sculpt. Will she become his lover? Most women seem to; and I cannot attract him with my stories it seems.

'No time. I might come to your room soon. I would like you to meet the secretary. We will finish early, so you can dress before he arrives. His name is Rainer Maria Rilke.'

A man. The relief is tangible. Rose, his other models, so many women, at least the secretary is male.

'Concentrate, the Paris Salon is in three months. We need to finish.'

'Finish.' My muscles tense as if to push away the word. I thought the pattern of my life was fixed: posing for my master and then others for funds, preparing my room and myself for his visits, enjoying the ecstatic pleasure of his lovemaking, and then painting fulfilled by his love. If he finishes the statue our life will be over too.

'Now that the day is ending, may I tell you another story? I have learnt the whole play Iphigenia by heart in the original French. So you will find my account completely accurate.'

He gives me a loving glance. Everything is calm immediately.

'I would like to hear, but do not move. A promise. After the Muse is finished, we will visit Rome together. I need inspiration.'

'My Master!' Possibilities are whirling. 'The weather will be fine, and I will wear the maroon dress you admire.' I cannot stop. 'I will take care of practical matters while you admire the classical statues.' A bright vision of the two of us, painting together in the Forum – a new dream. 'When we return to Paris, you will visit my room and be fully restored.'

'All in good time. Iphigenia can amuse me today.'

An hour later, the assistants are milling behind the screens. Their chatter is as regular a signal of the day's end as Sacré-Coeur's bell.

'We will cease for today. Get dressed.'

Rodin seems not to have learnt that conversations require questions, that questions and answers grow into relationships, but his sharp, barked out commands, are not so troubling anymore. At first, I thought a lack of questions implied boredom with me, or a refusal to share his life. Now his orders clarify the direction he wants us to follow, although sometimes I feel my own ideas are being ignored.

A voice floating over the screen sounds new. It must be the secretary. As I lace up my boots, Rodin washes the clay from his hands. How will he introduce me? Friend, favourite model? Lover will be impossible.

'*Mademoiselle* John, *Monsieur* Rainer Rilke.'

My name, nothing more. A frisson of disappointment is overcome by Rilke's warm '*bon soir*,' crossing with mine in mid-air. He smiles under a thin moustache. The dark eyes are almost as beautiful as Rodin's azure but have a gentle self-effacing quality. His smooth hair is greased back from his face, and a slim body exudes bashfulness, like a figure standing at the side of a painting, not the focus.

'So pleased to meet you, *Mademoiselle* John,' the scent of ink wafting from his fingers as we shake hands. 'I am writing a book about *Maître* Rodin. If you would be so kind, perhaps we could talk over tea?'

'I would be delighted,' and glance quickly at Rodin, but he

nods distractedly, which usually means he is intent on returning to Meudon.

'Careful Rilke, Marie can talk all day.'

He calls me Marie now to Rilke and the unease is evaporating, even though when we are all outside on the street, Rodin marches off to the station without another word.

'I will need to be at home with my wife and daughter by seven, will an hour's conversation be tolerable?'

Rilke's narrow face is intelligent rather than handsome, with none of Rodin's magnificent brow, but he seems pleasant. Knowing he is married and will not make advances, is restful after my encounters with strange men.

'Perfect. There is a café on the corner of the street, to the left. I am fatigued after modelling, and tea will restore me while we talk.'

The café is half empty, and tea and madeleines arrive promptly.

'Rodin calls me Marie. My name is Gwendolen Mary John, but Marie reminds him of his long-dead sister, he informed me. You can call me Marie or Gwen.'

'I will call you Marie as Rodin does. I changed my first name too – from René to Rainer. I was told René wasn't manly.' He blushes.

There is something endearing about men who blush, who reveal their emotions, their vulnerabilities.

'Which name does your daughter prefer?'

'She is two and switches from papa to animal names at will,' producing a bent daguerreotype from his jacket.

'She is beautiful; I was never a beautiful child.'

'The *Maître* said that you are one of his most graceful models.' Rilke looks surprised. 'When I look at his statue of you, I see a model and her maker sharing their souls.'

Is it true? Rilke's news fills the café with joy, banishing all the tiredness.

'I try to project emotions when I pose,' draining my cup.

'As I do in my poetry; emotions trigger our deepest sentiments. For my Rodin book, I would be grateful if you could speak more about your modelling and Rodin's work.'

There is so much to say – about how Rodin prefers to make armatures to stabilise the maquettes before scaling up to statues, and how my sensations connect with Rodin's when I model – and the hour passes too quickly. Chatting to Rilke is like swimming in warm water, lifting my body without effort, floating on a tranquil sea. Rilke is the brother I should have had – sympathetic, in tune with my feelings.

CHAPTER 19

PARIS THE DUCHESS

Next morning the concierge calls me into her apartment and hands me a letter. 'This arrived for you.' Given the size of her voice, she should tower over me, but she is tiny. The hall is decorated with flock wallpaper and a side table laden with unsteady figurines, like an interior in a Victorian domestic scene. Edgar is always tucked safely under my arm when we pass in and out. A large mirror hanging on the opposite wall shows the skin under my eyes dark with tiredness, my hand shaky holding the envelope. Recognising the handwriting, I rush up to my room, listening for footsteps in case Rodin is about to arrive. Often his notes come minutes before he does but the house is silent.

The note is not what I expect and certainly not what I desire.

'*The Muse is unfinished,*' he writes.

I know this, it is the key to continuing as Rodin's model.

'*I am starting another statue – a Bacchante,*' he continues, '*using the finest marble from Greece. You will not need to model for a while. Chère ami Rodin.*'

Rodin must have found another woman. What can she be like? Her skin must be so smooth if fine marble is required. He has evidently forgotten about Rome, about visiting me weekly, but what inspired the change? Bacchante suggests ribald pleasure; I have read Rodin's book of Greek myths, so I know about

Bacchus's dissolute life. The concierge knocks and asks what has occurred.

'Thank you but I need to rest,' as I throw myself down on the bed

Rodin always manages to work on several commissions simultaneously with many assistants. So focussing only on one is hugely significant; the new statue is using a model more important to him than me and I must find out more. I will never be able to paint until I do. I will go to the studio and peek around the door, so Rodin cannot see me. He is always too busy sculpting, and staring at his model, to take any notice. Pulling on my cloak, the folds almost knock over one of the concierge's little pieces on my rush to the street. As the cab rattles through the city to rue de l'Université, I wrestle with my decision. What if Rodin *does* see me?

Climbing out of the cab, with a flutter of anxiety, one of the studio doors is locked, and the other partially open. I will have to pass right in front of the porter's lodge but why worry? The porter has been friendly in the past, so I smile as broadly as I can.

'*Mademoiselle* John,' and the porter comes out from behind his desk, 'the *Maître* gave me instructions not to admit you today.'

He does not remove his cap and his face is blank, unmoving as if he is turning into an additional door to prevent my passage through to the studio. I take a minute, leaning against his office wall, to stare over his shoulder for an assistant I know, for anyone who can help, but the courtyard is empty. Sharp cracks and chisels tapping in rhythm, sear the air. Closing my eyes, I am immersed in the sound, as I always am in the dust of Rodin's work, in the smell of him. Before I sink to the ground, an arm supports my waist.

'*Mademoiselle* John – Marie, permit me to assist,' and Rilke hands me his silk handkerchief.

Tears are on my cheeks; my collar is damp. Rodin will hate such a public display on the doorstep of his studio. 'Thank you. I do not know what came over me.'

'I do. We must talk. You need a brandy,' guiding me across the street to the neighbourhood brasserie.

The plush bench absorbs my tremors and Rilke summons a waiter, asking for two brandies and bowls of soup.

'*Mademoiselle* is a trifle poorly,' as the waiter jots down the request, glancing sideways at me.

The mirror on the opposite wall places Rilke and I into a gold ornate frame – his thin, sensitive face alongside my flushed cheeks, the skin under my eyes puffy. The image resembles Degas's L'Absinthe with my absent expression. The brandy burns my throat, but it is down in one gulp and Rilke orders more.

'My cottage is in the grounds of Rodin's Meudon home.' Rilke speaks carefully as if about to describe a detective case. 'We all go to bed early after conversations, and at seven-thirty each morning Rodin and I discuss the day's correspondence before travelling together to the Paris studio.'

'I know this,' I say, blowing my nose.

'I am describing my day, so you will understand how much I see of Rodin, how much I know. I am his confidant. So, when I describe his feelings, his loves, it is the truth not a literary fable.'

A slim notebook is tucked into his jacket pocket.

As if noticing my glance, Rilke gives a faint smile. 'I might transfer my life into verse but never the other way around. What I am about to say are facts. I am afraid that your powers of endurance have to be further tried.'

The salt and pepper remain on the other side of the table. The soup is untouched.

'Tell me all, Rainer. Rodin has never pushed me to the edges of his life before. I once asked him not to describe his other women, but now I need to know.'

'Do you love him?' Rilke gazes straight at me.

'It is more than love. Strength rushes into me when I am in Rodin's arms. I am overcome by a capacity for living, which I have never experienced before.'

Tears threaten again, and Rilke holds up my brandy glass to my lips.

'My dear. I understand. Although my friendship with Rodin is not the same as a relationship, I too am overcome with joie de vivre every day with him.'

We are sitting side by side, silent for a moment, against the velvet bench. The restaurant is almost empty, and the waiters are congregating around the bar at the other end of the room. Could I lean on Rilke, have him cuddle me like a brother – but more tears would fall.

'Rodin and I are united in our thoughts, and in art.'

'Then I am sorry to have to say that you must prepare to wait for a time before he will see you again. He has another model – the Duchesse de Choiseul.'

'A duchess? She must be wealthy. Has she paid a good deal for her statue?'

'I do not know.' Rilke picks up his glass. 'She often spends money on clothes. She is a duchess by marriage – an American who has fallen for Rodin. Like us,' he adds, with a slight laugh. 'I fear our Master is mesmerised by her. She established herself in his building.'

Will she take Rodin away from me? There is the masculine Rodin, the man tempted by young girls, who thinks of conquest and of me. The other Rodin, the great artist in touch with world affairs, with life outside Paris, must desire travelled women like the Duchess. Women unlike me.

'She drinks. They talk all day, and she has installed a phonograph in his studio. They dance,' and he smiles, 'not very well.'

Dancing always seems so frivolous, and parties have those moments when talk spills easily from other people's lips and I am usually a wallflower. Am I capable of attracting him again?

'None of us like her. I prefer the company of women artists like you. My wife sculpts.'

I try to look calm. All I can hope is the Duchess drinks excessively and eventually disgusts Rodin. I want her dead. Perhaps she could cross the street drunk, and be run down by a tram, like the British member of parliament, whose name I can never remember, killed by a train. I pass over the handkerchief and Rilke pats my hand.

'Would you like me to accompany you home?'

'You are very kind, but I am well enough now to take the tram.'

∼

Without Rodin I will be alone like my paintings – pictures of isolation – usually one woman, in one chair, stuck in one room – a solitary being. I like to believe the works are about women's lives in modern cities but in truth they are about my own sense of loneliness. At the Slade, tutors described my art in terms of tones and McEvoy focussed on glazes; but the empty spaces around my figures are as significant as the techniques. Only my art can save the emptiness from taking over my life.

CHAPTER 20

PARIS THE DUCHESS (2)

The tram to Rodin's studio is muggy today; passengers have drained the air and left nothing for me. As if sensing my new purposefulness, the tram was timely and the tramlines rattle, underscoring my feelings. I know what I must do when I reach Rodin. My Master's responsibility is to public art like Whistler's Muse and hence to me, not to the Duchess. He cannot finish the Muse without me. The statue is a major public piece, will bring him even greater fame, so the Duchess must be instructed that I continue to model. My face in the tram window looks forbidding and the other passengers seem to glance away. My hands are clenched into fists as if about to crash my way into his studio, but it is her face which deserves a clout.

The tram stop is a street away from the studio but alighting now and walking there will calm my nerves. Around the corner into rue de l'Université, past the cafes, and the handkerchief square of green, the paving stones are shiny with early morning dew. A customer at the café is slicing his brioche into pieces; the silver knife glints as it travels back and forth across the risen surface. It is her puffy face I wish to attack. Shivering, clutching my coat tight around me, detesting how these emotions sweep over me, damping down my reason, I cannot seem to control myself. Should I have worn a disguise? It is too late now.

What will the Duchess look like? Rilke described an American accent, her propensity for drink and dancing, but not her face or height. Is she short like me? Or taller than my Master? Surely, he could not love an Amazon because he would hate being dwarfed. Does she dress stylishly? Almost certainly. She spends money on clothes, Rilke said, and my Master likes his women to be well dressed. She will wear a couture Paul Poiret dress, immaculate, chic. A flash of Rodin's face hovering above a beautiful woman, ecstasy filling his eyes, is right here in front of me.

The Duchess will apply powder and rouge after modelling, a vain, decorative appendage to Rodin. What else will she do to attract him? My Master enjoys new foods, so she will cook American meals – chowders and corn breads – offering many more skills than me. Is she clever? Most of his models act as his secretaries. I tried to translate English works for him, but my French is execrable he said. Tears are welling up again and I pat them with the sleeve of my coat. If the studio doors are locked, I will wait at one side until they leave; but she might step away in high-heeled boots, refusing to even glance at me.

I am right – ahead the high gates are barred. The workmen are locked in, sequestered along with my Master and her as if he is afraid to be seen. A woman passing stares sharply so I must be talking aloud. A respectably dressed elderly man walking towards me, glances curiously too. It has become second nature chattering away, practising my stories en route to Rodin. There must be a safe spot to wait. The café is too far up the street. I might miss them from there.

An artist's shop, directly opposite the gates, is perfectly positioned. Holding my notebook, as if intent on jotting down prices, glancing up every few minutes, time passes slowly. After an hour, my arms ache with the weight of my bag; but the plate-glass window feels cool against my face, and I try to avoid the eyes of people in fashionable narrow, gored coats with fur cuffs, hoping no one will stare. The studio gates remain closed. My teeth are clenched nervously together. A light mist is blocking out the afternoon sun; but in my rush my umbrella is at home. There is a striped awning over a laundry next door, partially covering the pavement and I nod to the ladies inside. They are too busy pummelling clothes to notice me.

When Rodin and the Duchess emerge, I will not be able to stay calm. Anger is bubbling up at an image of her spread legs and Rodin inches from her quim. I want to strike her, punch her so that she will lie unconscious, her face white and drawn. A shuffling sound comes towards me. A grubby drunk holds out a brandy bottle. Was I talking again? Turning, making a porthole in the now mist-covered window of the laundry, as if looking for my clothes, he is dissuaded and staggers off. The bell of Sacré-Coeur chimes five. I am faint with hunger and wet in the thin drizzle. A crack sounds across the street, and the doors open. My Master emerges, holding onto the arm of a woman. She is a stunner – wearing a tight-waisted emerald-green robe tailleur, and a wide-brimmed straw hat decorated with flowers crammed onto vivid red hair – and my Master smiles at her. I have rarely seen him seem so happy. As I rush across the street, oblivious of traffic, automobile hoots blare out.

'You are monopolising my Master,' my voice rises with each word.

They stare at me as if they have seen a ghost. I am a ghost to my Master now he has banished me from the studio.

'A little bird tells me.' And I stand right in front of her, screaming in her face, 'you've been exhausting my Master with high living.'

'You are hysterical,' and she frowns at me like scolding a bad-tempered little girl.

Rodin puts his arm around her shoulders, bringing her to one side, as if to push past me.

'You are distracting him from his art,' as tears pour down.

She is speechless, her eyes disdainful, as if I am an insect on her coat which she can brush off in a moment.

'Stop this,' Rodin is angrier than ever before. 'You must not appear in my studio without my express invitation.' And they sweep up the street to the station.

My best velvet coat cannot protect me from the stares of passers-by. What are they thinking? A harridan, or worse a prostitute? Drained and shivering, I thank goodness the tram is grinding to a halt to carry me home.

It is over, Rodin will never sculpt me again. A towel dries my wet hair but not my tears. What can I write to bring him back?

My dear Master

This letter is the most difficult I have ever written but my letters are my only contact with you. Today I stood in the street all alone, but you ignored me in favour of your American friend. It seems you have been claimed by society at the expense of your art. Please consider returning to your important public work like The Muse.

If it were not for my letters, I would be invisible, would I not? I have a spirit as well as a body.

The word 'friend' saves me from despair, from imagining the two of them in bed. I cannot mention the phonograph or dancing. Rilke might cease our friendship if Rodin is suspicious of my source of information. Tears trickle again, and I let a few drops drip onto the page to amplify the message. The letter is finished, and it is midnight, but I must end on a flourish – a phrase to attract him again.

All great men receive letters from the women who love them. Seneca was filled with pleasure, reading letters from his Paulina.

Votre amie, Marie

My Master will admire my knowledge. Through the window, the moon is obscured by clouds, with the houses silhouetted black against the grey sky. There are seven hours to go before the studio gates will open for the day, before I can deliver my letter, but sleep is beyond me tonight, so I dress quickly. Outside the quartier is empty, silent, allowing me to talk to Rodin in my head in the fresh air. In the next street, a few revellers, returning home, stare. I have forgotten my hat and gloves. Will men think me a prostitute? It matters little as long as they do not proposition me. Paris is emptying for the night with waiters stacking chairs onto tables at closed cafes. At least no one is enjoying themselves. Around the corner, the streets lead in the direction of the Seine, and the dark sky weighs down on my shoulders.

At the Left Bank, a cold breeze carries the dank scent of the slow-moving river, and the steps of Pont de l'Alma bridge are easy to climb to the parapet. The black water below reflects house lights and the lamps at the prows of moored barges, and I lean over to see the wake of the last barge tonight making its way to the coast.

'Careful young lady. Do not reach further.'

An elderly street-seller clad in a thick shawl, nods, an empty basket hanging on one arm. 'Why are you here?'

'Resting for a moment.'

'You are a foreigner?'

'English, and I am all alone in Paris.' Tears are dripping onto my lap. Moments of my times with Rodin surface, the odd words of tenderness like the isolated islands in the Seine.

'A pretty young thing can always find friends in Paris.'

The breeze is chillier here than in boulevard Edgar Quinet, and I shiver, pulling my coat tight across my chest.

'Take my other arm before a gendarme comes,' as I stare again into the black water.

'Thank you,' and climb down.

Above, a shard of light pierces the clouds, and the first rays of the sun are just visible. I can deliver my letter in an hour or so.

CHAPTER 21

PARIS, RODIN VISITS

Next morning at ten I am barely awake. The letter must be delivered soon to placate Rodin otherwise he will bar me for life. Last night, I dreamt of Rodin making love to me but as he was about to begin, Gus appeared. Neither man seemed startled by the surprise visit and Rodin immediately ceased lovemaking. Gus asked Rodin to accompany him to the station. 'Come back, come back afterwards,' I cried to Rodin; but he said no, dressed quickly and left. By the time I struggled into my clothes to follow, they had both disappeared, and I woke up. It will take me until lunchtime to recover but the dream's meaning is clear. Rodin does not want to be alone with me. How could he after my attack on the Duchess? And Gus would share his view. The dream spills out into the room, whose walls seem to close tight around. Through the window it is a cloudy day.

After two weeks there is no reply from Rodin. My modelling routine eases me through the day, posing for Hilda and other women artists, sometimes for Miss Hart next door, but always in the afternoons. Mornings are kept free for painting and in case Rodin visits. First thing each day, I carefully clean all the furniture and floors, water the ferns, and then freshen myself, paying particular attention to my hair.

Rodin loves my hair he said. Mornings are also for study – the books Rodin lent me: Schopenhauer and William James – so that I can be worthy of my lover, but the wisdom of philosophers is so far away. Any empty hours are filled with sketches using pencil and washes with delicate tones but dynamic forms, consoling me by their novelty.

Today Miss Hart is dressed more conventionally in an almost feminine floral smock and slim ankle boots; rather than the workmen's boots she normally favours. Even her loud voice seems softer today and she is being very gracious as we finish the modelling session.

'Stay for liqueurs and madeleines,' and hands me a crystal glass. 'You are pallid and need bolstering. What do you enjoy in the afternoon when you are alone?'

'Tea and cake. Marmalade cake is my favourite, but the madeleines are delicious. Thank you.'

'After all this time, you are resolutely English.'

Rodin prefers English women, he told me once, so I cling onto my English accent, style and preference for tea, but the liqueur is relaxing. Is this why Miss Hart is pouring me another glass? We sit on her sole two chairs in companionable silence, listening to the tip tap of pedestrians in the street below, drifting through the open shutters.

'Are you modelling still for Rodin? You have made no mention of him for a while.'

'He is busy finishing another maquette.'

'I heard some idle talk about Rodin from Hilda Flodin,' she stares hard at me, 'when I visited her last week.'

Placing my glass on the table gives me a moment to breathe.

'There is always gossip about Rodin. Because he is so famous, people like to claim they know him in some way.'

'It is about his latest lover, the Duchess. It seems she has taken charge of Rodin's finances, become his manager, arranges his exhibitions.'

The liqueur is too warm, and the madeleines are too hard.

'He often asks his models to be his secretaries, especially if Rilke's away. I translate Rodin's English letters for him.' It was true once but months ago.

'What do you think of her? They say she cannot bear children, and her fiery red hair is a wig.'

Rilke made no mention of any of this, but a woman knows what matters to other women. So there can be no child to bring them closer, keep them entangled and my smile is instantaneous.

'Another glass?' Miss Hart scrutinises my expression.

'You are truly kind, but no thanks.'

I am already tipsy and must concentrate on tonight's letter to Rodin. The letters take hours to write because my French is too banal, and to impress Rodin letters need a more literary vocabulary. At that moment, there is a tap at my door across the corridor. Perhaps the concierge has a note from my Master. At last a reply to my letter.

'You have a visitor, I think,' Miss Hart pours herself a third glass.

'It is probably the concierge. Edgar may be up to mischief.'

With Miss Hart's door firmly closed behind me, ahead there is a burly dark shape wearing an immaculate jacket and shiny top hat. I have rarely seen Rodin so clean, normally clay spatters everything. Is he trying to impress me? My heart flutters and my key misses the lock needing both hands to steady it into position; and manage to guide him into the room like a normal visitor.

'It is good to see you again,' and he hangs his hat on a hook. 'Forgive me for my abruptness the other day. The event was so sudden I had no time to think, and since then I have been besieged by clients.'

'You might have written a note. I did apologise by letter immediately,' desperately trying not to nag, but I cannot help myself. Edgar is mimicking my irritation, pawing at Rodin's shoe. Normally, I would have rushed her into the kitchen, but today the scratch on the polished surface seems appropriate. Rodin glances at me, as if uncertain what to do or say. The last rays of the sun collect on his face making him golden, handsome, and suddenly his mouth is on mine, and his arms are around my waist, pressing himself against me. His lips taste of cigars. I scarcely hoped he would want me again and cannot resist. He holds me tight as if I am a spirit about to fly away.

'I have missed you Marie,' his voice thick, deep, as he releases me to undo his jacket.

I want to be distant, appear unwilling, but I cannot wait, and slip out of my clothes quickly while his eyes are on my breasts, and I am in his arms, as he pushes me down on the bed.

Later at dusk, Rodin stands and dresses. It is the first time he has stayed for more than an hour. We must have dozed for an age; the moon is shining in the window. He watches me, examining my body, as if reluctant to leave.

'I have decided to pay rent on better accommodation for you. Try to find an unfurnished room. Then you can make it your own and I will cover all the costs.'

'I cannot let you pay for furnishings as well as a room. But I will buy exactly what you like, with the savings on the rent.'

I am the sole mistress to have an apartment paid for by my Master. I will learn to tolerate the Duchess and other lovers; they can never be as much a part of his life as me. My Master wants me to live in a beautiful room especially for him. It will be almost as good as a full-time lover. Perhaps even better.

'I will try to visit every week,' and puts on his hat, 'but I cannot promise.'

'I will write to you. We will be together in print.'

'And I am returning to the Muse next week. Be at the studio on Monday, at the usual time.'

As the door closes behind him, the whole room is moonlit. My Master wants to be with me every week and will make love to me after modelling as before. His studio is floating in front of me, candlelit, our bodies intertwined on the couch behind the screens. Here, the moon is full and very bright tonight.

CHAPTER 22

RUE ST PLACIDE, PARIS

It is a warm spring and tramping the neighbouring streets to find an apartment the air feels humid and heavy. I would prize a place nearer Rodin's studio, but his quartier is expensive, and at least here Bon Marché is close by, the tea room a tantalising prospect in today's temperature, although I cannot afford to be tempted into buying things en route to tea. Last week's Bon Marché velvet shawl cost the equivalent of five afternoons of posing.

Rue St Placide's busy traffic between wide pavements, reminds me of Malet Street and walking down to the British Museum with Ursula. Shutting my eyes, in an instant I am back. London places and people often appear so shiveringly real as if I can reach out to them, like the first sighting of Rodin. At the end of the street, the Luxembourg Gardens' last few cherry trees in bloom scatter their pink blossoms over passers-by. At my left, a decorated window sticker catches the sun. An apartment for rent. Number seven. Something about the flowers, or the pretty little shops makes me feel at home, as well as the proximity to Bon Marché and the gardens. A few minutes later, a concierge, whose bosom enters a large, empty room before she does, lists all the features.

'You overlook a courtyard, Mademoiselle; and the wallpaper and pink floor suits a young woman.'

The yard will be ideal for Edgar's exercises.

'You may take the room for as long as you wish.'

'It is perfect. Who else lives in the house?'

'My house is quiet and respectable. *Mademoiselle* Pelletier next door is a laundress but does not do her washing at home.'

An odd reply. Laundresses always work in laundries never at home. The concierge looks impatient but at least she is friendly, with no lewd husband visible.

The wallpaper is pretty and the pink floor. The curtains are simple white muslin.

'I will rent the room.'

With luck, rue St Placide will be as serene as its name.

For days, every evening after modelling, I carry items from Hôtel Mont Blanc until everything is moved. The new concierge has kindly placed a plank as a windowsill for my ferns and flowers, and I thoroughly clean the pink floor until it shines. Rodin's first visit will make the room truly beautiful.

∽

'It is a pity you have moved.' Miss Hart is waving her chisel. 'I will miss seeing you each day, but we should celebrate your new apartment all the same.'

After posing for her all afternoon my legs are cramped and stiff. Another morning passes without a visit from Rodin to my new home despite him initiating my move. But in a note which the concierge pressed into my hand as I left for Miss Hart's, he did say that he would sell my drawings for me. His care, his thoughtfulness makes me content.

'May I move?' and stretch my legs.

'Of course, apologies. What about joining me and the girls at the Gaîté-Montparnasse tonight? I can promise free champagne and amusements galore.'

Sudden invitations are unsettling. Every day must have its own pattern mapped out the evening before, otherwise my anxiety rises like a violent storm, but the evening sounds an adventure.

'That would be delightful. The Gaîté – is that a Sapphic bar?' I can be open with Miss Hart. She knows about Rodin.

'There are couples, singles, men dressed as women, women

dressed as men. Artists and actors carouse with everyone. Return here at nine pm. Miss Gerhardie and a few other women are attending. You remember her – the German painter?'

'What shall I wear?'

'Anything bright. Please not your old browns. See you at nine.'

At night, Paris resembles a Canaletto painting of Venice, with lights dancing on the Seine. Ahead, Miss Gerhardie is linking arms with Miss Hart. I have already forgotten the names of the other two women, but formality is not important tonight, and they seem friendly enough. By day, Montparnasse is full of artists bustling back and forth, but now the streets are empty, and our perfume wafts us through the dying smells of pommes frites. In my excitement I forgot to eat, but the cooking smells from the concierge's flat deter any hunger.

At the Gaîté, there is already a queue surging through a baroque entrance. Inside, the café hums with chatter and singing, and oil lamps in red lampshades cast a warm glow over top hats and glinting jewellery. The windows are drowning in greenery, turning the room into an intimate bower. A few women are extremely tall, and Miss Hart leans over, whispering 'female impersonators'.

'Slade students often dressed up as the other sex; and at Whistler's ball here in Paris.'

My voice betrays me, too nervous to sound sophisticated. Miss Hart winks.

At a piano, a singer taps out a lively tune and the glasses of champagne the waiter delivered to our table are immediately refilled.

'Who is paying for all this?' I whisper to Miss Hart, but she is engrossed with her friends.

'The dancers are next,' Miss Hart strains her voice to be heard above the hubbub.

Women with tight corsets file onto the stage. It is a tarantella. Jerking, twisting bodies fill the entire space, threatening to fall off the platform. Their thick, tinted hair and black-rimmed eyes startle as much as their crimson, voracious mouths. Toulouse-Lautrec's posters pale in comparison with these three-dimensional erotic women.

'I can see you're intrigued.' Miss Gerhardie smiles.

Is my flush from the sight ahead, the heat of the room, or the champagne? It is impossible to say. My models are always demure, wear grey, many with downcast eyes, and their breasts resemble mine – flat and small. I want to stroke the skin of these women, feel their ample breasts, with nipples firm like little pebbles. A top-hatted man thrusts notes into a dancer's cleavage, and she blows him a kiss. Before my hand can follow his, the showgirls are high kicking off the stage. A hum of voices hovers over, enclosing me in a bubble of happiness. In a blink, Dorelia's breasts are in front of me – the early mornings when I woke lying on their soft mounds, but this is different. It feels as if I have walked into an erotic book, whose pages I am desperate to turn for the full sensation of voluptuousness.

Miss Hart kisses me on both cheeks when we reach rue St Placide.

'I am delighted to see you enjoying yourself. You must spend evenings more frequently with us girls.'

'I will. It has been an amazing few hours.'

Rodin's note about my drawings is still there on the table but I push it to one side, and slip naked between the sheets, spreading my legs, reaching for my quim with a finger, and keep the rhythm regular and even, rubbing up and down. Tonight, the crescendo is immediate. I can pleasure myself.

∽

After posting a letter to him next morning, the erotic feelings substitute for breakfast. An hour later, after dusting and watering the ferns, the room is restored to itself but in a new way. The wardrobe's full-length mirror reveals a contented woman, surrounded by my beloved objects – my wicker chair – a Dutch interior. Placing a stretched canvas on the easel, it is time for a new self-portrait. The muted early light blends everything together as if a gentle melody trembles through the air. I am painting again with last night's pleasures filling my mind and my figure is dynamic, original in its clear detail and surfaces and my careful, layered construction.

CHAPTER 23

A THREESOME

Rodin is furious. His note almost flings itself from the envelope. In future you must sleep with your hands crossed on your chest, he writes. Like the other Mary, the virginal one. Rodin switches emotions as brutally as he turns off the water tap in his sink, and I am uncertain what to reply. Mentioning masturbation should have triggered his desire. Instead, it seems, he is infuriated yet again; but at least my room is a haven, and my Master will admire my painting.

My canvas stands in one corner reflecting another corner with my wicker chair and table. The self-portrait contains a woman reading, sitting as I do when reading Rodin's books. Somehow, as I paint, my fingers have a kind of energy, stretching out to fill the room, pointing to feelings, thoughts. After a couple of hours, the pose seems more certain, a good contrast with the shadowy background.

'*Mademoiselle*,' the concierge wearily opens the door. 'Another letter.'

Disappointingly, it is Hilda Flodin's scrawl, not Rodin's but perhaps she is offering me some modelling and it will be pleasurable to see Hilda again. We can talk about our latest work. Sometimes Hilda's Sapphic cravings are in her eyes, and erotic poses are tricky, but art discussions are safe ground, and I can talk about my self-portrait. Every new painting encourages my growth, and I have managed to create meticulous layers.

Her message is urgent. I am to come immediately to her studio, not for modelling but because Rodin is there. My latest green and white gown is stretched across my nervous stomach, and I pray that he will be kind today after his harsh note, especially in front of Hilda my friend. The tram to the studio will take too long, and as a cab slows to a halt, my mouth is almost too dry to say the address clearly. Often cabbies are loquacious but luckily today's is silent because it is impossible to speak, and I need to practice controlling myself so as not to appear too eager.

With a deep breath, I gently knock on Hilda's door. She beams seeing me, taking my hand. Hers is hot, sweaty.

'He wants you; he wants both of us,' pushing me into her studio.

All the irritation about Rodin's abrupt notes, his temperamental emotions, drains away at the sight of him gazing at me, and when I scan his face for clues, he smiles. His frockcoat is dotted with clay, and my hands ache to pick off the tiny bits, stroke his body and lean into him, waiting for a kiss.

'Marie, you are beautiful today.' Rodin's cologne wafts over me as he kisses my hand. 'I want to make love to you, with Hilda looking on. She has agreed.'

Hilda nods, and tension flows between all of us as if we are on the same electricity current. No need for conversation. Rodin undresses first. In his studio, I am always first, naked for modelling, displaying myself for his pleasure; now, I clumsily swish off my cloak and unbutton my dress. He likes to slide his hands up my leg underneath my chemise. So, I wait for instructions, wanting him to pick me up like a doll and throw me down on Hilda's bed. She sits in a chair opposite, skirt pulled up, playing on her quim, staring at us.

'Take off your drawers and everything,' his voice is thick with desire, and I roll down my stockings slowly, feeling wet already.

Hilda's gaze is fixed on his member. The smell is intoxicating as Rodin gathers me in his arms. He knows I cannot resist his passion and he thrusts between my thighs. Hilda moans simultaneously, as Rodin turns my face away, as before, and enters me from behind. My arms are splayed out as if on a cross, with his arms on top, nailing me to the wall. His heart beats against my back and I climax as his hot stickiness drips onto the floor. Withdrawing carefully, he lifts me onto the bed as delicately as one of his maquettes.

'Hilda, please undress too, and be with Marie.'

She lies holding me, running a trembling finger over my breasts, then my thighs while Rodin dresses and reaches for his sketchpad.

'Place your breasts together; cupped by your hands.'

He sketches, using quick charcoal gestures, his eyes dark, dreamy. Absorbed in the work, his member grows large again in his trousers. The mirror opposite reflects Rodin's touch – the red marks on my arms, and the blush on my face – while he draws. Page after page drop on the floor speedily until at last, he stops and takes out a cheroot, studying us as if we are completed statues at his workstations.

'The past hour been one of the most erotic of my life. Again?' crossing over to him, wanting to sit on his lap, have him thumb me, take the ache away.

'I am exhausted, but Hilda will stroke you for certain.'

Kissing us both on each cheek, he stumps out his cheroot and leaves. Hilda and I are naked, shivering not with cold but with excitement, lying together and covering ourselves with a sheet. She brushes her lips over my breasts, reaching her hand between my thighs. Her fingers are not as strong as Rodin's thumb but stimulate me into a second crescendo. Hilda sweeps her tongue over my belly. She is not Rodin, but the sensation is pleasurable.

'You are delightful. We should make love when you next model,' as Hilda and I dress.

Her touch was intoxicating. After Dorelia left me, I renounced women, but Hilda's blonde hair on her body, a lighter shade than on her head, gives her an attractive glow.

'Perhaps,' and button up my coat.

∽

A note from Rilke is waiting when I return to rue St Placide. An invitation to drinks and conversation this evening in the brasserie near Rodin's studio, the place where Rilke first heard about my secret feelings for my Master. He has returned from Germany and wants the latest news. Intriguingly, he must trust me more than Rodin to tell him everything, but Rilke respects women artists. Few men do.

'You seem rested,' and slide onto the velvet bench opposite Rilke. 'Was the trip successful?'

'Perfect. My wife and I met old friends who discussed philosophy into the small hours.'

Ordering drinks from a passing waiter, he continues, 'We talked about the difficulties of creation and about romantic love; and naturally, I thought about you and Rodin. I do hope you are not immured in an abyss of love for him. You need to save yourself for your art.'

Rilke stares at me, as if his dark eyes could drill into my feelings, bring my emotions to the surface. He understands my sentiments. Talking with Rilke is like walking through a sunlit meadow – open to sensations, feeling the warmth of the sun on our backs. He has a wife and is completely unthreatening.

'The best news is that Rodin has returned to sculpting my Muse.' I will not describe today's event.

'Be careful not to be subservient to him, you need to work. Solitary artists are authentic creators. You are a genuine solitary, and I believe people will come to see you as a great artist.'

Rilke understands how important being independent is to me; but he cannot feel a woman's desire for a man, especially one as brilliant as Rodin.

'It is difficult to explain. Even when my moments with Rodin are infrequent, they excite me, fulfil my desires, inspire my art.'

After an hour's easy conversation, he beckons again for a waiter and orders pâté, bread, and olives. 'Is this simple dish of hors d'oeuvre acceptable?'

'Yes, thank you. For once I am extremely hungry.'

The olives are perfect. Their acidic, exquisite taste adds to my happiness. The afternoon with Hilda and Rodin was like drinking a fine wine and I can eat well for the first time for months. As we finish, Rilke leans over, patting my hand.

'I will make sure, if I can,' draining his glass, 'nothing will intimidate you in Rodin's studio. I can placate his temperamental outbursts. And all our discussions will be completely confidential.'

It has been discouraging not to be able to talk freely about Rodin with anyone else. Most of the women I sketch are besotted with him. Gus would scorn and I miss Ida and Ursula.

'Thank you, I do work best alone, but it is wonderful to have a protector. Augustus used to care for me at the Slade, but I rarely see him now.'

Rilke takes my arm as we leave the bar. 'Talk whenever you want to,' tipping his hat as he hands me onto a tram.

What an extraordinary day.

CHAPTER 24

PARIS, MADEMOISELLE PELLETIER

A sultry Tuesday summer afternoon, and it feels as if I have lived in rue St Placide for ever; I am completely at home. Today the canvas paint is drying too quickly. The room is breathless, humid, like the summers when we started swimming nude in the sea at Tenby. Only a chemise covers my nakedness as I paint. My pink dahlias are hanging their heads, as if their petals are dripping with perspiration. Edgar has flopped in the heat, and it is too hot to paint anymore – the Bon Marché tea room will be cool and shady. The canvas can do without me for an hour.

Last night, *Mademoiselle* Pelletier in the next-door room, was with a lover for the whole time. The squeaks and banging of her bedstead against the wall accompanied their cries and her squeals. Each day different men tramp up and down the stairs at odd times. Yesterday, Pelletier was leaving my room holding a key as I climbed the stairs, probably exploring more interesting venues for sex.

As I pick up my purse it feels thinner. Where is the twenty francs Rodin pressed into my hot hand at his last visit? I wanted to throw the money at his departing back, screaming I am not a prostitute but an artist, but twenty francs is enough for a week's food.

'Madam,' knocking on the concierge's door, 'money has disappeared from my purse.'

'Have you checked everything in your apartment?' her enormous breasts bristling with annoyance at the interruption.

'Yesterday, I saw Mademoiselle Pelletier leaving my room with a key.'

'She said she wanted to compare the rooms. We must call the police. Have her room searched.'

'It will be too late for the police; she is not at home and may be spending my francs now.'

I reach the brasserie at the end of the street in seconds, Pelletier's favourite haunt, the concierge added. The brasserie's interior is bright and busy with luncheons. At the end of the room, past the hors-d'oeuvres chariot, Mademoiselle sits, leaning against her lover, cigarette in hand, lips bright red. A white silk blouse is open down to her breasts, with gleaming artificial pearls nestling into the crease. Their table is strewn with empty oyster shells and two, almost empty, flasks of wine stand perilously close to the table edge. I picture smashing a flask down on her head.

'Are you enjoying your luncheon with my money?'

Startled, her hand shoots to the pearls as if praying on a rosary.

By good luck, the admirer is drunk, and the table hems them both into their bench against a wall. They cannot possibly reach me. The flasks rock when my hand slams down in front of her.

'Twenty francs now.' I am surprised by my ferocity.

Like an impressionist painting, the mirror behind the couple reflects the other diners' faces, their eyes widening. There is laughter behind my back, but they are staring at her not at me.

'Now.' She nods, removing a purse hidden up her skirt. The titters behind increase.

'So who will pay for the meal?' the lover slurs, his face whitening as if to vomit, and he slaps her hard.

A good aim. The twenty francs are damp from her sticky fingers, and I turn my back before she can change her mind. As I walk back to my room, the street shop windows show me enjoying my life. I am.

There is a letter from Gus waiting for me. Ida and Dorelia are travelling with him to Paris next month together with the six children – Ida's four and Dorelia's two. Ida is pregnant with her fifth. The family is welcome but only if they do not interrupt my painting.

∽

Ida's belly is more swollen than with earlier pregnancies.

'I trust it is not twins,' and kiss her on both cheeks as I welcome them all to my rooms.

'As do I,' Ida embraces me carefully. 'When I walk out, I am a great event.'

She seems exhausted.

'You are grand,' Dorelia smiles, 'like a moving mountain.'

The phrase is not kind.

'How is my little sister? What is the latest news?' Gus takes out a cheroot before clasping me to his chest.

'I spend much of my time in pleasurable pursuits. I have bought lovely materials from the Bon Marché.'

My new dresses boost my morale. I tried out the faille dress, wearing it without a coat, on the way to Rodin's studio. An elegant diner, smoking outside the brasserie called out 'beautiful woman'.

'That is not what I meant,' Gus stares quizzically. 'How is the modelling? We saw Rodin's study of your head at the Salon. He has captured your fiery spirit, and your alabaster skin.' Is that irony?

The sculpture's surface is as smooth as any I have seen in his studio. There was no invitation to the Salon's private view but to hear Gus's approval fills me with happiness.

'And your own work?' You should be sending paintings to the New English Art Club exhibitions.'

Only a half hour and already he nags. The boys are clutching his legs, interrupting his flow.

'A tisane will be good for your stomach.' I say to Ida, ignoring him. 'Let me make you all tea.'

'Thank you. Remember those sugar-coated biscuits we used to enjoy in Montparnasse?'

The boys, having failed to catch Gus's attention, brighten up at the word biscuit and start plucking at Ida's skirt, jumping up and down.

'Cease,' Gus says, wearily. 'We have an hour, no more. I have arranged to pick up the keys to our studio.'

'I am going to live in my own studio with my two boys, but we are all close – in rue de Château.' Dorelia adds. 'We can see each other often.'

She is as serene as the first time I caught her glance across the Bloomsbury room; but I feel no desire anymore.

As they all leave, Ida's swollen legs cause her to waddle down the stairs, and she clings onto my arm.

'Augustus has another woman. You have never met her. I am desperate. Do come and visit if you can.'

'I will. I promise.' I hug her. 'And I will bring those sugar biscuits.'

The boys are scampering around like terriers. Thank goodness my paintings are all the children I desire.

CHAPTER 25

PARIS, IDA

Another disturbed sleep after Gus and the family departed. He is right – I should be exhibiting more often. Modelling for Rodin stimulates my senses, and helps me to new ideas for painting, like last week's fresh colour co-ordination; but it is impossible to sleep with the dog in next door's courtyard howling all night. The noise is more than a whine, more than Ida's children crying for their mother's attention. There is an anguish, a torment as if the animal is in despair. As I wash and dress, Edgar is pacing in a circle in sympathy. There is a kind of feeling which different species share wordlessly. The howls must cease, and I will write to the Société Protectrice des Animaux for advice.

Later, armed with their reply that dog beaters can be prosecuted, I knock at the house next door with its intimidating façade.

The concierge is even fatter than mine, with unwashed hair, roughly pushed into a knot on her head, cigarette ash dripping onto the newspaper in her lap.

'Who has a dog in this building?' as I try to avoid her foul breath.

'I have two poodles. Who wants to know?'

'Me. I am Gwen John, an artist living next door. What is your name?'

'Why do you need my name?' and returns to her newspaper

'You have been brutalising a dog.'

From behind the concierge, a maid pushes her way towards me. 'We adore our dogs,' as her face reddens. 'We feed them with a silver spoon, and they sleep on satin cushions.'

Her dress, under a pinafore, has a tattered hem and her shoes are scuffed and grimy. Silver and satin are unlikely.

'I am reporting you both to the Société Protectrice.'

The maid turns to a tall man with a swarthy face, who emerges as our commotion becomes louder. He is bulky with wide shoulders.

'Tell her we are not dog beaters,' the maid yells at the man.

He looks me up and down.

'Stupid woman,' and points a knife directly at me. 'The noise comes from the street not us. Be off.'

The knife has serrations all along its length as if for sawing bones, and the man holds it close to my bodice; the concierge and maid are alongside, the dog straining on its lead gripped by the maid.

I slip backwards, one small step at a time. It is twenty feet to my door.

The three figures do not retreat, and the man slowly wipes the knife up and down his jacket arm as if sharpening the blade. His mouth is moving but I can only hear the blood in my ears. We stare at each other for one last second then I turn and run. The pavement is still wet with the early rain, and I force myself to move with exaggerated care around the puddles. I must not stumble.

'Be off with you,' I hear this time and dare not turn.

At last my house porch is in front, and for once the concierge has left the front door unlocked. As the door bangs fast behind me, I stand, breathless, my back to the door, listening for any sounds. The street is silent and back in my room, my face in the mirror reflects the passion I experienced. There is a new energy, a sense I can accomplish anything, and I report them to the Société.

Today's letter to Rodin will include a story about the dog. Often, I write to my Master in the form of a diary about whole days, to fix them on a page. It is as if I am creating a total picture of myself in print, as well as in paint, to preserve the days for ever and ever, for my life story. Tonight, time smooths out the minutes while I write, feeling unhurried, expansive, enjoying reliving the day's event. Someone working in a future archive will analyse my letters, seeking to understand my art, my life, and everything must be clear.

∼

'*Mademoiselle* John, *Mademoiselle* John,' the concierge is shouting outside my door, 'there is an urgent visitor.'

I slept sounder than ever before. Yesterday's event gave me a new sense of self.

'Coming,' and throw on a dress, arranging my hair in the mirror, confident that Rodin will be standing eagerly in the corridor, but the visitor is Ida's mother Ada, in tears. I last saw her at the wedding, and she has aged, her hair is completely grey.

'Come in, please come in. Has Ida had an accident?'

Ada slumps onto a chair, pulling a handkerchief from her bag.

'She asks for you. Ida gave birth and is feverish, in great pain. The doctors say the fever is peritonitis. She is near death.'

'But Ida is thirty.' What an idiotic thing to say; but I am scarcely a year older. Death seems such an impossibly distant future. 'Were there complications at the birth?' my tears welling up.

'No. Henry – the baby's name – was born safely,' and Ada stands. 'Please come now. I must return to my daughter. I moved her to a better hospital – the Maison de Soeurs – but she has not rallied.'

A cab will take too long in the traffic. The hospital is on my tram line, and we mount a tram, holding hands. Ada's are sticky, hot and she continues to cry. I cry too, desperate to see Ida and Gus.

'Augustus is with her; he will not leave her side.'

Perhaps my brother has become the husband Ida always wanted. The tram brakes at every stop and the fifteen minutes to the hospital seem interminable. Ada is exhausted, clinging to my hand as if, by bringing me to Ida's bedside, she will bring fresh energy. I must hope. I quickly buy some violets at the entrance to the hospital.

The Maison de Soeurs's large sash windows throw sunlight along the corridors as we hurry to Ida's room; the nuns guiding us are cheery; everything is so incongruous.

'She is delirious,' Gus rises from his chair to clasp me. His eyes are red, his beard uncombed. 'She has not slept since the birth.' His shoulders slump and tears trickle into his beard. Ida is pale grey, seemingly unconscious. Death must be near and an ache like a scream almost reaches my throat.

Ada sinks back into another chair beside the bed, and I clutch Ida's hand, lean close to her face and murmur in her ear.

'Ida, Ida, it's Gwen. We are all here. We love you. Please, please rally.'

Part of me knows it is ineffectual. I have no desire to live, she told me on the last visit. The children and Gus's affairs drain all her vitality.

'She has asked for all manner of things,' Gus says. 'I dashed around Paris buying perfume and those particular beef lozenges she loves. You know the kind.'

We stay with Ida for the next hours stroking her hands, taking turns to rest.

'I wrote to her sisters, but told them not to visit unless I wired,' Ada seems almost too weary to speak. 'If Ida sees them, she will know that she is at death's door. She must pull through.'

By late afternoon, rain lashes against the windows, rattling with a storm. Lights above the bed flicker, giving Ida's face a blue tinge.

'This morning she rallied and asked me to toast "Here's to love" with Vichy water; then she went far away.' Gus's eyes are brimming.

One of the nuns enters and wipes Ida's forehead with a damp napkin, taking her temperature. 'She cannot live much longer,' and checks the thermometer. 'God's will be done.'

A close-fitting white coif smooths away her hair but not the frown. She is as apprehensive as us.

Gus flings himself on the bed, howling like the dog next door to my apartment. Ada and I rub Ida's hands again and again, but she is unconscious, gives a little whimper and it is over. I am numb, watching the nun's lips move in prayer.

'We prepare her for the undertaker,' the nun places my violets in Ida's hands, kissing each in turn, before putting a large crucifix and candles next to the bed.

My body is cold, shivering, it is impossible to think of anything but pain. I have never seen a dead body and I never wish to again. The nun is gesturing that we should leave, and I help Ada to her feet. She tucks Ida's white sheet under the bottom of the mattress as if Ida is a little girl again. Gus watches, frozen.

'I cannot leave her.'

'*Monsieur*,' the nun says. 'The nuns will take turns to pray with her until she leaves the hospital; and we will pray for you too.'

Outside, the storm is over, and the evening sky is extraordinarily bright as if we have all been locked in a dark cell for months. My body has never hurt as much as this before and my head is completely numb. Gus hugs Ada and me and hails a hansom for her. 'I must become drunk Gwen. I will come to you when I surface. I may be several days. Dorelia is caring for the children.'

As Ada climbs into the hansom, she touches Gus's arm. 'I will book the cremation for Saturday at Père Lachaise cemetery and return now to assist Dorelia.'

'Thank you, Ada, – you have been so kind-hearted to Ida and me,' wiping his eyes with his sleeve. 'I will not attend the cremation,' Gus whispers to me. 'I cannot bear fake sentiment and exaggerated grieving.'

'I will attend,' and reach for his hand holding it as we watch Ada's hansom disappear. 'And your friends?'

McEvoy's name is almost on my lips.

'I told them not to come. None of them can match Ida's spirituality and honesty.'

It is certainly true of McEvoy.

∽

The cremation is as sparsely attended as Ida and Gus's wedding. Gus's current mistress had the decency to stay away. McEvoy attended but was already drunk on the train. The Rothensteins took Gus at his word to remain in London. Henry Lamb, Gus's new acolyte, places flowers on the coffin and promises to carry Ida's ashes to Gus and hold a memorial tribute to Ida in his rooms. Unsure about attending the funeral, I am glad I came. No one this time criticises my sombre dress. How else could I dress in my melancholy? My prayers fill the void, but it is so much more painful to witness the coffin slide into the flames than anyone had warned. I feel like jumping into the Seine or under a tram. When I am unhappy it seems to comfort me, momentarily, imagining a gruesome and more totalising torture than the one I feel. A more terrible fate would be to mirror Ida, married with five children, ceasing painting, and dead at thirty. I am Rodin's lover, but I will never bear his children nor abandon my art.

CHAPTER 26

PARIS, AUGUSTUS'S STUDIO

Time to check on Gus. He returned from a three-day bender in a peculiar state, he wrote. Ida's death is casting a darkness over us all but if I try to let go of my grief it will hit me harder when I see Gus.

'I cannot talk to anyone else, Gwen,' as he opens the door. 'You knew Ida better than most, and you are the most utterly truthful soul in the world.'

His red eyes are wild, glancing back and forth as if he is catching sight of ghosts slipping in and out of vision. Has he washed since Ida died? His dishevelled clothes smell like a homeless vagrant's.

'I will stay with you until you recover.'

'You must understand; I did love Ida more than anyone believes. Their sympathy now is meaningless.'

'Well, McEvoy had the decency to be drunk by the time he appeared, so was perfectly charming. I cannot speak for the others.'

'Rothenstein has turned into Uriah Heep. I instructed him not to visit me, but he keeps writing full of remorse for not attending.'

'He has a generous soul. Take a bath while I make soup and light a fire?'

Gus's resentment, his malice towards his old friends is nothing new; but his inability to care for himself is almost childlike. We talk intermittently over the next few days while he continually groans and berates himself. Every moment makes me more resolved to continue working.

'Rodin telegrammed.' I wonder how much to mention. 'I thought you would like to hear of his concern for you.'

For me not Gus. The telegram was a surprise. Rodin said he had to travel abroad and so would not be able to visit or sketch me for weeks; but that I was in his thoughts continually.

'And Ursula sent condolences, saying Ida is in a better place. Ursula promises to visit.'

'Ida has rejoined her spiritual lover, Christ. He was my most serious rival when we first met.'

Gus is impossible. The childlike emotions are becoming maudlin. At least he promises to paint again.

'I will need to return to my room today. I do not trust the concierge to care adequately for Edgar.'

∼

Edgar is well. Her coat shines and she is not gobbling her food so has obviously eaten.

The concierge is consoling as she hands me my post. 'I am so sorry for your loss. Edgar has been no trouble, I love cats, *Mademoiselle*. Mine is fifteen years old.'

Everything in my room has black edges. My ferns survived but their leaves are sharp, serrated, pointing upwards. The sky is dark, and I light a fire. Everything is too raw. Thank goodness, Ursula arrives tomorrow.

∼

'I visited Augustus en route,' Ursula removes her hat and coat. 'He is painting again, which he said was a comfort. How are you?'

'All the better for seeing you.'

'We have always supported each other,' and hugs me. 'We must think to the future. Ida would want us to continue working. I am trying to sculpt.'

'You are always braver than me at essaying new techniques,'

offering her a cup of tea. 'Do you remember the day Legros ordered us out of the studio. You immediately said we should change direction and sculpt? And we went to the BM.'

What I remember most of all, is my first sight of Rodin then and the intensity of his gaze.

'I do. It has taken me several years to finally decide, but here I am. I would like to study with Rodin. You have spoken so highly of his work,'

How can I tell her Rodin rarely sees me and he might even refuse to meet Ursula?

'Rodin is a perfectionist. He only sees dedicated people, so you will need to show him some work. But he is travelling abroad at the moment.'

'Then I will be free to sculpt you. I will set to work once I find accommodation.'

'You are most welcome to stay here. The concierge has a spare room.'

'I am particular.' Ursula laughs. 'Living with my parents has kept me bourgeois. I will look for a larger space nearby.'

It is for the best. Painting on my own allows me to stare at one spot for hours imagining what colours I could use; but having Ursula near at hand will settle me; we can talk about ideas, have sympathetic conversations – special moments.

At last we find a suitable room five minutes away. As soon as she unpacks, Ursula plans her sculpting. She chooses terracotta as she did in the British Museum, and I am to pose three times a week.

'You have one of those faces,' Ursula says, a few days later, 'at which one can gaze for ever without growing accustomed to it.'

'*Gentil*. When your head is finished, we can take it to one of Rodin's open Saturdays. Ladies are invited to inspect his maquettes to encourage them to buy.'

I often wonder if there is an alternative reason for invitations to ladies; but at least the Duchess cannot bar me. Everyone is welcome.

'I would appreciate his opinion, but the head is merely ten inches tall. Would he be interested in such a small sculpture?'

'You are English.' I smile. 'He is always interested in English ladies.' Even me when it suits him.

∼

A few weeks later, as we walk down rue de l'Université to Rodin's studio, my hands are trembling, glad Ursula is carrying her terracotta. The bar where Rilke and I enjoyed our reassuring talks is directly ahead. Rilke's keen sympathy would strengthen my resolve, but the bar is almost empty. His sleek head is not visible through the window, and I heard he is visiting Germany again.

'Perhaps we should drink after we have seen Rodin,' Ursula follows my glance. 'It would not do to arrive with wine on our breath.'

'I was searching for an old friend. We will celebrate once Rodin has praised your work.' Who knows if Rodin will even see us, let alone speak? All I want is a warm glance. There can be no kiss in front of a crowd.

The studio gates are fully open today and the porter looks me up and down. His focus is on me because Ursula is hugging her statue like a habitué and I shift my weight from one foot to the other, trying to look bold. He must remember me, and with a shrug, he nods us through into the courtyard and I can breathe more easily. The first hurdle is over.

'The whole space is enormous, I never guessed he would be so productive. How do you concentrate when you are modelling?'

'With difficulty. I am often distracted.'

Not from the space or even the usual bustle of assistants, but from Rodin. We step cautiously forward through the throng, searching for Rodin. Is he even here? A bead of sweat pricks my eye and is impatiently transferred to my sleeve. The visitors are clustering closer now and I find myself breathing in delicately as if making myself smaller.

'There is Rodin.' Ursula points to the platform.

He is as vigorous as ever, his face animated in conversation with an expensively dressed lady. The Duchess is standing at one side as if she is at heaven's gate tapping the chosen few on the shoulder and pushing back the rejected. Her face is covered with makeup, and she wears a long velvet gown, adorned with jewels, reflecting the startling red of her hair. If the hair is a wig, I could knock it from her head.

The back of my dress substitutes for a towel to wipe my sweaty hands. If she sees me, I will be barred, but what explanation can I give to Ursula if the Duchess pushes me away? 'We need to edge towards him, trying not to antagonise the ladies waiting in line.'

A weak excuse but Ursula nods her head.

Closer to the platform, I keep several women between me and the Duchess, with their wide feathered hats acting like overlapping screens. Ursula is alongside, clutching her terracotta, hopefully unaware of my fears. When we reach Rodin's side, I will have to speak. In front Rodin shakes hands with another guest and looks around. Time to step forward.

'*Monsieur* Rodin,' my voice almost too soft to be heard. 'May I introduce my English friend Miss Ursula Tyrwhitt the sculptor,'

Standing four-square directly in front, I focus on Rodin's face, not the Duchess, not daring to even glance in her direction. Ursula is smiling broadly at Rodin, holding out her terracotta. He nods at us both. The Duchess stands frozen, disdain sweeping across her face. Please do not let her take Rodin's arm, try to conduct him away from us.

'I am honoured to meet the great master at last. This has been my dream.'

Ursula is not normally so effusive, but the tone is exactly right. Rodin adores to be admired, and the Duchess will not dare to deflect his pleasure; and I try to enjoy the moment.

'*Enchantée*, Mademoiselle.' Rodin's face is unsmiling, but at least he seems calm about our interruption, and lighter in mood, as if happy to gaze at Ursula. Will he acknowledge me, touch my hand?

'I would be so grateful for your opinion,' and Ursula holds out her statue. 'The statue is of my dearest friend Gwen John,' gesturing to me.

Rodin stares at me and then at the terracotta, taking time to compare the likeness for several minutes. Ursula sculpted me as I was when we were younger, together at the Slade, with my long girlish hair. Will Rodin remember the first day he took the pins out of my hair, sweeping it down between my breasts?

'*Continuez, Excusez moi,*' as the Duchess touches his arm, but he nods his head, smiling in my direction.

It is sufficient. Shepherding Ursula out of the mêlée, before the Duchess can speak, we escape her impending wrath, visible in her eyes, darkening at the sight of me. There was no humiliation; he smiled at me.

'Is he always so abrupt?' as we walk out through the gates.

'Often. It is not his way to waste his words or his time.'

'But he did not offer me a critique.'

'He gave you the greatest compliment. He said *continuez*. You are officially a sculptor now.'

Laughing, Ursula nudges me into the bar opposite.

CHAPTER 27

CHERCHE-MIDI, PARIS

One evening in March 1907, after Ursula returned to England, I find a beautiful attic in rue Cherche-Midi not far from my house. Rodin asked me to move again to a bigger, more comfortable room. He will still pay my rent, although he is not inviting me to model for months.

This new concierge is younger than most, with a welcoming face.

'*Merci*, Mademoiselle, the deposit is exactly right,' as I place a fifty franc note in her hand.

Reluctant to return home immediately to pack, I stand for a moment admiring the view, and then the wide spiralling staircase as we descend, because the light is perfect, not too harsh for my pale greys and blues, and the space is ideal.

'I will move this weekend,' smiling in turn.

Saturday afternoon and the two removal men and cart are due to arrive. Everything is in boxes except my canvases and hats which I will carry myself. The men said four in the afternoon, but the clock is at seven already. In the room, the bed carries memories of Rodin's passion and next to it the wicker chair on which he sits to remove his shoes. Glinting on the far wall is the small mirror which reflects his head when he combs his hair after we make love. I will put the mirror in the last box without looking at my face in case I resemble a careworn woman; but I have an odd feeling that the new room will settle me in some way, allow me to stretch my wings, paint better than before.

Two hours later, I am guiding the cart to Cherche-Midi. The removal men are drunk, their faces an unhealthy green as if about to vomit, and their voices are brusque, angry. They damaged the box containing my ferns and plants and insisted on dangling the wardrobe through a window although I measured every inch; and the stair width seemed adequate. The new house is so much grander, in a wide boulevard. The concierge stands on the steps, smiling.

'Welcome, Mademoiselle,' as the removal men brush past her without a glance. With the boxes piling up in the hall, the men lean against the balustrade in an apparent state of collapse.

'We need fifty centimes more for a drink; it is customary.'

'It is not the custom at all,' the concierge replies.

'Thank you, Madam, but I will pay if it means they complete the job tonight.'

I cannot risk antagonising my new neighbours. A half hour later, the men stagger as they carry the last box and my wicker chair into the attic. The slender, younger man falls over my bedside table.

'The wardrobe will have to come through the window again,' the older man pronounces. His face is puce, and the extra drink seems to have befuddled them both.

The concierge carries ropes from her apartment, and the noise brings other tenants onto the landings. Their faces are friendly. There is no time for introductions from the concierge but one slim man in workman's clothes is already on all fours, assembling my bed. The wardrobe is hanging perilously from the window as the men haul it up. An older gentleman translates my requests for the men into a French too difficult for me to follow. Perhaps he only seems older because of his bald head, and his lively face is full of expression above a well-tied cravat and perfectly tailored jacket, as he shakes my hand with a firm grip. Two little old ladies climb up from the floor below with oil lamps, but the light gives the removal men's faces an even sicker, yellow tinge. Tense with anxiety, I am ready to sink onto the bed, but the old dandy is remonstrating with the men, bargaining them down from thirty-one to twenty-one francs, ignoring angry rants from the younger man.

Handshakes and thanks all round, and I am the proud owner of a beautiful space. Through the window, a sizeable courtyard is visible, circling a plane tree. Even a liberating act, like moving to a larger room nearer Rodin's studio, hurts even though it heralds a brighter future. It is hard to place an important part of my life behind me without pain. Coping with the day's events emboldens me to eat out this evening in a nearby restaurant and I order wine with lamb and beans. I am an independent woman enjoying dinner *tout seule*. Edgar will enjoy the meat I carry home in my serviette.

Next morning at six, the light slants through the half-open blinds, falling in grey, soft diagonals across my bed; and the houses opposite, are silent and peaceful in the early hour. The mat alongside is new and feels thick and springy on my bare soles. A new room does need a new model. Last month, Hilda introduced me to two English sisters and one, Chloe Boughton-Leigh, promised to sit. Her face has a kind of openness and with a lively quality in the way she poses as if she is about to rush out of the frame. Today I can start the background in her portrait now I am settled.

The painting will be more of the room than of Chloe – in honour of Paris, an unmistakable Parisian interior including my front door key. No house in England has such large, heavy iron keys, with a handle at the top big enough for two fingers. When I open the lock, it feels as if the key is more appropriate for a château. The keys will be the focus as much as Chloe. I must finish the painting quickly because Gus wrote asking me to send a new work to his dealer for exhibition and sale, so the portrait is a wash, not oils. Gus may scorn but the technique has a freshness.

'Why are you sketching me from behind? Do you dislike my face?' Chloe is younger than me and her body is graceful despite her dishevelled dress.

'You tease; you know you are attractive.'

'My sister is always telling me I am too bedraggled,' and Chloe smiles, 'and that I should not let my hair fall loose around my face.'

'At the moment, the way light catches the folds in your skirt is all that matters to me.'

'Tell me more about your work, I need to learn.'

'I do not have one set technique. It is more about the tonal subtleties than being too fixed on one approach. Why are you asking? Do you want to become a professional painter?'

'I am uncertain but would like to learn more; my sister suggests attending Colarossi's atelier. Do you know the atelier?'

'Colarossi is one of the greatest. I may return to studies myself. We could attend together.'

'You are a wonderful painter already. Why would you need further lessons?'

'All painters never stop learning,' trying to hide my pleasure.

There is a warmth between us I appreciate which will turn to friendship; I need another friend with Ursula so far away.

∼

Next week, Paris is icy cold, with snow inches deep, piled high in drifts at both sides of the streets. The trams are cancelled, so we walk to Colarossi – only a few blocks away with the snow feeling smooth like velvet until your feet become insensibly frozen.

'My sister said a year at Colarossi,' Chloe says, 'is worth three at the Royal Academy with its lack of attention to modern art.'

'Your sister is quite right; but I do not intend to remain at Colarossi for long. Just time enough to study any new techniques. It is hard to develop as an artist in isolation.'

'I wish to be a full-time artist and will study the entire day.'

'My plan is to study there in the afternoons and work until late.' Rodin never visits in the evenings, and I paint in the mornings.

Ahead, our breath is misty, a white veil in the cold and we stay silent until Colarossi's tall building looms ahead.

The hall is full of dripping coats. Removing our galoshes, we step inside a warm studio, smelling of fresh paint, perspiration and damp, the oily smells overcoming the dankness and are directed to two free easels by the tutor. The room is smaller than Whistler's atelier, but men and women are working side by side, as before. A man next to me smiles, puts down his brush, extending a hand.

'I am Hugh Ramsay,' he has an Australian accent. 'Welcome.'

'I am Gwen, Gwen John.'

He seems such a callow youth after Rodin. The face is too smooth, lacking Rodin's luxurious facial hair, but his eyes are kindly.

'I have heard the name before. I travelled to London before Paris and visited galleries. Are you related to Augustus?'

I am about to say his sister, but the words stick in my throat. I refuse to stand in Gus's shadow, and I will be a better painter than him one day. 'John is a common surname in Britain. I am Welsh like Augustus.'

As the models enter, Chloe looks alarmed. A line of nude men slowly advance. Each springs onto the model's platform, takes a pose for a moment, and then jumps down until the tutors choose one for the day. It is hard not to compare their members with Rodin's unfavourably. Chloe places one hand over her mouth, and rushes from the studio into a latrine at the rear. After five minutes, she emerges, her face is white, handkerchief at her mouth.

'I was sick,' she whispers, and I clasp her hand.

'It is your first time. Rest a little.'

All afternoon, we sketch and erase with our bread crusts, then switch to oils, while a tutor in a velvet suit gives instructions. Whenever he leaves the room, horseplay develops with male students throwing crusts at women, imitating cockerels, all so different from Whistler's and Rodin's studios. After Rodin, it feels as if the studio is a kindergarten.

'I found the tomfoolery odd at first,' Hugh glances over. 'My family is religious, and I was the church organist at home.'

'I am not prudish; the noise is just distracting.' I want to say juvenile, but Hugh is no older than the others. 'I will become accustomed to the clatter,' eyeing the model, wishing Hugh would cease his conversation.

'I am determined to exhibit at the Société Nationale des Beaux-Arts within three months.'

The last place in the world where I would wish to exhibit. My paintings will appear in avant-garde galleries, not those dedicated to fashionables attending to preen; Duchesses being the ugliest. 'I am here to learn, and a slow painter. Let us work.'

Hugh blushes and returns to his canvas. His image is passible. He has caught the model's differing skin tones with the lower arms a sun-kissed red, but the portrait could have been painted ten years ago. Mine transposes the light into blended tones using space to highlight the figure rather than representation and feels modern.

The studio is close. The smells of unwashed people and clothing are becoming overpowering, and I splash my face in the sink studiously ignoring the male students surrounding me as if intent to win a wager.

As Chloe and I leave, the cold is intense on our faces.

'Today was informative,' Choe says. 'I learnt a good deal.'

'Your technique is excellent for an amateur,' and she blushes. 'I will return too and attend for a few weeks.'

The day was significant. I learnt to believe in myself, to know my art is good, even perhaps superior, but none at Colarossi will be as fine an artist as Rodin.

'May I continue to model for you? You are more serious than these students, a real artist.'

For once my intensity is appreciated.

'It will be my pleasure,' kissing her cold cheek before turning in the direction of Cherche-Midi.

CHAPTER 28

RODIN VISITS (2)

Not long after I begin studies at Colarossi, a letter from Rodin promises a morning visit. Today I sweep the floor and wipe down all the furniture (the ferns are thriving) and watch the sun stroke the top of the courtyard tree. If only Edgar Quinet was here to share the sight with me; her disappearance two weeks ago left an emptiness in the room and in my heart. My only hope is that she will enjoy the warmth of the sun wherever she is; and my consolation is to sketch her again and again, with my emotions creating fine lines. Watercolours are catching the varying tortoiseshell shades particularly well; and I am tempted to write a poem celebrating her life.

Today is cold so the window is closed but it also blocks out any outdoor sounds so that every squeak in the house, including Rodin's, will be clear.

'Marie,' Rodin sweeps in without knocking and gazing round. The kettle whistle must have masked his steps on the stairs. 'The room is charming. It is perfect.'

'I arranged everything exactly in the way you preferred in my old apartment.'

If only he stays longer than his customary hour, with his presence filling the whole space, there will be more to remember in the empty hours.

'Will you take tea?' Helping him with his coat. 'The kettle is boiling.'

'No, all I want is you,' and he starts to remove his shirt.

It is all happening too quickly. My usual routine is to savour each moment.

'Do you like my new dress?' Twirling before him, spreading out the pleats in the sunlight. I will not undress until he is clear about his feelings for me.

'I do but please remove it. I have little time. Clients are due in rue de l'Université.'

He is aroused I can see and seduced by my body, but he must see me as more than a body.

'You said you liked well-dressed women,' my voice is rising uncontrollably. 'Why do I buy new clothes, if all you do is to ask me to remove them. I will wear a cotton dress all winter, rather than take another franc from you.'

I cannot stop although all I desire is for him to disrobe me, hold me, take me. Why am I becoming irate?

'The nude alone is well dressed. All I desire is for you to be content.'

'I am when I paint, or when you visit, and when I model for you. But I see you so infrequently.'

Why am I scolding? Rose must nag not me. The morning is turning into a nightmare. I am intelligent, not a shrew.

'Be tranquil. When I am absent, study, paint, focus.'

He is fully undressed now, and delay is impossible. In a moment I am naked, my skin glowing in the sunlight. He first sucks my nipples, and then smooths his hand over my breasts and I moan in anticipation.

'*Ma chèrie*, Marie.'

His member presses against my motte and I writhe as he pushes me down on the bed. He climaxes quickly, and I rub myself against his thigh to silently climax too, although I moaned at the same time as him. We kiss, and he reaches for the towel I always have ready on the bedside chair. 'I must leave. I will be late for my clients. The money is important.'

More than me, evidently. As he dresses, everything hurts, as if I am a new-born baby. The sunlight is too bright, the air too cold, and his rapid breathing as he puts on his boots, hurts most of all.

The anger surfaces again. 'You no longer listen to me.'

'It will pass. Keep calm. Take care of yourself for me.'

'All we have in common is our history together.'

This resentment will antagonise him, and his kisses will cease if he sees a harridan so why am I unable to stop? It seems as if I am covered by a painted wash – tinted green with jealousy.

'Forgive me,' and he kisses my cheek, 'I mean well.'

'You are forgiven,' managing to keep my emotions in check.

He reaches for my head and holds it tenderly between his hands as if smoothing a young child. All I can hear is the pounding of my heart in a deep cavern.

'I am concerned about you because I care.'

His voice is no louder than a whisper, but his touch is calming.

'Next time bring me poetry; I can translate for you. Read aloud while I model.'

He nods and closes the door softly.

Who am I angry with – Rodin or me for succumbing so easily to his desire? Later, the letter paper lies crumpled in the waste basket and the sunset dissolves into night.

∼

A basket of plums is outside my door when I leave for Colarossi two days later. I tap on the concierge's window.

'Thank you a million for the plums.'

'Oh, the fruit is not from me. A Monsieur Rodin brought them. He said to mention his name, but I was so occupied yesterday I quite forgot.'

All afternoon in Colarossi's studio, I plan menus involving plums to make them last all week; picturing Rodin plucking the fruit from his trees in Meudon and fallen plums from the ground underneath. The autumn is so bountiful after the heavy spring snows. I will have plums tonight before painting.

'You are using an interesting shade,' Chloe stares at my canvas rather than at the model. 'Purple is unusual for figures.'

Rodin's gift is shimmering over the studio and into my art so what I had planned – to show emotions through arrangements on the canvas – has vanished. Instead colour is everything; juxtapositions of vivid colours will surprise the viewer.

'Monsieur Rodin gave me a huge basket of plums.'

'Are you in a relationship? I do not mean to pry, but I noticed when I was modelling for you, the figure in your self-portrait holding a letter, is so incredibly alive. I wondered whose letter could make you so vibrant?'

'Yes, my lover is Monsieur Rodin.'

Chloe puts down her brush and stares.

'Is a relationship wise? You must know his reputation?'

'He is so knowledgeable and a great artist. I learn a great deal.'

'But he has a wife – Rose – I understand.'

'They are not married. Rose is Rodin's housekeeper'

'But Rose and Rodin are seen together in public,' Choe's disapproval is etched across her face, 'they must be in a close relationship.'

'As his housekeeper, she means nothing to him he told me.'

'And you believe him?'

'I have to. I love him.'

Thank goodness I have told no one else except Ursula. Gus would scorn.

'Please keep this to yourself.'

Choe puts her arm around my shoulders. A couple of nearby students turn to stare, but the class ends soon, so they quickly turn back to their canvases. I will take the train to Meudon.

~

By the time I arrive in Meudon the sky is black. The moon is surrounded by a halo of mist but offers enough light for my way up the hill. A soft breeze cools my flushed face. The climb up the hill is tiring. Reaching a convent, I keep to that side of the street. No one must see me. My Master cannot be embarrassed by village gossip about a strange woman.

The convent door creaks, and I freeze against the wall, pulling down my hat, and remain motionless, listening for sounds. No one emerges. The air is cooler here than in Paris, filled with pine and cherry scents. The forest surrounding seems immense and I continue up the street. As I pass the last group of cottages, a dog barks and I stand silent, holding my breath. No lights are turned on. The minutes before I can walk further seem interminable. The bark is not repeated. I have no idea how much time has passed since I left the station. No convent bell has tolled as if the evening has paused, waiting for me to enter time again. At last I reach Rodin's house.

The whole of the valley Fleury spreads out in front of the house, dotted with small cottages, like the land surrounding Gus's house in Matching Green. The hedge is thin, winter snows must have denuded its buds. Rodin's garden is full of statues now, like a small factory. Over to one side, there is a new pavilion with three glass doors as if each might lead into a different studio. Through one door, an oil lamp flickers showing shadows moving back and forth but none are his shape. Rodin must have transferred maquettes from Paris for assistants to work late into the night. A spreading horse chestnut drops a few leaves onto a patio table and an unkempt elderly woman emerges and wipes them away with a corner of a napkin. It must be Rose, in slippers as if she is as much part of the house as its furniture. She beheads some dead buddleia flowers putting them into her apron pocket, and smooths her hair, smiling as she steps back inside the house. She will be here too until kingdom come.

∼

At last Rodin invites me to model. The plums were a signal of affection and, although a couple of months have passed since our last encounter, we will be in harmony while he recreates my feelings in a maquette. The morning has a brightness and the Seine, down a side street, is blue today, even, and tranquil. As the tram slows to a halt outside the studio, the familiar sounds of chisel striking marble, and the smell of wet clay wafts into the street. Soon I will smell Rodin, his lemon cologne, feel his warm breath on my cheek, his soft lips kissing every part of my body.

I will part my thighs as soon as I am naked, see his member pushing upwards, pointing at me. Even the assistants look cheerful today as I swiftly step across the cobbled courtyard. Their chatter always stops when Rodin enters the studio. I think it must make him feel powerful. He swells in height walking through the room. Now, in the silence, I swing my skirt waiting for instructions. His other models probably undress quickly but I need the tension of waiting, building up an erotic charge, slowly removing my bodice and stockings. First, he gives instructions to Eugène about the sculpture to be finished for the client in Le Mans, and seemingly invigorated by his trip there, his blue eyes sparkle.

'Marie,' and points to the platform.

Will he make love to me today? Caress my body when the Sacré-Coeur bell strikes five? I see the Duchess standing in the doorway. She does not speak, and, after the brightness of the street, I cannot read her expression. Rodin is arranging his tools in a row and spitting on a maquette, delaying the start of sculpting, ignoring me still dressed on the platform. I feel as cold and wet as the maquette. Without moving, the Duchess watches us both as if she can control the whole morning with her presence.

'Why is the Duchess here?'

Rodin continues to fuss with his workstation, ignoring me.

The Duchess's voice floats over, 'Gwen John you are not welcome here.'

In a moment she is next to me, moving quickly like a wolfhound about to spring, pointing to the door.

'What do you mean? I have been asked to model today,' and due to be loved later by Rodin I want to add.

But Rodin just sighs as if unwilling to confirm the invitation; so I start to unlace my boots, hoping that he will intervene, ask the Duchess to leave.

As quickly as she appeared at my side, the Duchess steps over to the phonograph, opens its cupboard to reveal a row of shellac records, their case torn at the edges, obviously well-used.

Clearly knowing the exact place of each, the Duchess pulls out one, placing it on the turntable and winds up the handle. Stock still, Rodin avoids my gaze as if transfixed by her. A Brittany folk tune fills the studio with the sound of tambors and violins and I stop untying my boot laces. I will not move unless Rodin tells me to leave, but it is as if he and the Duchess are on a theatre stage with me a sole spectator looking on from the stalls.

Swaying in time to the drums, the Duchess wafts her black shawl back and forth over her ample breasts, smiling enticingly at Rodin. I can smell her expensive Guerlain eau de parfum, sweet and cloying, displacing the smells of the studio and men's sweat. It is as if my world is being erased, my comforting miasma dispersed by her. I glance at Rodin, but his eyes are only for her like King Herod watching Salome, as she swirls around. Will she expose her belly?

Rodin has clearly forgotten my existence. He holds out his hands to the Duchess, places an arm around her waist and they waltz like two dolls on top of a music box. Rilke was right, they dance very badly. I cannot bear to watch any longer. The folk song reaches a crescendo, and I throw on my coat and run out of the studio, across the courtyard to the street. She is within and I am without.

CHAPTER 29

RILKE, PARIS

The next few months, I focus on drawings and the swift gestures needed to fix a line, which calm my mind, giving me hope that my life as an artist is still developing. The paintings are serene, harmonious. This is now my aim – to move out of Rodin's shadow into my own light.

One afternoon in the brasserie, celebrating a new taupe colour and fine brushstrokes with a glass of wine, Rilke enters but does not recognise me, evident in the way he glances around the room. When you first enter a restaurant, you scan as carefully as possible so as not to miss a friend, but Rilke's eyes pass over my table as if embarrassed to be staring at a strange woman. My pad on the table has a letter to Rodin, as usual written here in rue de l'Université, in case I can see him emerging from the studio. In one of his billets-doux, he told me not to visit without an invitation, but the sight of his studio encourages me into stories, tales I would have told him if I was modelling.

As Rilke seems to adjust to the darkness, he waves at me over the hovering waiters' shoulders.

'May I join you?' and leans over and kisses me on both cheeks.

'Of course, I am delighted to see you,' Rilke's conversations were always such a comfort. 'How was your trip home? Tell me all the news.' I must avoid mentioning the reason for Rilke's return to Germany.

Rodin fired him; Hilda told me. Erratic in his visits to me, Rodin grew impatient with Rilke, said Rilke was intent on burnishing the brightness of his own small light by joining it to Rodin's shining sun. The friendly kind man I know was unrecognisable in Rodin's description.

'A successful trip. I published a poetry collection, but that is not why I am here. First, how are you? What are you painting?'

The intervening year, since I last saw Rilke, has consisted mainly of drawings and Colarossi and a few paintings. But the paintings and drawings are good, and that is all that matters.

'I continue much as before. So why are you in Paris again? You seem excited?'

'I am. As you know, Rodin's rented a new studio in rue de Varenne, and keeps merely a few assistants and statues here in the old place.'

I am speechless. So, Rodin has been sculpting elsewhere, not inviting me to the new studio or even mentioning the place, keeping me at arm's length. Luckily, Rilke is engrossed in his account.

'I found the building for him. We are reconciled. We had a heart-to-heart talk.'

'I am so happy for you,' wondering why on earth I am writing to Rodin in a brasserie opposite his old studio. I push my food around my plate, counting the peas.

'I had occupied my wife's old studio in the building, Hôtel Biron, and wrote to Rodin about its charms – bay windows and a secret garden. When Rodin visited, he could see the possibilities and rented the ground floor immediately. What do you think of it?'

What can I say? I cannot tell Rilke I know nothing of the studio. He will guess at once that Rodin has stopped sculpting me; and I can never lie convincingly.

'I model for Rodin here in his old studio.' I tremble on the word 'old', but the statement is true although there has been no invitation to model for a year. My wobble seems unnoticed, and the words are masked by the clatter and laughter of diners.

'Do you want to visit Hôtel Biron this afternoon? Rodin might not be there, but I have a key.'

My heart misses a beat. What if Rodin *is* there and ignores me in front of Rilke? Or worse, that the Duchess is ensconced in Hôtel Biron? The shame and the consoling look Rilke would inevitably display would be unbearable. Glancing anxiously at him, do I dare? When I brought Ursula unexpectedly to Rodin's studio that Saturday, Rodin was distant but at least polite. The risk is worthwhile.

'Of course, I would be delighted to visit with you.'

The new place, Hôtel Biron, seems run down. The garden is overgrown; wooden arches are collapsing under the weight of roses, wisteria, and jasmine, but Rodin would find the jumble of flowers irresistible. Assistants are scurrying back and forth as usual, and the metallic ring of chisel on marble floats through the rooms. Is Rodin here? Or the Duchess? What shall I say if he is working? He hates to be interrupted.

'This is his favourite place now, to meet potential buyers and the press; even though he initially said he wanted it as a refuge from the world.'

I glance quickly around the room. The assistants are smoking indoors, chatting to each other, which they never do when Rodin is about, so he must be absent, and the Duchess too. Am I relieved or sad not to see him? I realise my breath seemed to stop when we entered the studio and breathe out slowly. The space is perfect with trees tapping at the window, making a feathery background for the statuary and his favourite Renoir is the one painting decorating the walls. It is all quite simple, a few selected pieces of polished furniture and his maquettes. None of the mess of rue de l'Université, with its mass of sculptors' tools, half-finished statues, and dust.

'It is like an empty gallery; I prefer the busyness of his old studio.'

'Perhaps that is why he sculpts you there.'

Rilke obviously does not know.

'I have a present for you. One moment, I will run upstairs to my studio.'

With Rilke absent, I can look around more carefully. My statue is not here but there are no maquettes of other women. There is an open door at the end of the studio leading to a bedroom with a narrow bed and a coverlet thrown to one side as if Rodin slept here last night – because he always disapproves of sleeping during the day. So there are nights now without returning home to Rose in Meudon? The bed is too slender for him to sleep with the Duchess given that Rodin is quite rotund. What to think? Sadness because he never slept all night with me when it would be so easy; or happiness that Rose's place in his life is evidently diminished, and possibly the Duchess's too, and now I can focus on my painting?

'Here, *Love Letters of a Portuguese Nun*. I know you like writing letters to Rodin so I thought the book might be inspirational.'

Is this how Rilke sees me – a nun? I might as well be one, given how infrequently Rodin visits my room.

'I will read the book immediately tonight, thank you so much.'

'Let us leave a note for Rodin to say we visited,' Rilke says. 'Nothing as baroque as the Portuguese!'

We laugh as I take a piece of paper from Rodin's desk, turning my back to hide the scribble, but Rilke tactfully crosses the room to study the sculpture.

'*Rilke suggested I write. I am calmer now and look forward to seeing you. Votre amie Marie.*'

I cannot say more in case the Duchess somehow reads the note or Rilke guesses at Rodin's absence in my life. With the melted tip of a candle the paper is sealed. '*The Master*' in large capitals will take his eye when he returns. As Rilke escorts me out, the streetlamps are being lit and the early evening *flaneurs* pass by. It will be a starry night and I pat Rilke's arm.

'Thank you for today.'

~

On Christmas Eve, ice is thick in the courtyard. *Le Figaro*'s weather report predicts more snow over Christmas, but I manage to concentrate on painting despite the cold. I experiment with different yellows to catch a range of lights from lamplight to window light. A letter from Ursula helped, although there is little news about Gus. Not seeing Rodin until the New Year, would normally cover me with a thick cloud of unhappiness but, in a paradoxical way, not having to constantly anticipate his visits to my room allows me to focus. I have time to rearrange objects, allowing the placement of a chair to freshly inspire a different set of angles on my canvas. It feels as if I can complete a whole portfolio of new work. My usual objects – the wicker chair, the bed, are in shadow with grey tones. Each object is distinct with its own subtle colour and identity. The paintings feel fresh, distinctly modern. Exhausted, I should eat but first a note from my purse goes into an envelope.

'A small present for Christmas, Madame,' and I hand the envelope to the concierge downstairs.

'Thank you, Mademoiselle,' she seems surprised. 'A thousand thanks.'

'You have been so kind. I have gifts from England. Happy Christmas.' My sister sent a ribbon and necklace and Ursula sewed me a jacket.

In the morning, I wear my new jacket and necklace. The streets to Notre-Dame are slippery with ice but Rodin sometimes attends mass, he told me. Rose or the Duchess will probably be with him, but I am resigned now to their presence; and he sent me a Christmas note saying he loves me. It is snowing lightly and very cold. Outside the cathedral door the lame and blind appear mysteriously from nowhere as the bell tolls for the early mass. Inside, the West window's aquamarine on my jacket is brighter than my palette paints and a colour I must memorise. The choir is fuller today, and the cathedral heavy with incense. Walking down a side aisle, the beauty of the cathedral is overwhelming. Rodin is absent, but I can pray for him and more importantly for my art. Finding a space in a pew near the alter, I kneel and place my hands together.

CHAPTER 30

RODIN'S PRIVATE VIEW, PARIS

The New Year ushers in a new decade. I am oddly optimistic about 1910, although the constant rain makes me feel as grey as the sky. Ursula is still sculpting in England and writes asking me for Rodin's ideas about art. Rodin talks rarely while sculpting, but I can tell Ursula that he does say he loves Nature and such virtues as patience and humility, although I am the patient one not him. December was his last visit.

My last visit to Bon Marché was before Christmas, so perhaps buying a new dress today will encourage my art, a different shape I can incorporate into a painting. The younger women in the streets are dissimilar to a few weeks ago, now with coatdresses straight to a hemline stopping at their ankles. Are they wearing corsets? It is hard to tell, and they seem oblivious to the drizzle, making me light-hearted in turn, skipping into the store.

Back home, clutching my parcel, the concierge is waiting.

'A gentleman in a top hat left this package for you.'

An artist's portfolio, black imitation leather with a label, bearing Rodin's name. Carrying it upstairs fills me with welter of emotions, irritation being the most conspicuous. The one morning I venture out and he visits. Why no letter of warning? Almost a month has passed, and I want him to see him, but any dismay must be my secret; his other women probably quarrel with him but not me. I have learnt to accept them, I think, because I feel my art progresses and art is the focus of my life. A collection of Japanese prints slides out of the portfolio, but no note. Has Rodin swept his hand over the surfaces, but there is no trace of his eau de cologne? The prints shine, spread all over the table. The colours are brighter than my usual greys and browns and each image is so definite and clear. They are figurative with women in landscapes, but the marks seem spontaneous and expressive. I could learn from these brush marks.

All afternoon my fresh quick, clean drawings feel uncluttered and erotic matching the prints, with the washes a cold brilliance of colour. I am moving forward. Today's letter will thank Rodin and tell him of my work, certain he will be happy with my new self-discipline. Sure enough next day, a note arrives from him. Too excited to open it immediately, I sit for a moment until I cannot wait any longer.

Come tomorrow to the old studio and remember to bring this note to give to the concierge.

No signature, no *cher ami*.

～

Rodin's studio is full of assistants. The enormous space rings with the sound of chisels. I hoped for some privacy with screens, but he is sketching me today so there is no need for nakedness or to touch my body.

'Will you sculpt me later?'

'It is the intelligence which draws, but the heart which models.'

Does he mean his heart is not involved with me today? He is distant, his hand moving across the sketch pad in a series of swift gestures. What is different? The room is as full of dust as ever, and as noisy, but Rodin has changed. If he continues to work up his maquettes from sketches, he will never need to feel the shape of my body, my thighs, the way my skin stretches flat across my belly.

'I am so grateful for the prints. Your present pushed me in a new direction – into sketching with gestures rather than outlines'.

'Good – new work is the most important thing,'

'Do you want to know more?'

'I am sure you will tell me.' And he smiles. 'But I need to focus.'

I am treading on eggshells again.

'I am using quick lines. It helps to overcome my anxiety when I put brush to canvas.'

'Good. Stay still.' But he gazes at me as if we share ideas, share techniques as creative partners. The Duchess cannot paint, I heard. My skill makes me special.

'*Mon Maître*,' an assistant is hovering behind. 'The gallery director awaits you in the next room.'

'*Pardon, ma chère*; our time is over for today.'

This is my first modelling for weeks. I hoped we would make love when the assistants go home but Rodin must find me calm.

'There is to be an exhibition of my drawings and I would like you to attend. I will send you an invitation to the private view.'

He is willing to see me in public. He might take my arm, touch his champagne flute against mine. The drawings could be of me – perhaps those he drew of Hilda and me embracing. I will wear my new gown and he will be amazed by how well it fits under my bust now I wear brassieres, not corsets, like the fashionable women. 'Please send the invitation as soon as possible.'

He must not change his mind.

∽

Rodin's exhibition invitation is on my mantlepiece for me to stare at while I eat although today, the day of the private view, all I can manage is coffee. Will my new gown be correct? I have no decorative feathers which I read women wear on such occasions but in any case, I would be uncomfortable with extravagant ornaments. The blue-grey fur-lined coat, a Christmas present from Ursula, is my most showy accompaniment. Its full collar stands proud over the other clothes in the wardrobe as I flick through. A cab tonight to the private view. My wide-brimmed decorated hat needs protecting because, through the window, rain seems certain. Hilda suggested I parade with other men to encourage Rodin to pay me more attention, and Hugh from Colarossi accepted my invitation. My occasional dinners with Hugh kept me in touch with Colarossi techniques after I stopped attending, although Hugh might like a different kind of relationship.

The cab is stuffy; happily, Hugh does not smoke.

'Thank you for the invitation. I must say it came as a surprise.'

'We are friends, and I thought you might like to meet dealers, gallery owners.'

Was that too patronising? I manage to sound so superior sometimes.

'Well, I admire Rodin's work, but I do not understand his figures, but then the modernists do not appeal either.'

'Rodin is a master,' but stop in case my voice betrays me.

As we enter the salon, Hugh takes my arm and walks me over to Rodin's studies of young women.

'I am astonished. What an overwhelming number of people to see drawings.'

'Rodin's drawings carry hints of sculptures to come, and the critics wish to see his latest ideas.'

In each drawing a woman is exposing her quim to the viewer, drawn in by a thigh line. Rodin's sketches are powerfully and unrepentantly drawn by a man, down to the tiniest gesture. Are these sketches of his new mistresses? Or past discarded lovers? I am blushing as I check the dates, hoping the drawings predate me, but also wondering if there are any of me.

'The depictions are making me uncomfortable too,' Hugh glances at my face.

'I am not embarrassed.' Perhaps I should have come alone. 'They are naked because his drawings are about true intimacy. It is as if all the layers of clothing have been stripped away from the bodies to expose the souls. That is the point.'

'Well, I will be far away from all this soon. I return to Australia. I will miss you.'

I touch his hand in reply but cannot bear to talk to Hugh anymore; Rodin must be here, it is his private view, but the crowd is dense. Walking into the next gallery, with Hugh in tow, one man is without the obligatory top hat, standing surrounded by male friends chatting and laughing together. It is Rodin and thank goodness the Duchess is absent. The stuffy air seems to fill my lungs, but I manage to saunter over without hesitation.

'Who is it?' Hugh trails after.

'Monsieur Rodin,' I call out.

Rodin is deep in conversation and my voice was too tiny, so I wait for Hugh to draw level. Hilda is right, I need an admirer for Rodin to notice me and Hugh will have to suffice.

'Monsieur Rodin,' I call again, and he turns to face me.

'How are you Mademoiselle John?' A few of his companions stare. Do they know about Rodin and me? Obviously, Rodin would not reveal our relationship. He glances at Hugh, at his smooth skin and slim body.

'Thanks to you, my painting goes well,' pleased the other men now show a flicker of interest.

'I have missed our modelling sessions. We must make an appointment for next week.'

Hearing the word model, his companions turn back to their conversation, but I am relieved. He wants me in his studio and soon.

CHAPTER 31

PARI S FLOODS

A week later, a scribbled note from Rodin asks me to come to rue l'Université but without giving a date. I will visit immediately before he changes his mind. Has the Duchess installed herself in the Hôtel Biron studio and so the old studio is safe to visit? At least, this time, I do not need to hand his note to the porter for inspection before being allowed entrance, he wrote. Rain has fallen incessantly morning to night for weeks and the sky is cloudy again today. The metro is flooded and closed so I take a hansom cab. Horses can clip-clop through anything.

'You might find yourself knee-deep in water, Mademoiselle. I heard that rue de l'Université is flooded.'

The street is near the Seine, and flooding is inevitable, so what will have happened to my statue? If the Muse is damaged it will be as if our time together is blemished, washed away.

'Please be speedy. I can pay more for a difficult journey.'

Normally traffic is congested in this arrondissment, but today there is scarcely a horse to be seen. With every pause of the cab, my hands clench and unclench. All my usual worries about how Rodin will receive me, what to wear, what to say, are overwhelmed by my fears for the Muse. The image is not just my replica. It is a visible reminder of me, every time Rodin enters his studio.

Water almost reaches the cab door as I pay the cabbie so what will I find in the studio? A pond spreads across the whole place with the surface several inches above the floor, and a few marble statues are lying on their sides. None are the Muse.

'Marie,' Rodin is wading across the studio towards me. 'You came. How brave. You have damaged your dress to see me. Apologies. At the time when I wrote, the studio was clear of water.'

He acknowledges my courage, my spirit. The warmth from his words counters the water's freezing temperature.

'I was anxious about you. How much is damaged? May I help?'

'Everyone is working hard.' And he sweeps an arm towards his assistants.

The water is over my galoshes, and I step carefully in case a valuable art piece is submerged.

'And the Muse?' my voice is trembling.

'So it is not only me you wish to see?' Rodin laughs, taking my hand, steadying me. 'The Muse is in the corner. We fished the statue from the water, and there is no long-term damage.'

'The Muse is me,' keeping tight hold of his hand. The statue's face is as full of passion as mine when Rodin and I first met.

'At least you are drier than the Muse and I will be able to restore it. The flood simply caressed my works. It came to my studio as a friend and not an enemy. I found one of my favourite drawings floating in the water and the drawing is not damaged in any way.'

Is his favourite drawing of me?

'Apologies for your wasted day. The concierge will hail you a cab. You must not catch grippe; and journalists are about to arrive to photograph me knee-deep in water.'

As he tenderly kisses my cheek, I breathe in his smell and feel the warmth of his lips. There is so much work to do righting the studio, and I should not make any demands, but one slips out.

'Write to me when you can. Take care of yourself.'

'I will never abandon the Muse.' He smiles.

∼

Gus writes insisting that I send work to the New English Art Club – again. You will never be renowned, he writes, unless you exhibit frequently. I have been painting diligently since visiting Rodin. His calm response to the flood settles me, as did his devotion to the Muse. His notes are brief, scarcely more than a line, but the Muse's restoration requires more modelling sessions. Perhaps the rhythm of our lives will become more secure. Short encounters where we share thoughts, and I paint inspired. So I sleep well and eat regular meals. There are drawings and watercolours which I could dispatch to the NEAC. Gus will be surprised at my productivity when I write tonight.

~

This Paris morning my plants are bending towards the light as I water them, and, through the window, a tall lanky, bearded man, in a sombrero, is climbing out of a sleek car below. The hat is unmistakable. No one in Paris wears something so flamboyant. It is Gus and only Gus would immediately tip his hat at a passing woman as if he is her closest friend. Scarcely three weeks since his last letter and yet here he is. His gold watch glints in the sun as he checks the time and glances up. Our smiles meet in mid-air. Gus might be demanding but there was a time in our lives when painting alongside each other as children filled me with bliss, and seeing him, it is as if such simple emotions, without me asking for them, return.

'I am here with excellent news.' Gus tosses his hat as neatly as ever onto the door hook and hugs me. 'The New English Art Club will take all your drawings. Perhaps your calm interiors settle people's fears about the future? Who knows? Or maybe grey interiors are the fashion *de nos jours*.'

Is there a hint of jealousy in his voice? Grey is not a colour he often uses.

'Whisky please,' as he waves away my proffered teacup.

Gus never changes, but there is something about the size of his beard, the broad shoulders, the certainty of his voice which fills the room with energy.

'Thank you for the news. I am always grateful for your assistance,' handing him the bottle and a glass. 'But surely your long journey is not simply to tell me about the NEAC?'

'That is true, but I thought I should start agreeably.'

Sitting square in front, he holds my gaze as if about to paint a difficult client. He cannot be concerned about what people say about him. Titillating stories follow him around like cats do a fish bone. Or is it worse? Has he found a new mistress and will leave Dorelia with all the children, half of whom are her stepchildren? He knows how I would react. Tense, I place my cup down. Dorelia deserves better; she is so faithful.

'There are rumours.' His expression darkens. Despite his bohemian lifestyle, Gus is surprisingly conservative when it comes to women's behaviour. The gossip must be about me and Rodin.

'What rumours?'

'I had luncheon with Ursula last week, and she told me about your affair with Rodin. I will be forthright here. You know me.'

Ursula would never betray my confidence. Gus must have browbeaten her or plied her with wine. Or both. He cannot forbid me to see Rodin. I am thirty-four, an independent woman artist living in Paris. I will never return to England, and Parisians take such liaisons in their stride. They even have a term for me – *cinq-à-sept*, although, with Rodin, it is more often eleven to twelve in the morning, if at all.

'Rodin is my Master.' If only there was a language to describe the significance of Rodin for my art, the blazing intensity of that as if I always hold a ruby jewel in my hand, even if there is no art for peering into the secrets of his heart.

'This may seem hypocritical from me,' and slowly sips his whisky, 'but social standards are different for men and women. All I want is for you to succeed, to be the famous artist you deserve to be which means,' and he stares hard again, 'having an unsullied reputation.'

'And my happiness is not in this scenario?' my voice gaining strength. 'My friendship with Rodin stimulates my art, enlarges my world, my life.'

'But he has many mistresses. He could discard you at any moment. I worry about my little sister,' his eyes softening as he reaches for my hand.

'Rodin's most significant work, the Muse, is of me and he

continues to sculpt the statue, so he depends on me as much as I learn from him.'

Not true, either about the continuation since the minor repairs are complete, or needing me, but Gus knows the demands of creation, the all-consuming desire to keep working, and how his own art depends on relationships. He has hundreds, Ursula said. So many, he pats any passing child on the head in Chelsea in case the youngster is one of his.

'I,' we say simultaneously, and Gus smiles. 'It is true. Art and life are inseparable. I should not be so dictatorial. But sometimes I feel I must substitute for Father's inadequacies as a parent. I apologise.' Finishing his whisky he stands and hugs me again.

'Forgiven,' I murmur into his chest. This is the first time he has apologised so worth a lie from me.

'Let us enjoy some time together. I will take you in my splendid, hired car to Versailles for luncheon.'

Everything is excessive in Gus's world, including driving to Versailles just to eat.

'Oh. I had no time to change my English money. Lend me some francs and I will reimburse you later.' And he sweeps us down the stairs with his sombrero.

∽

We travel southwest out of Paris in the open car, and the streets rush past as Gus drives fast towards Versailles. In Tenby, he sped through the town on his bicycle with the same lack of care. For an hour, there are occasional sights of isolated figures until pedestrians blur and shop fronts merge into one shining glass expanse: Gus roars through unknown parts of Paris, houses without gardens flat up against the road. His open jacket flaps in the wind. A swaggering manner seems to have taken over his whole body. Out of the city, an avenue of tall poplars lining the road propels us into the distance, and woods and villages zip past, with the clear sky above pressing down on the horizon. It all resembles an impressionist painting, with cows and hillocks dreamy in the sunlight, stroking the rolling fields, giving way to the outskirts of Versailles. I would speak to Gus, but in case he answers and takes his gaze off the road, I hum one of Father's organ pieces to keep calm – the only hymn Father published – and my singing voice is stronger than my speech. Gus roars with laughter, thankfully still gripping the wheel, and deftly swerves the car alongside a brasserie with outside tables sheltering under a long tassel-fringed blind. The summer sun gilds the brasserie's gold lettering, and the subdued grey paintwork gives the restaurant an affluent air.

'This is all I have until my next modelling job,' slipping him a five-hundred-franc note. 'Try not to spend it all.'

'Only the best for my little sister,' and greets the *maître d'hôtel*.

'I am not inordinately hungry,' I say, studying the menu, 'An entrée suffices,' but Gus has already ordered us oysters with Muscadet. Happily, the cost is low.

'Gwen! Fancy encountering you here. I did not know you frequent Versailles?'

As I glance up, Hilda is beaming at us both, together with a younger woman clutching their two portfolios. Hilda's usual tatty smock and boots are discarded today in favour of a smart broadcloth coat and pumps, but she is still irredeemably mannish.

'Hilda, how lovely to see you. This is Augustus my brother.'

'And this is Ruth Manson; my new artist find. Gwen and Augustus John.'

Gus is still drinking, ignoring Hilda and Ruth. I have mentioned Hilda's sexual preferences in the past, so is he assuming Ruth is of a similar tendency? He is only friendly to women he thinks he can conquer.

'Do join us,' and I raise a hand for a waiter.

'If you can match our drinking,' Gus slurs.

As he leans back in his chair, Ruth gives me a little pout as if to say all men are tedious. A petite face peaks out from lush black hair falling to her shoulders. It is not a conventionally beautiful face, but her grey eyes are startling against the hair.

'Thank you but we have already eaten, and Ruth needs to return to her daughter in Meudon. We have enjoyed painting *en plein air*.'

'I have heard a great deal about you,' and Ruth blushes and smiles at me while avoiding Gus. 'If my request is not too impertinent, Hilda said that you sometimes give painting advice. I would be honoured if you could visit me in Meudon on one occasion to see my work. Meudon is only a half hour from Paris and situated in beautiful countryside.'

Resting for a few days with someone who admires me is an attractive prospect. 'I would be delighted. The country air will do me good.' Hopeless at lying, I keep silent about my visits to Meudon.

'We must make haste, Ruth. The train departs soon.'

I am about to say we can drive you home, but Gus, seemingly bored, is ordering another bottle.

∽

The next weekend in Meudon I climb up the hill, past Rodin's house to nearer the Observatory. Ruth's building is two stories high in the grounds of an old chateau with tall beech trees and long, shining paths facing the Seine valley.

'You can see the Eiffel Tower.' I am still puffing after the climb. 'Thank you for inviting me.'

'You can see right across Paris; and the rent is cheap I understand though the owner is kindly not charging. You could consider moving to Meudon.'

What can I say? Rodin would not pay the rent on anywhere near his home, he would worry I might visit Rose; but the thought of being near him entices.

'And this is Rosamund my daughter.'

The little girl must be seven or eight. Thick black hair, like her mother's, falls to her shoulders as she curtsy's before shyly taking her mother's hand. She has a sweet face. I wonder who the father is, how Ruth became pregnant, as Rosamund stares up at me.

'Do you think you will grow up to be an artist like your mother?' as Rosamund peeps around her mother's skirt.

She nods, still too shy to speak but gives me a big smile.

'Hilda made no mention of your choice of art,' turning back to Ruth. 'Do you paint or sculpt?'

'I paint, but I have much to learn.' Her features are handsome but guarded as if her inner life needs protecting.

'We all learn, all the time. I recently took extra classes at Colarossi.'

'But you are already such a fine artist! I would be so grateful if you would look at my work, but first we should eat. You must be hungry after your journey. I cooked a cassoulet.'

Later that evening, as I examine her paintings, Ruth's intensity, and willingness to listen, attracts me. One portrait of a nun stands out.

'She is from the convent, down the hill. The nuns are so kind to Rosamund after Sunday mass; the painting is a small return.'

'It is a fine portrait. Being a single mother it must be difficult to find time to work; the constraints on your time,' remembering Ida surrounded by clamouring children.

'We are so close to Paris, I find there many supportive women artists,' her cheeks glowing.

Ruth's obvious enthusiasm and sincerity is refreshing. 'Let us sketch together tomorrow.'

The weekend passes quickly. Rosamund is evidently used to playing quietly with her toys on her own, while we sketch each other and her in a warm circle of friendship.

'I will saunter around Meudon later; I may take your advice and see a few houses.'

'May I accompany you?' Rosamund shyly glances up from her dolls.

'Of course, we will explore together,' and Ruth approves.

It feels as if I have been invited into a new kind of family, one without hierarchies, without a demanding father or brother. Ruth shares Dorelia's calm, the same ability to manage meals, children and painting simultaneously; but with a seriousness all her own.

Rosamund and I step carefully down the steep slope into the village, her little fingers warm in mine. As we pass Rodin's house, I glance quickly through the hedge, pretending to search for a bird, but his garden is full of marble statues, not humans, and curiously I am relieved. Ahead, in the high street, nuns are leaving the convent church and beam at us both.

'The nuns resemble playing cards,' Rosamund whispers, with the clarity of a child, 'in their black and white clothes.'

As we make our way back to Ruth, after staring at a few

cottages, the long, winding street takes us in a different direction to the Observatory. At the top of the hill, stands an old house, nearer the forest with a spectacular view of Paris and overlooking Rodin's house. From here I could see Rodin in his garden when he is at home and breathe clean air walking the forest paths. The countryside is fragrant, with sweet-smelling chestnut trees and grass with herbs, soft underfoot. The birdsong is clamorous. If the rent is cheap, as Ruth claims, I could have two homes. Like my Master.

∽

Back in Paris, there is another letter from Gus. The New English Art Club exhibition was a success for us both. An American collector John Quinn bought one of my paintings. Infuriatingly, Gus does not say which, but I am to expect a letter from Mr Quinn apparently. Quinn must be eager because there is an expensive thick cream envelope here already, lying under Gus's thin one. Quinn has a loose, swooping hand covering the whole page, leaving no margins, like a man who wishes to take over the world. He writes he is a lawyer, friends with many artists and writers. A few names like Picasso and Yeats I know. As Gus wrote, Quinn is certainly generous. He mentions a ten-pound commission for Gus, and, for me, a one-thousand-franc advance on future paintings. I can exhibit anything, he writes, before delivering to him.

Much to reflect on, sitting in my wicker chair sipping tea. Of course, exhibiting my work gives it a provenance, allowing a painting to have a higher price when Quinn sells, but he makes a generous offer. The amount will cover almost all my expenditure, apart from the rent which Rodin pays. I can model for fewer clients, focus on my paintings, and now I could rent in Meudon. The chill I have been trying to cure all week, seems to be disappearing.

CHAPTER 32

MEUDON

Not long afterwards, I find an apartment in Meudon. The street name is auspicious – 29 rue Terre Neuve – although the house is old. I keep my Paris address, which Rodin pays for, because the room can be a studio. Ruth promised to ease my move.

'This is spacious,' and Ruth rolls up her sleeves. 'I hope you are content with Rosamund assisting our cleaning?'

The little girl's expression is serious like her mother's; fiercely clutching a brush in one hand and her doll with the other.

'You are as good as your Mama,' and stroke back Rosamund's tousled hair. 'There are three rooms and the kitchen,' turning to Ruth, 'even a grenier downstairs. But the grenier is for storage; we can clean it another day.'

'I love the way in which the morning sun dapples your floors,' as Ruth sweeps, 'and there is no traffic noise here. Outside our house the horses snort all the time when they reach the top of the hill.'

'And the convent bells ring,' Rosamund adds.

'I am used to bells. When I was your age, bells tolled us into church and out again twice on Sundays.'

'How boring,' and Rosamund sits to play with her doll.

Ruth is smiling at us both. Conversations with them are less stressful than with anyone since with the Slade girls in Bloomsbury. 'You said there is much to explore in Meudon.'

'I will be your guide.' Ruth is blushing.

'And me. You are my Aunty Gwen.'

Being an adopted aunt to Rosamund is tangible, somehow more real than with Gus's ever-increasing brood, and she is much friendlier. Meudon is meant to be my refuge from the world, but it also offers new experiences, new friendships. 'When we finish, I will treat us all to the tea room in the forest.'

After our late meal, the evening is cloudless. The moon hides behind the trees, ready to slide higher into the night sky; Ruth carries Rosamund asleep and her doll dangles in my hand. The walk and tea cleared my mind, and Ruth seems happy to wander down from the forest in silence, without questioning me about my life, unlike the women I model for in Paris who constantly converse. Ruth's calm is refreshing. Parting at the crossroads, I gently kiss Rosamund's curls so as not to wake her, hand over the doll, and Ruth's lips touch my cheek, making me desire more.

'Tell me when you next arrive in Meudon. I can decorate your flat. It will free me from my painting anxieties.'

'Wonderful – thank you! I intend to keep the rooms simple, with a few rugs on bare floorboards. Perhaps whitewash the walls.'

The Meudon flat will replicate Rodin's unfurnished studio but without his half-completed sculptures and dust.

As Ruth turns away, I walk straight to the back of Rodin's house on the other side from Rose's kitchen, so I will be invisible. After a few minutes, dogs scamper into the garden followed by a cloud of smoke. There he is, smoking a cigar, staring up at the sky. We are sharing the moon with its silver stream holding us together in the dusk like an Impressionist painting, but one ready to be hung on a wall – framed and distant.

∼

Meudon encourages my art, I write to John Quinn. Quinn is anxious about my work, wondering when a painting will arrive for him in New York. I can stop apologising that I paint very slowly and say that Gus is sending my painting direct from London. Quinn is so generous, telegraphing his payments regularly to Brentano's bookshop, which makes them simple to collect. Letters to Mr Quinn are easy to write. In those old letters to Rodin I needed to describe my feelings in intriguing ways and include fascinating intellectual topics. For Quinn, chatty accounts of Parisian cultural life keep him content. So I describe Henri Rousseau's exhibition who, at fifty years old, started painting not knowing at all how to paint, and yet the pictures are remarkable works.

Quinn's reply is not encouraging. A bad picture does not become good merely by growing old, and he is still waiting for one of mine. What can have happened? *Le Figaro* said the *Titanic* sank. Was my painting aboard? Gus reassures me the painting is on its way in another ship and should arrive shortly. *Le Figaro* is full of bad news. The art reviewer attacked my Master for praising Nijinsky's erotic dancing in the Ballets Russes. Rodin is so true, so honest. If he could see them, the journalist would be aghast at Rodin's drawings of me and Hilda embracing; I imagine myself posing again, because Rodin has asked me to come tomorrow to rue de l'Université.

∽

As I step off the tram outside Rodin's studio, the tall doors of the studio are ahead. The porter in his little office nods, recognising me, but with no indication I should enter. So I wait, scuffing my feet. It is a bright day with a cloudless sky. The street is full of couples, a few arm in arm, others wheeling perambulators. Inside me there is a kind of ache at their happiness, although I do not wish for marriage, or children. Women artists cannot complete great work with a perambulator in the hall. Workmen repairing a window in the café opposite whistle, but I practice a conversation with Rodin. Should I tell him about my new friend Ruth and her little girl? No, I will ask him how he is, what he is working on, and describe what we share – our love of *Pamela*.

As the scenes flash through my mind, Rodin is walking towards the porter's office. He smiles at me, putting a finger to his mouth.

'*Ma chèrie*. We have only a few minutes. The Duchess is in the studio today.'

Of course she is. She never leaves you for a moment.

'How are you?' The first question on my list. 'What are you working on?'

'Not the Muse, I fear. The commission has been terminated by the International Society due to my protracted delay. They are asking for the funds to be returned. I wanted to tell you in person.'

Tears well up. We created the Muse in unison, and its presence reminds him of our history.

'Of course you are upset, *ma chèrie*, but I will visit soon. Take care of yourself and keep calm,' and disappears indoors.

My stomach is empty as if I have been without food all day, and people, pavements, cabs seem devoid of colour, with hard edges. My old life is in the Muse, my body too. Sculpting was the reason we came together. The Society's decision is absurd. Ahead a cat arches its back at a dog. Both animals disappear, and tears are falling. My coat sleeve is as damp as my cheeks and a voice says, 'May I assist, Mademoiselle? Are you unwell?'

A thick-set man in a bowler is leering at me. Despite his friendly questions, he is probably thinking of something other than support. Jumping onto a passing tram, steadying myself on the platform, I reach home and my canvases.

∽

The first day of June 1911, and a month since Rodin did visit. He scarcely stayed an hour, but there was little time to discuss our art. Somehow those discussions have become more significant to my work than our passion, and I miss his ideas; but with the beginning of summer, today is for leisure, visiting the Louvre and meeting Ruth and Rosamund for luncheon outdoors. There is always a peculiar lightness in the air whenever Ruth and I meet. The streets are crowded today with open cars gliding past, some being driven by emancipated women in beehive veils. The world is changing, moving on, carrying me with it. At the Seine, the beauty of the Ile de la Cité takes my breath away and, on the other side of the river, the Louvre's cupolas shine in the sun. The bright colours could have been borrowed from Rousseau's palette and I stand, imagining for a moment how the effect would look if on painted glass.

The Louvre is emptier than usual, I suppose, because it is Monday. The few spectators are tourists, it seems, from their foreign languages. When I visited with Ursula and the other Gwen, we rushed through quickly to see the Mona Lisa. Today there is time to stand before other paintings assessing techniques, especially those, like mine, with surfaces conveying subtleties of light and atmosphere. Poussin converts light to colour in stimulating ways; the paintings are so luminous. Yet, I wish my figures to have inner lives, floating in my spaces. Somehow today the pictures seemed not old friends but, old teachers whose judgements I had already moved beyond. Ahead, the Venus de Milo stands alone at the end of a corridor waiting to usher me into the Renaissance rooms. She is cold but magical. The strangest thing is that no one misses the arms, as though arms are defects in a perfect woman. Perhaps I should persuade Rodin that our Muse needs no arms? Have the commission renewed?

It is tempting to sit after all the hard work of staring, and I will rest in front of Mona Lisa, my last picture of the morning, but her room is entirely full. What an overwhelming number of people, as if the room has drained everyone from elsewhere in the Louvre. The gallery was too crowded to look carefully at the art, as if everyone had come to see each other.

'Why are there so many visitors, especially on a Monday?' I ask a guard at the entrance. 'She is never this popular.'

'Haven't you heard, Mademoiselle? It is because she has been stolen.'

Standing on tiptoe, a blank space on the wall is just visible. The crowd in front is silent in homage as if the Virgin Mary has disappeared.

'More people are coming to see her missing than ever came when she was here.'

A kind of melancholy pervades the room. I will write about the event in a letter to Rodin, creating a story. Art has never been this significant to so many people. But the clock on the wall shows nearly one o'clock. Ruth arranged to meet me with Rosamund in the Luxembourg Gardens for our luncheon. Rushing down the Louvre's wide marble staircase and outside, the sunny day is an antidote to the gallery chill. Ahead, in a passing omnibus, Rilke is riding on the top deck as if in a trance, oddly out of place amongst the other burly passengers with his sweet, pale face. What a coincidence. Rilke deserves a visit but not today – Ruth and Rosamund are waiting. Across the Seine the gardens are busy with children. We are meeting at the lake, and all around its perimeter, boys roll hoops or spin tops, and schoolgirls in black pinafores, more circumspect, sit together on benches sharing ices. Ruth is at the far end, holding onto Rosamund's coat as the little girl guides a miniature boat with a stick and hook. Ruth is dressed in green silk with a matching cape embroidered with pink flowers like figures in the Japanese prints Rodin gave me. A man across the lake examines Ruth with the eye of an art dealer appraising an auction item.

'Apologies for my lateness. You are particularly stunning today, Ruth.' And I kiss her on both cheeks.

'Clothes I can manage; it is painting as fine as you which is unobtainable.'

'Aunty Gwen,' Rosamund throws her arms around my hips.

'Careful, Rosamund,' Ruth says, 'you will lose your sailing boat.'

Before the voyeur can chance an intervention, I grab the stick, bringing the boat alongside the pavement.

'Bravo,' Rosamund claps her hands.

'Time for food and drink,' walking us over to the café. 'Ruth – would you like Japanese tea? You have the appearance of a Japanese lady today.'

'Ugh, not tea.' Rosamund frowns. 'May I have ice cream?'

Ignoring Rosamund for a moment, Ruth blushes at my compliment. 'Your thoughts are as interesting as your paintings.' I blush in turn.

Her hand holding mine is firm like a protective shell.

'Shall we all have ice creams?' I ask.

CHAPTER 33

MÈRE POUSSEPIN MEUDON

The new portraits for Quinn are finished at last. Gus told me to send the paintings to the New English Art Club for exhibition, and the club would then send them onto Quinn. It is not only my drafting and redrafting which is time consuming, I wrote to Ursula, but sometimes painting models you dislike is a punishment worse than Sisyphus's rock. Hard to find an inner self in a model when their conversations are boring, so several days in Meudon will help me recover.

Meudon's high street has a sleepy holiday air today except for a crocodile of schoolgirls dreamily walking down the hill. The long line of serene faces atop matching grey cloaks is like a strong gesture on a canvas. Their tranquillity must stem from their faith.

'Good day,' I say to the nun at the rear who pats my arm as if giving a benediction. It is a comforting sign. 'I attend mass in Meudon, Sister, and make my first confession tomorrow.'

Not a full confession; Rodin must not be mentioned, at least not our past relationship.

'You will become God's child,' the nun says. 'Like all of us.'

My prayers in the church next to Gus's house, the solace of Ida's memorial, and the transcendental Notre-Dame, seem to have led me here, to the mass in Meudon. It is not the mass alone which appeals but the whole spectacle. The nuns wear black aprons matched by the black dresses and white collars of the little girls, and the clothes resemble workers in Bon Marché or restaurants, with the nuns' headdresses the starched napkins on tabletops. Sketching them each Sunday has its rewards – a sense of belonging – which I will enjoy for longer than my Slade years, I am tempted to tell Gus, but he would never understand.

'I need to learn more,' following the line as it takes a right turn and stops in front of a convent door.

'Then enter,' she says pulling on a rope attached to a bell by the gate, 'our Mother Superior will be happy to give instruction. She is as knowledgeable about life as about prayer.'

The convent's interior is musty and chilly after the street, a damp smell as in the village church but without the incense. While the girls hang up their capes, the nun conducts me along a cloister corridor and knocks at an open door.

'Mère Poussepin is always available. She keeps her door open for everyone,' ushering me inside.

The room is surprisingly small, not much bigger than a cell, and bare of decorations other than a large cross above the desk on which a bible rests in front of the Mother Superior.

'Be seated my child.' Mère Poussepin smiles.

She is short and dumpy, the picture of a country woman with rosy, shiny cheeks in a romantic painting by Ernest Walbourn, not a painter I admire. I had imagined an imposing, severe lady, but a long narrow nose gives her a more learned air and her eyes are bright, welcoming.

'Thank you for seeing me. I would like to have instruction in the faith.'

'Why?'

The question strikes me like a slap. Her eyes are friendly, unblinking.

Gus married in a registry office not a church; and although Rodin does attend mass in Notre-Dame from time to time, it may be more for show. Ruth is too free-spirited. But I need spiritual assistance, to understand my desires, and to persevere with my art, to learn how to grow.

'I find difficulty,' after a moment, 'in setting plans for myself.'

With rules for living, for my painting, everything will be less stressful. So far, my art absorbs some anxieties, but life escapes beyond the frames.

'Be uncomplicated, my child. Expect nothing from circumstance. My childhood was difficult with many obstacles, but when I turned to prayer everything became lucid.'

'I do say my prayers. I try to simplify my life. The stars in the sky and the plants on my windowsill console me, but sometimes life overwhelms.'

'I have watched you drawing during mass.'

Is she cross? I am quiet while I sketch; and it is easier to capture images when everything is so calm.

'Your life can be a work of art,' putting her fingers together as if in prayer. 'Be patient and wait for the colours to emerge.'

The room brightens as if the weather agrees with the prioress and encourages me to be composed. I will continue to be dedicated to art, to see Ruth and be open to what emerges.

'I will try to show my faith.'

'Every moment is holy. Do not soil the moments.'

Has she guessed about Rodin in a mysterious way? Does she have some divine insight? My past with Rodin was ecstatic but months go by now without a visit or modelling and my painting is my life.

'I am not certain I should say this since we have only just been introduced, but may I paint your portrait?' the idea unexpectedly in my mind. Painting will show commitment to the church, to the convent.

'I am too humble for grand portraits. But the nuns did ask me to consider the notion, and here you are. God moves in mysterious ways.'

'I work very slowly but it would be such an honour.'

'I will need to ask the priest's permission, but I am sure we can arrange sittings.'

'Thank you,' keeping a flash of irritation out of my voice.

∽

This spring, while I paint Mother Superior, a letter arrives from Ruth, inviting me to join her for a few days in Brittany. She has rented a house in Pont-l'Abbé which I will appreciate. Rodin is away yet again, selecting a London site for his sculpture *Bourgeois de Calais*; and the nuns seem happy for me to go. They are probably relieved to have their Mother Superior more available. She blesses me, laying her hands on my head in benediction, her cheeks rosier than ever, as if by becoming her child in faith, she blooms in turn.

With all the windows open, the train to Pont-l'Abbé is cooler than the air of Meudon. Trees seem to shrink in height as the train nears the coast, bending their trunks away from the sea as if auditioning for a painting by Van Gogh. On the station platform, Rosamund is clutching Ruth's hand, but the doll which always dangles from Rosamund's other hand is absent today; instead, she strokes the head of a black poodle. Rosamund is almost at her mother's waist already, as slim, and elegant as Ruth.

'Aunty Gwen,' she calls out, as I pick my way down the train steps, and I am the centre of two sets of arms as Ruth and Rosamund hug me tight.

'We have hired a diligence; we will be at the house in a trice. Our rooms are in a fisherman's cottage.'

'And this is Pluton,' Rosamund adds, as the dog leaps up. 'He barks but never bites.'

Do I like dogs? Edgar has disappeared, so there is no worry or guilt for befriending another animal and, as I rub behind Pluton's ears, he licks my hand to squeals of delight from Rosamund.

'You see Aunty Gwen. I said he is a good dog.'

Unforeseen tears are in my eyes; it seems as if I held in my feelings about Rodin for years and now, they could flow away into the day. Ruth puts a comforting arm around my shoulders as the cart horse trots into the village. Everything is peaceful. The granite houses are austere, but our house is protected from the sea wind by others opposite. Yet there is a sense of the sea in the glow of the sky, a freshness in the air, making me happy to be so close. In my room, I lay out brushes on the bookshelf to persuade myself that here, in this house, any remaining thoughts of Rodin can be banished. I am in a new place and the light is brighter than in Paris. A good sign.

After dinner, Rosamund disappears to bed and Ruth pours us both another glass of wine in front of a blazing fire.

'We can swim tomorrow if you care to, the weather is mild, but the waves can be high.'

'Waves never deterred me in Tenby. I will complete a sketch in the morning before the beach.'

'No need to work. We are free here to do as we wish.'

But work is what I need. If I succumb to hours without sketching, how will I manage without a pattern to the day? Draining my glass, I gently stroke her wrist. Rodin always made the first move; now I do and with it comes a new sensation – stronger, powerful. Emotion untroubled by tension. 'Let us walk down to the sea.' She holds my hand.

At the pierhead, we watch waves cresting sideways onto the beach, slapping the sand into lumps, white spumes rising into the drizzle.

'It *is* like Tenby! When I was a child, I used to sit on rocks resembling those ahead, waiting to be swept away.'

'I do not wish you to be in any danger, just to be content here with me and Rosamund.'

Her cheek is cold, wet with sea spray and my lips taste of salt after our long kiss. Ruth puts her arm around my waist, guiding me home. We go to bed together as soon as we are indoors although it is not completely dark. Leaning into her, uncertain if the kiss means she wants more, her breath is warm on my cheeks and she takes my hand, placing it between her legs. No need for words. My fingers rub up and down as rhythmically as I can, and her quim becomes wet, open. She moans and reaches for me in turn and her ardour streams right through me, reaching my heart as if desire has become love in an instant. With my last cry, we embrace and drift into the most comforting sleep I have ever known.

In the morning, drying myself on the beach, I watch Ruth and Rosamund run in and out of the water. The tide is in, and the waves are calmer, dark blue. I felt exuberant swimming, wanting to swim far out to sea. As I towel my hair, two little girls in school uniforms with their hair in plaits, perhaps a year younger than Rosamund, walk past on the promenade.

'*Bonjour*,' Rosamund calls out, waving her hand, and turning to me. 'They're Odette and Simone, our neighbours.'

In the distance their dresses are black oblongs. Charcoal, or the point of a brush, would capture them perfectly and I could leave the faces blank. Ruth picks up a towel, rubbing Rosamund dry, and I pull Ruth close to me with the subterfuge of enveloping her in my towel. The air feels heavy, electric.

'We can sketch the girls.' Ruth leans against me. 'They are happy to model; their parents need money.'

With Ruth and Rosamund on either side, it is a slow, but delightful walk back to the house.

A few days later, my sketches are complete with forceful, pleasing lines, and Ruth asks me for a final walk along the cliff path, overlooking the beach, empty now with the tide far out towards the horizon. An hour before my train to Paris.

'Will you be returning to Meudon?' keeping my hands in my pockets in case the trembling betrays my feelings. The certainty that Ruth lives a few streets away from my Meudon apartment means so much more to me than seeing Rodin in his garden.

'Yes, if I can continue to stay rent free. I do not wish to impose on my landlord too much.'

'If the owner needs to house a paying lodger,' trying to keep my voice level, 'you are both welcome to live with me.'

There is a wild poppy near my foot, and I pick the flower to avoid looking into her eyes until she answers.

'Thank you, I would like nothing better. Rosamund has become fond of you. As I have.'

Handing her the flower, I turn to kiss and my foot slips on the wet grass.

'Take care,' and she grabs my arm and pulls me to her.

We hold each other, the flower crumpled against her skirt.

'Let us pick a bouquet,' I say, 'for Rosamund.'

Ruth's lips brush my cheek, and we turn back towards the village. A new start.

CHAPTER 34

RODIN

This winter is biting cold, with a penetrating icy wind seemingly blowing all the way down the Seine from the sea. Christmas was a solitary affair in rue du Cherche-Midi, as well as New Year here in Meudon, but it is too cold to travel to Ruth and Rosamund in Brittany again, to their holiday stay. I will miss loving Ruth. With my chest tight with an infection, I stay indoors, and I can focus on painting because Quinn's generosity frees me from regular modelling. Meudon is my refuge; on Sundays I can attend mass and make my confession and the success of Mère Poussepin's portrait is encouraging me to paint several versions, each subtly different. In one, her chair seems like a throne, in another her habit is darker, and evening clouds are massing in a rear window. It is amazing how even little differences help me to create new relations between the figure and the foreground. The nuns want a portrait for each room as if Mother Superior is like the President of France hanging in every public building; but our conversations are delightfully informal. We talk about our childhoods and how prayer can become significant in my life.

This morning a blanket of snow covers the cottages and forest trees in Meudon, although the main road is already clear. The reflected light is as bright as a full moon on a cloudless night and the village is a Christmas card. Last week Rodin asked me to meet him at the station today so that we can travel together into Paris and to my apartment because he cannot visit me in my Meudon house – too close to Rose. Perhaps her proximity makes an erection impossible. The snow crunches under my feet like sugar crystals en route to the station; my breath is misty on the air, but my body is warm. After five minutes according to my watch, Rodin's car mutters into view, the black paint sleek, shining in the sunlight. As his chauffeur helps Rodin onto the pavement, it is like seeing a stranger, bent over a stick, clutching his chauffeur's arm for support. Strange how much he has aged over the past months. I would offer my shoulder, but the chauffeur is already guiding him onto the platform, and we all stand together, side by side, silent until the train puffs in.

'Thank you, Marcel,' Rodin releases the servant, after he and I are safely in the carriage.

Sitting opposite Rodin, the change in his appearance is startling. His cheeks are sunk downwards like one of his dogs. The hair is in white curls and thinner, but his skin's grey pallor is more shocking, as if the portrait of Dorian Gray is cracking in front of me.

'My dear, we will take a hansom directly to your apartment when we arrive. I have much less strength these days for walking.'

Is it simply old age or is he hinting at more – at some major illness? I should reassure him of my support. Today he seems more a father.

'Your eyes are as bright as ever, and your mind.'

He shrugs without smiling; seemingly not what he wants to hear. As he shrinks into his thick overcoat, he leans against the carriage wall, closing his eyes, and takes my hand. The train journey has never been so long.

Paris traffic turns the snow into slush and the horse splashes all the way to my building. The concierge's window is completely covered over inside with condensation, so thankfully no awkward explanations or conversations are necessary as we slowly climb the stairs. Rodin rests on the bed, and his eyes close again, while I bustle about lighting the stove, and make tea.

'Have you brandy? To take away the chill.'

Will alcohol make him sleepy and diminish his conversation? So I give him the square bottle together with the tea, leaving only an inch at the top of the cup for the brandy. As if guessing my thoughts, Rodin ignores the tea and slugs directly from the bottle, and mimes I should remove my bodice. Oddly shy, like the first time, my sash and the buttons take longer to undo, as Rodin removes his clothing. The white hair around his balls is even thinner than on his head, but his member is erect as ever. Kissing my arm from wrist to shoulder, he murmurs 'your beautiful arms,' and embraces me. His chest has even more grey hairs, but he has an old man's breasts, drooping down, almost the same size as mine. His pleasure seems brief; mine is negligible but the moment is sufficient. As we dress, he is deep in thought.

'I must leave soon for England. Is there anything English you miss?'

Gus, my friends, particularly Ursula, British newspapers.

'Tea – Earl Grey.'

He takes small steps to the door; his patent leather shoes must be pinching with his spreading feet. 'Take care of yourself.'

'When do you return?' For once I am unconcerned at his absence.

'I intend to travel straight to Rome. With the talk of war with Germany, I must see Rome's statues before too late. I will miss you.'

The parting comment I always longed to hear. Almost as much as 'my dear,' or once, 'my darling'. Rodin is never loquacious, so his few endearments are credible, but something has changed. The thrill when he touches my body, when his eyes glance at mine, has vanished replaced by the urgency of painting and my need to see Ruth again. The end of Rodin in my life, but now it has happened, it seems too hasty, too swift, like something out of a romance. An old man closes the door.

∽

'Rodin is vanishing from my life,' I say to Mother Superior, as I put the final touches to her second portrait. I have an odd sense of liberation, a sadness overlaid with freedom to fully explore life, at least on canvas. Switching from one painting to another of the same person allows me to experiment with techniques: keeping the overall shape and arrangements constant to give the works a solid pattern but taking risks with differing kinds of light which brings out the skin of the figure. Will she like my style?

'Great men,' she says as she stares straight at me, 'become great by prayer and hard work.'

I cannot say that Rodin became great through his attention to women's bodies. 'Perhaps so. For me, I work each day and abandon myself to God's kindness.' True but painting means more to me than God.

'My child, you are your own person; be separate from Rodin. You can take charge of your life.' Her fingers tremble as if she is about to pray.

'I am stronger now, I think,' feeling her maternal warmth, 'thanks to your advice and guidance.'

By working together we share our lives like a mother and child and, as children do with their mothers, I do not mention anything about my life which would trouble her. Her face is sweet; and when her lips curve upwards, dimples appear in her cheeks. The hours pass easily as the light changes, casting beams first on one wall then on another.

'I must prepare for Vespers,' as if reluctantly. 'You are very welcome to attend. We are delighted you come to mass so regularly, even if you sketch more than kneel.' She winks with a beatific smile; the dimples reappear.

'Thank you, but I am promised to a friend for dinner. The portrait has developed well today.'

As I finish gathering my paints together, she puts two fingers on top of my head. 'Bless you, my child. We will resume tomorrow.'

The sun's rays are low in the sky on the walk up to Ruth's house. Now winter is over, we enjoy the terrace, surrounded by pots of geraniums, under a magnolia tree, as if on an exotic island, created for the three of us.

'Dinner is only Rosamund and me. No guests.'

'Perfect. All I wish to see is you, and Rosamund of course.'

At the sound of her name, the little girl hurls herself at me.

'Aunty Gwen.' Wrapping her arms around my legs in her usual firm grip. 'May I show my painting? Mama and I worked side by side this afternoon. I will be an artist too, like you and Mama.'

'How will I contend with the competition?'

Rosamund's eyes grow wide with pleasure, and grasping my hand, she leads me indoors.

'You are such a tease,' Ruth whispers, 'I would appreciate your advice too.'

A miniature easel in front of a child-size basket-weave chair is alongside Ruth's easel. Both paintings contain a view of the garden stretching out into the forest.

'You have captured the trees' deep green very well.' Leaning down to assess Rosamund's picture.

As Rosamund blushes deep pink, she strokes the dog's head. 'Pluton helped, didn't you, you lovely dog?' And they run out into the garden.

'I do appreciate your kindness to Rosamond,' when her daughter was safely out of earshot. 'Will you be sweet to me too?' pointing at her canvas.

Oddly, Ruth has painted the garden covered with snow as if true observation is beyond her; or does the snow represent feelings inside her which she cannot reveal to me?

'It is charming, charming.'

Ruth's blush is less pink than her daughter's. 'I wonder, could you send my painting to John Quinn when you next send your own work?'

What can I say? Ruth's is a pretty picture but Impressionist, not the avant-garde works Quinn seems to prefer from his letters.

'Of course, I will send him my portrait of Chloe, together with your painting, and the drawings I made during mass.' Perhaps the mixture of genres might persuade Quinn to buy a few – hopefully, Ruth's.

'You are my dearest,' and she squeezes my hand.

Pluton bounces yapping around Rosamund who is gesturing at us, beckoning us to join her in the garden. No letter from Rodin for months. Has he returned from England or reached Rome? Somehow his absence is immaterial when Ruth is now in my thoughts.

'You are my family now,' squeezing her hand in turn, as something falls into place inside me.

CHAPTER 35

A TURNING POINT

Yesterday, the Seine was full of coal barges steadily gliding to military depots and today there is a change in the air, a kind of oppressive damp refusing to rain. My plants are bracing themselves to enjoy their daily watering, but suddenly Rodin walks into my Paris room without knocking. I had already cleaned the furniture, made my bed, but he only watches me not the surroundings. Today's gown is new – a white tea dress shaped in a narrow column, modern the Bon Marché assistant said, and I hold his gaze for as long as I dare, with the air between us seemingly sucked out of the space.

'Ma chèrie,' Rodin frowns, 'I need so much to see you, to talk with you.'

What can it be? Need can mean so many things: desire, obligations, demands. He reaches for my fingers, and an old rush of passion from his touch should return but is absent. He does not pull me down onto the bed this time, and I am pleased. Talk is sufficient. His face is worn and fragments of plaster dot his beard as if he has just finished a day's work.

'You are the very creature I desire.' His hand now by his side. 'The only person who understands my pain.'

I should be offering up Hail Marys that Rodin wants me for my understanding, my mind, not just my body. Hearing that Rodin desires conversation first and with no one else is incredibly fulfilling. I feel surprisingly poised and confident, as if I can take ownership of the day.

'May I make you some tea?' wishing the phrase were less banal but I need time to think.

'Thank you,' wiping his forehead, 'It is hot outside.'

In the kitchen, my finest cups and saucers are already clean. They always carry a stain of sadness as a gift from Ida, but as I place one carefully next to Rodin on the bedside table, what should I say, what would Rodin want to hear? Sentences are forming in my mind, words of praise for his sculptures, for him, and I glance around the room as if the right phrase might be nesting among the plants but Rodin rushes into a speech before I can speak.

'It is the *Gates of Hell*. I can never finish. I began the sculpture long before we met. One of the figures grew and grew and escaped, turning into *The Thinker* and I worry that other figures might escape, that I cannot contain all my ideas.'

Taking a sip of tea, he stares at me. He is right, the sculpture is overpowering, full of squirming, intertwined men, and women. It was the first piece I noticed when I entered his studio; everyone does. The figures wail like lost souls.

'The sculpture is magnificent, stunning,' thinking he must want more, something knowledgeable, something only an artist would see. 'The bodies cling so intricately together; they touch at many points with perfect balance. It feels as if you have captured the whole world of Hell – the surfaces seem unending. Surely there cannot be additional work?'

He takes my hand again and his trembles, with the same dampness as his forehead.

'*The Gates* are part of me. There is no boundary between me and the sculpture.'

He approaches all his female models in the same way, but now is not a time for flippancy.

'The sculpture absorbs all my fears. I worry that if I finish, the fears will take me over instead, but if the figures escape what will remain?'

Normally I can never have my fill of his thoughts but today he is vulnerable.

'You seem so changed. You always counter my anxieties, just with the feel of your hands.' I place his on either side of my face as if my soft cheeks can absorb his emotion.

'It is the *Picture of Dorian Gray*. If the sculpture disintegrates so will I.'

I remember he agreed to meet Oscar Wilde in Paris. It was the talk of the Slade, of London. I admired Rodin enormously for seeing Wilde in public; we all did. In every life there is one moment which is the source of our outcomes, lying beneath the layer of the present, forming our future self. As a student, hearing about Rodin's bravery and enjoying the strength of his gaze in the British Museum, was that moment.

'*Dorian Gray* is a novel, not real life. Wilde's death had nothing to do with his art and your art will be famous for ever. Your studio is full of half-finished pieces; there are many works you can turn to. Let your assistants work on the *Gates*, push the piece away from you for a time.' I want to say why not return to the Muse.

'You are right,' he says sitting up straight and gazing at me. 'I need to free myself more often.'

'Right' is such a surprise. Somehow, I know that this moment will become the beginning of the rest of my life, like the sexual passion which triggered my love. Rodin recognises my ideas as if I am equal in art, and I am happier than I have felt for many months.

'I have also freed myself from the Duchess.'

Stunned, a feeling of unbelief slowly turns into pleasure.

'What happened?' I cannot say more because my voice might reveal delight.

'A box of drawings disappeared, and she accused my assistant Marcelle. But when I examined Marcelle, her honesty was transparent, and I realised then that the Duchess had been making money from my work. I told her to leave immediately.'

Rodin once dismissed Rilke abruptly too, but they are now reconciled. Can he really be free of the Duchess?

'I refused to see her again and she returned to her husband. This month has been tumultuous.'

'How can I best assist?' I do not want his answer to be 'let me enter you'. My work and Ruth are my constants.

'How do you remain calm to paint when you are anxious?' He smiles still holding my hand.

'I focus on everyday things that no one notices, and that can become significant and beyond measure in my pictures. Like the chair you are sitting on.'

Laughing, Rodin kisses my hand, resting it on the arm of his chair.

'And I write my diary. I become self-possessed every time I write as if my older, sensible self is writing.' Not the reason I write but I do not know all the reasons. Love could be one or more likely fixing my life firmly in print.

'Marie, you are so perceptive, as well as beautiful.' Smiling again, his face close to mine.

The Duchess is no more. I am the only woman he can talk to; ours is a true friendship not just a sexual relationship. His other women can never understand the pain and fears of creativity. I am a painter and I do.

'You have put me back together again, ma chèrie,' as he stands and takes his hat. 'Like that English children's character.' I cannot tell him Humpty Dumpty remained in broken pieces.

The room is flooded with colour as he bends over, pulling me to him. The kiss is tender, and, as he leaves, it seems as if a breeze wafts him out and gently closes the door.

CHAPTER 36

AUGUSTUS

Soldiers sometimes parade along my street en route to the Gare du Montparnasse, with their horizon-blue uniforms blending with the sky. I am not tempted to paint them, and my room is a quiet sanctuary. There are still reminders of Rodin – *Pamela* on the bookcase, his portrait above my bed – but Ruth now haunts the room – the smell of her on my coat hanging on the door near the easel. Since I met Ruth, my work seems swifter, the brush knows where to go all by itself. My brushstrokes are looser, catching the effects of light. Two hours of painting and I sink onto the bed realising that my last meal was yesterday. The café on the corner may still be serving breakfast croissants with coffee at the usual reduced price for late arrivals.

At the bottom of the stairs, a soldier is standing between me and the street door, his greatcoat dark against the fanlight, an incongruous bushy beard atop the uniform.

'Gus! Why are you here and what on earth are you wearing?'

'To see you of course. Do you like my outfit? I bought this myself. It is called a walking-out uniform. The service dress the army offered was too tight-fitting. I prefer the Australian slouch hat, but the Canadian cap does keep out the rain.'

'But why are you in uniform?' A knot of tension is in my empty stomach. 'Surely you have not enlisted?'

Nothing in our wild lives in Tenby or at the Slade should have led to this – a soldier brother.

'I am an official war artist for the Canadians. I would never fight and certainly not for that warmonger Kitchener.'

'Thank goodness,' kissing him on both cheeks. 'Otherwise I would disown you. Join me at a late breakfast. I have been painting all morning and am ravenous.'

Gus stands for a moment, scrutinising me as if he wants to memorise me for a portrait.

'I am pleased to hear that. I worry that you will use the excuse of war rations not to eat proper meals.'

Taking off one leather gauntlet, he holds my hand as if we are little children again walking along the promenade for a late swim, and gently steers us out into the street. The morning working crowd have left the café's outdoor tables free – the smoke from Gus's endless cheroots can waft away thank goodness.

'So where are you painting if this is not a war secret?' The waiter places a large basket of croissants and bread on the table. 'Not near the front line I trust?'

'No – nowhere too dangerous. I am becoming too deaf to hear the guns but, in any case, my batman tells me where to go.'

'A batman! You have become the very model of a major general.'

'But I cannot hum all the fugues.' He laughs. 'Some French soldiers thought I was George V because of my beard; we are the only two allowed to keep our facial hair. Generals' portraits are my current project, and generals are never near the front lines, but it is difficult to paint each with any individuality when they are all in khaki covered in medals.'

'I wonder what Quinn will say about war pictures?'

Gus avoids my gaze. 'At least war pictures have more meaning in life than those indecipherable post-Impressionists.'

It was the same when we were young. Gus just drew what he wanted, usually odd strollers from the streets and I was always defending his choices to Father. But what can I say? Ursula told me Gus has had no shows recently. Now Quinn is probably paying more attention to me. Quinn has certainly been generous in the past months.

'The bakers still use butter for the croissants,' I say quickly. 'It will not be for long; we have been told.'

'I am glad to see you enjoying food,' watching me move a wet finger over the last loose flakes. 'I do care for you.' And he reaches inside his knapsack. 'Here, I brought a Jaeger blanket to keep you warm.'

'The colour matches the clothing in my portraits,' stroking the grey wool. 'Thank you, and you find me well, although the lack of coals is a problem, so the blanket is the perfect gift.'

'I should not be in Paris – the detour was to see you. I go south tomorrow but when I return, in a few weeks' time, why not visit England with me?'

The invitation is tempting. I have read so much about Virginia Woolf and the Bloomsbury Group, who seem to share my views about pacifism, about life. Perhaps Gus could arrange a meeting. He claims to know everyone who matters. But I cannot leave Paris. The city is a kind of dictionary of human life which I can open at any point and find subjects and views. 'My home is here, and I have new friends who stimulate me, help me to paint.' He means well but I am my own person now.

'Are you not with Rodin anymore?' He stuffs out a cheroot, glancing up quizzically.

It is Ruth who gives me a fresh purpose when I paint, not Rodin.

'Rodin is more of a supportive figure these days. We share ideas, our thoughts about art. Somehow our discussions are more significant than whatever came before.'

'Well, Quinn's suggestions are not forthcoming now. He takes little interest in my work.' He picks up the bill. 'That is why I have become a war artist – pastures new, to the letter. I will pay. I owe you for our last meal.'

'Thank you. Perhaps it is the war. Quinn is probably cutting his expenditure like the rest of us.' I cannot tell Gus I had a hundred-franc note from Quinn only last week. Quinn seems to take anything I send because the work is good. Every portrait.

'Well, at least the generals pay well,' and Gus stares down the street as if expecting a garrison to march towards us.

Gus and I are becoming an old companionable couple, second

guessing each other's thoughts. His dominating style, his influence over me, is fading into the past. And me? I have never felt more alive, waiting in the wings to take my place on a well-lit stage.

'Do think about returning, I worry about your safety although I have every faith that the war will end soon now that the Americans and Canadians are here,' kissing me goodbye. 'I'm off to buy crates of wine.'

Is it me he really wants to see or acquire cheap wine? Or to grumble about Quinn?

'You look splendid,' smoothing down his greatcoat. 'Really imposing. Take great care.'

CHAPTER 37

1914, RILKE RETURNS TO GERMANY

Rilke's oval-shaped apartment with its soaring ceilings and terrace onto the gardens is almost empty. A few packing cases rest along one wall. The bust sculpted by his wife, and the wide oak table, where he always writes facing an open window, are gone, but the smell of apples still overwhelms the space like an old country house.

'Thank you for coming, apologies for the late invitation. I had little time for farewell calls,' and Rilke gestures at the packing cases.

'Are you really leaving Paris for ever?' hearing a slight tremble in my voice. '*Le Figaro* reports that the Germans will never take Paris or much of northern France.'

'But I am German. That is my predicament. My ill-health exempted me from war service, but it is only a matter of time before the French start rounding us up as you English are imprisoning Germans.'

'It is true. Sometimes I am ashamed to be English, to be somehow associated with all that. Are you not sad to leave? I am unhappy to lose you.'

'It will be a sadness.' He takes my hand. 'You are such a good friend. Paris is a magnet and in this city three years has been but a single day.'

'Paris *is* the centre of the world; and you have been such a support to me since Rodin first introduced us.'

'I have been able, unfortunately to do so little for you. But you will flourish even in wartime.' He smiles. 'You are one of the aristocrats of art; and Rodin will stay in Paris too, I imagine, at his age.'

Somehow Rilke's praise for my talent far outweighs the reassurance about my Master. 'You are kindness itself. Did you finish writing your book about Rodin?'

'Yes, and it is being published in Germany so another reason why I must return. But I am being remiss, would you like some tea?'

'Thank you,' sitting on the one remaining chair, placed near the window to the street. Outside a blind woman is singing. A black poodle tugs on her left hand and as a coin falls near a dish at her feet, the poodle takes it in his mouth and tosses into the metal basin. Then she launches into another verse as if entirely sure of an audience.

'I *am* flourishing,' I say holding the full teacup carefully.

'I too,' Rilke laughs, squatting on the floor. 'I am beginning to behave like a proper published poet. I wear a fashionable black coat to readings, remove my gloves very slowly, keeping my eyes on the audience, daring them to look away. You would find the spectacle amusing.'

'Your poems are works of art.' The cool air from the garden smells now of grass cuttings mixed with the apples. The laziness of a fine afternoon fills the room where two friends respect each other, and seemingly can discuss anything.

'I have always wanted to ask, what first impressed you about Rodin's techniques?'

'His candle test,' Rilke replies, without hesitating. 'He holds a candle to a sculpture and moves around the contours to check any flaws. It seems as if he is honouring the body just as people place a candle before a church statue.'

The first evening in Rodin's studio, after the assistants left for the night, when he lit candle after candle around the couch and kissed me, delicately, tenderly, is as bright as the sunlight on Rilke's face. Was Rodin honouring my body? How long ago that seems and how changed I am from then. 'That is how he assesses movement – with light and shadow. But I too have learnt how to create light around my figures in paint. They are sometimes as luminous as Rodin's sculptures.'

'Art is your true calling. Not modelling for Rodin.'

True. Rilke always reads my thoughts, as if I am a child; although, sitting on the chair, I tower over him on the floor. A pair of rimless glasses balances on his nose, giving him a professorial appearance, but behind the lenses his eyes beam.

'To love is crucial too,' he adds, after a moment. 'For one human being to love another is perhaps the most difficult of our tasks; it must be learnt.'

'I will miss your wisdom. I am still learning to love.'

'Sometimes I experience other people's passions with such painful acuteness,' he says, 'I have to lean my head against the gate of the Luxembourg to breathe in the cool evening air.'

'I too. I often take evening strolls in the gardens.' Walking along the paths strewn with leaves, with their damp, fusty smell, used to settle my nerves.

We are so similar in some ways, yet I am not as good as Rilke, but what does it mean to be a good person? Perhaps goodness is different for men and women because there are so many set expectations about women's behaviour. Rilke is a good man – kind, sympathetic, supportive – more so than Rodin or Gus; sometimes Rilke seems like a young priest or seminarian.

With a quizzical glance, he rises, washes both cups, and wrapping them in newspaper, places them in a crate.

As he stands, I wonder what it would be like to be his wife. Why have I never wanted love from Rilke? It is something about his dreaminess, his separateness from the world like that sight of him one day – solitary on a crowded Paris omnibus. Rilke is a brother but so different from Gus – self-effacing, sensitive, making me feel like a serious artist, encouraging me. There is a quiver in my stomach, like the pages of a newspaper blowing away in a breeze but it is not disappointment about him. The quiver is nothing to do with missing the kind of life Rilke would share. That life is unpredictable, constantly on the move around Europe. No, the quiver is the excitement of possibilities with Ruth, about what life with Ruth might become.

'Rodin is growing old,' and Rilke glances at me. 'He wanders around sucking sweets, with important letters sticking out of his pockets, unanswered.'

'Whatever Rodin and I share is not intoxication anymore but a kind of peaceful regard.'

'You must realise that you will grow as a painter, that life has not forgotten you, that it holds you in its hand and will not let you fall. You will have a great future,' and kisses me goodbye on both cheeks. 'Take great care of yourself Marie.'

CHAPTER 38

WORLD WAR ONE

The pen is scratchy today, but new nibs are hard to find. A glass of wine holds down my paper on an outside table in the breeze. The inside of the café is too full and stuffy. Gus has written again asking me to return to England, not to stay in Paris during the war.

Taverne de la Brasserie Dumesnil Frères, Boulevard Montparnasse, Paris
Dear Gus
Isn't this a dreadfully ugly piece of café paper? It is cold in my room, and I have no coals for a fire, so I am here to write to you. There is a band playing and a lot of startling-looking ladies among the men. I have my sketchbook and writing paper all over the table to deter visitors, so they think me a mad Anglaise. Perhaps I am but Paris is my home now.

He has kindly researched boats and trains to return via Boulogne. Newspapers carry blank spaces now, so that no one can discover where the Germans are massing, but I will stay. A strange resilience is in me today and writing it down makes it real.

'It's a Taube,' a gentleman calls out.

Everyone stares up at the sky. Against the sun, a short plane has one wing stretched across the whole of its body.

'The Germans bombed near Versailles,' his female companion adds. 'We should go indoors.'

A few customers carry glasses into the café, but there is no danger because the plane is slowly moving west. The wing resembles one of the sycamore seeds falling into our garden at Tenby, its wing almost translucent against the darkening sky, except the plane does not twirl as it disappears into the distance. As the plane banks away from Paris, the sunlight picks out a black cross highlighted on a white background. The customers are right, a German plane. Putting down my pen, the wine shakes in its glass as I raise it trembling to my lips.

'The plane has disappeared,' and the same gentleman emerges from the café, carrying his drink. 'Let us raise a toast. Vive la France.'

He stays calm while I feel embarrassed – a habitué of Paris, thirty-seven years old, quivering like a child at a Halloween monster but we all dread this moment – bombs raining on Paris. Except there are very few bombs and the Germans are still far away.

The French are surprisingly stoic. Ruth is in Meudon. She will be making a meal for Rosamund with Pluton bounding back and forth across the lawn, playing with the little girl. Will she hear the plane or see it from the house? The winter sun glances off the glasses on the café tables. How strange that sunbeams pay no attention to what happens elsewhere in the sky; they keep shining on our bodies, warming my back. Smiling, I raise my glass to the gentleman. The letter's conclusion is in sight.

Your letter gave me great pleasure. You told me things I did not know about politics and thank you.

Much love

Gwen

'You are calm, Mademoiselle.' The gentleman clinks his glass against mine. About my age, his bowler is shiny with long wear, but his camel coat is smart. For once a man is treating me as a passing acquaintance, rather than voyeuristically as a prostitute. It must be because his female companion is nearby.

'My brother in England wishes me to return, but I assist the English troops here, translating for them at Gare de Montparnasse. Many are young boys.'

'Bravo, Mademoiselle. I admire your soldiers.'

Finishing his wine, he tips his hat and strides out erect, as if imitating an English officer, his companion in tow.

Earlier this month I wrote to Ursula about the soldiers. How often they lose their luggage at the station, seem unconcerned, and invade the souvenir shops, grabbing whatever takes their eye. I do not approve, I tell them, but they seem pleased to hear an English voice.

After helping at the Gare de Montparnasse, I savour some peace in my studio, but today, finishing my wine, a telegraph is more urgent – to alert Ruth of my arrival because my hands are still shaking despite my bravado in the café. Ruth matters more than anything and I can be with her by late afternoon.

'I needed to see you,' as I reach Ruth on the terrace. 'The Germans are flying over Paris now.'

'I saw the plane too.' Her voice is tense, giving off a kind of nervousness, a restlessness she usually hides from Rosamund. 'It circled before flying away to the west.'

Just the two of us. Is the little girl missing today? Ruth points up the staircase, placing a finger on her lips.

'She is playing with Pluton in her room. Do not disturb her. We need to talk. I have decided it will be sensible if she and I return to England.'

'But they say the Germans won't invade Paris. They have too many unhappy memories of the 1870 siege.'

True. My concierge repeated the story not newspaper propaganda. Concierges know everything.

'It was forty-four years ago. In any case shops here are closing, and wounded soldiers are reaching Meudon. I do not want Rosamund to be scared.'

'Have you already booked tickets?' I am trying not to sound upset.

'I have rented lodgings for two days near Boulogne, ready to board the first free ferry. There is plenty of room for you. Please travel with us.'

She wants to be with me, be her companion. The lawn outside the window shimmers in a breeze.

'You know I love you.' This is the first time I have mentioned love, a word I wanted to hear first from her. Is it too soon? Will such an open declaration dismay Ruth?

'Then you will travel with us,' and beams. 'We are a family. We should stay together.'

No word of love in return; 'family' will have to suffice. 'When the plane flew over, a strange feeling like a thrill went through me this morning at the café. I sensed it in others.'

'They will flee at the sight of the Germans. You should escape too.'

'I am not certain. In any case, when I read *The Times*, England seems a foreign country to me now.'

'I will miss you,' and Ruth grasps my hand.

'Is Aunty Gwen going away?' Rosamund skips into the sitting room, pulling Pluton behind her.

'No dear,' Ruth drops my hand and cuddles her daughter. 'Gwen will stay in Paris, but we are returning home just for a few months. The generals say the war will end quickly. By Christmas the newspapers promise.'

'So we will see Aunty Gwen at Christmas,' Rosamund beams. 'We can pull crackers together.'

'I do hope so.' A snowy landscape surrounding a cosy cottage. Ruth, Rosamund and me warm by a blazing log fire, after snowballing; Christmas stockings hanging from the mantlepiece. A banal Victorian image but bright, enticing.

'Three months at most,' Ruth says.

In the garden a solitary squirrel flicks his tail madly from side to side as impatient as me.

'If Meudon is threatened, I will consider leaving, but I am helping the curé care for soldiers, as well as still painting the Mother Superior.'

It has taken three years to find a place, a safe community. Rue Terre Neuve is a haven; the cosy cottage will have to wait.

'In any case, the Germans plan to invade England,' I whisper to Ruth. 'You might not be safe for long.'

'Lord Kitchener is organising a huge volunteer army. I am not particularly patriotic, but I trust the English more than the French.'

Evidently, she has been reading about all this for some time without mentioning it to me.

'Some of the English soldiers here and at Gare Montparnasse are volunteers, but they are brave.'

They will not be able to save us, but I am at home here. I have lived in Paris for over a decade; the French are good to me. Sometimes I think this is where I will die.

Rosamund has fallen sleep on the sofa behind us with Pluton's head in her lap and Ruth tucks a rug over Rosamund's legs and looks directly at me.

'I do hope we are not discussing politics, as a way of avoiding talking about each other?'

Her directness is surprising. The honesty must show she cares.

'My love for you will survive any separation.'

Is this what she wants to hear? Is she worried about Rodin as if I will be overcome by fresh adoration of him as soon as she leaves? Impossible; he and I are partners in thought, in intellect not in lust.

'I will never give you up,' she says.

She is jealous but independent too. Her worries about Rosamund trump staying with me. It should be so. The squirrel has disappeared, and the garden is a solid black through the window, cut through with a single shaft of moonlight.

'Stay the night with me, Rosamund will be happy to see you in the morning.'

We carry the sleeping girl upstairs. As she settles under her eiderdown, she smiles with her eyes closed, as if giving us her benediction. The moment we sit on Ruth's bed, everything falls into a pattern as if the steps are all planned. Her touch is transforming my irritation into lust. I want very badly to remove her clothes and she lies back as if in unstated agreement. Leaning over, my fingers feel her wetness. She is a canyon, a ravine, taking the fingers into her and our voices synchronise. 'Yes, yes.'

CHAPTER 39

PARIS, A GYPSY

The Rotonde café has a pianist tonight, the concierge said. It will be good to be surrounded by revellers with Ruth away in England. The empty streets are still damp with the morning's rain. Is it raining in England too? Rosamund loves jumping in puddles although Ruth disapproves. If only we were both holding hands with Rosamund right now, swinging her high over any pools. A hansom cab dashing past, as if frightened to be exposed to the sky, splashes my skirt. My favourite maroon dress; drat the war.

Paris is unnaturally quiet since the declaration of war. At least most of the shops are still open and the cafes are full. With emptier streets I can walk freely everywhere – to modelling for Hilda and other women, shopping, caring for wounded soldiers at the Gare de Montparnasse. Yet with my constant grippe, it is as if my body is telling me the war is not proceeding well. *Le Figaro* continues to print blank, white spaces among the non-news items.

The Rotonde's lights blaze out as they did before the war. Smoke fills the bar, and a pianist taps out a rapid beat, underscoring laughter, and conversations. Ahead there is one empty table with room for my sketchbook and I order a glass of wine. From my seat opposite a gilded mirror, my cheeks are flushed with the heat of the room, and the maroon dress is cherry-red in the glare of gas lights. After a sip, I sketch the lady at the bar with her tight, black lace bodice reflected in her mirror behind. The figure is not in the new elongated shape I have essayed with my models but has the effect of contre-jour from the mirror and in front couples are embracing and clapping the last notes of the pianist.

'May I join you, Mademoiselle?'

He resembles a gypsy. His brown moustache is luxuriant over a soft mouth and his long curly hair is pushed behind silver hooped earrings. A welcome sight – something to write about to Gus who would love the gypsy outfit. Glass buttons, sewn randomly, speckle his jacket and silk pantaloons are tucked into knee-length leather boots.

'You may, as long as you do not interrupt my sketching.'

'You seem sad. I merely wish to lighten your mood.'

'It is the war.' Being solitary during wartime is less appealing than before, and for one evening having company will be agreeable. 'My brother Augustus knows Romany. He bought a gypsy caravan for painting trips.'

The man smiles, waving two fingers at a waitress, and within seconds two glasses arrive on a tray. 'Then you will know that we carry good luck with us everywhere we go.'

Reaching into a deep pocket he produces a bouquet of heather tied with a white ribbon.

'For you.'

'On London's streets, gypsies expect coins for heather, but I have no more francs with me I fear.'

'You could sketch me instead, while we finish our wine.'

'I will,' quickly drawing outlines of his head and face.

'I worry too about the war. The Germans imprison gypsies.'

'My brother taught me to respect you all.'

'Then you will allow me to read your palm?' sipping his wine.

His eyes are warm, and the wine is relaxing. My palm is on the table and, scrutinising it, his eyes crinkle at the sides as if he has smiled all his life. Tracing a finger along each crease in turn, he frowns. 'I have sad news and good news, Mademoiselle. Which would you prefer to hear first?'

'The sad news as long as it is not too shocking.'

'It is not alarming, Mademoiselle, but you may feel dismay.

Someone you used to care deeply about, but do no longer, will become seriously ill next year and die soon after. This is in your heart line.'

Not Ruth, she is young and healthy, and I love her – very deeply. And I love Gus and care for Rodin. Perhaps it is McEvoy. Would I feel distress at an announcement of his death? Given how much McEvoy drinks, an early death is to be expected but I would feel a frisson of sorrow.

'And the good news?'

Smiling now, he draws his finger vertically again down the palm. 'You will have a long life and become famous one day.'

'Thank you,' handing him my rough sketch. 'You have helped me forget the war for an hour,' pushing my sketchbook, along with the heather, into my bag.

The gypsy remains seated, stroking his moustache, as I button up my coat. I will write to Gus about the gypsy but without mentioning my future fame. His exhibitions are receiving poor reviews, although he seems to make more money than ever before.

It is too late to walk back home alone through the dark streets. A tram glides past as I exit the bar and, seeing me about to jump on board, the driver, a woman stops. The first woman driver I have seen. The stars through the window have yellow haloes across the sky like Van Gogh's painting.

∾

I must have slept late. Sorting through my wardrobe, the maroon dress smells of cigarette smoke and wine and needs cleaning. In any case I wear it often so, and the new mustard blouse, set off by the wide black satin bow I bought in Bon Marché, needs a turn.

A gentle tap at the door, followed by 'Mademoiselle John?' A man's voice. 'It is Eugène Guioché.'

The name is familiar. Eugène is the assistant who first directed me to Rodin. My Master has sent one of his assistants in public to collect me. A surprise.

'One moment, I am dressing.'

'Apologies, Mademoiselle, if I woke you.'

'No matter,' pulling my mustard blouse over my head, 'enter.'

There are new lines around Eugène's eyes and some grey hairs. How extraordinary that a decade has passed, since the glorious moment when Eugène led me into the studio and Rodin first kissed me.

'I can wait if you need breakfast.'

Rodin is back in Paris and impatient to see me.

'I am not hungry. Which studio has the Master asked you to bring me to?'

'Dépôt des Marbres. I have been given money for the tram. The Master has a gift for you.'

Eugène is taking me to our traditional place. This must mean something. The Dépôt is crumbling, but Rodin still uses it for larger sculptures. It is where he first sculpted me after Eugène handed him my card and every detail of the day is still bright in my mind. The other model dismissed rapidly by Rodin when he saw me, Rodin stroking my thighs as he measured me with the compasses, the lighting of candles, and his request to kiss me after the assistants left for the evening. The start of our life together. The Muse is in the Dépôt des Marbres, so he must want to work on the sculpture again. Perhaps the day when we discussed art, sharing our thoughts, has energised him?

The tram draws into every stop, there are so many requests. People crowding into the carriage have worried frowns, half-empty shopping bags, grubby clothing, and continually glance anxiously up at the sky. The war has turned Parisians into peasants. Eugène stares straight ahead, silent, and I am on the bench's edge, eager to reach the studio.

When we leave the tram in front of the studio, I walk briskly ahead of Eugène to the doors. One is closed and inside the other a man is brushing down a horse, smoothing the skin as if readying it for Rodin's carriage. Perhaps Rodin is spending the day with me, driving north into the countryside, away from the war. He will whisper bon mots in my ear, telling me I am his muse, his confidant. We will halt outside a quaint country inn, and, over luncheon, he will toast me again and again. We will discuss art and life as we do now in our new kind of relationship. But I miss what the groom is saying to Eugène.

'Yes. The Master has left an envelope for you with the groom.'

'Is he not here, to give it to me in person?'

'No, Mademoiselle, the war you know. He has these things to follow.' The groom points to a cart laden with boxes parked in front of the studio.

'But he asked to see me. Surely, he will return today?'

'You must have misunderstood,' Eugène says. 'Apologies if I was unclear. The Master is leaving the country. He is en route to England with Rose and his secretary. The groom is to take the cart with his luggage to the port.'

'Yes, the Master gave me this for you,' and the groom hands me an envelope.

The envelope goes unopened into my bag. Eugène and the groom saddle the horse, leading it over to the cart and I manage a quick 'thank you' before leaving.

The old brasserie is across the street, and I order brandy at the bar, taking out the envelope. The barman gives me a consoling glance. Perhaps he thinks I have a telegram with the news of a relative killed at the front. Breaking the seal, and with a quick swig of brandy, I open the envelope and pull out the contents. A hundred-franc note but no letter, nothing. In a way it does feel like a death. The death of our affair.

CHAPTER 40

PARIS, THE HOSPITAL

Today is freezing, and the concierge is limiting all her lodgers to two shovels of coal a week, so I am wrapped in blankets trying to paint without a fire. At New Year, John Quinn sent me an advance for a new painting, together with an encouraging thought – the Germans will not conquer France because they failed to advance last year; but Quinn has not seen the queues at the bakers – or the new National Bread.

'If we are forbidden croissants,' the concierge said this morning as she delivered a few coals, 'then we cease to be French.'

'The National Bread is nutritious,' and offer her a cup of tea. 'It reminds me of eating granary loaves in my brother's caravan in the countryside.'

'That is the trouble,' and she shakes her head, 'the government is turning us all into rustics,' and pulls her overcoat tight against the cold.

We are all shivering today. How many more years of war will there be? Ruth is still in England so perhaps I should join her; but I must keep working. The new painting is an interior of my Meudon home – the room with a mantlepiece. I am cropping the picture and the table, encouraging the viewer to step into the frame, a new kind of angle. My slippers are too shabby to include in the picture, so I am putting Rodin's favourite *Pamela* on the bookshelves. I wonder if he will ever see the completed painting.

He is back in Paris to check on his studio, but he has not renewed our significant discussions about art, so I put him out of my mind to paint.

The papers say the Germans are within thirty kilometres of Notre-Dame, but the threat of capture seems outside of any frame. Mornings are much better spent now, helping the English soldiers who are filling hospital wards across the city. It is hard to tell their exact ages and most resemble children. They refuse to reveal full details, probably underage when they signed up. Their bodies are so emaciated, the pyjamas are suits hanging on thin wire. Bony wrists protrude from the sleeves, and I am to feed a watery potato soup to those who can swallow food thicker than pure liquid. Today Matron tells me to feed a man who just had his lice removed and head shaved.

'Private Blackford,' I say, glancing at his bed label as I sit down holding a bowl of soup.

'An angel is what you are. We have been eating raw berries and anything we can dig up from the fields.'

I feel the heat of a fever as I hold a spoon to his mouth 'We will feed you well as you recover. You are safe here.'

'So you can send me back to the front.' He eats until the bowl is empty and exhausted lays back on the bed.

'Let me make you more comfortable,' and as I settle him on the pillow, his heat seems to intensify, so dipping some muslin cloths into his bowl of cold water, I smooth one after another across his brow.

'Thank you,' and smiles. 'That's just what I need Miss, along with my young lady. May I ask a question?'

'Nurses are not fully informed about patients' medical histories so if something troubles you, I will call a doctor.'

'It's not that. I shouldn't ask about personal things, but you seem kind. Do you have a sweetheart?'

I cannot mention Ruth. I will have to pretend I have a male sweetheart. Rodin was my suitor once. 'I have a lover.' I will not see the soldier again, and somehow talking to a stranger would be a comfort. No names of course, just general descriptions.

'Is he French? Do you canoodle in French?'

'Usually,' and smile. 'But the last time was too brief.'

Mademoiselle, the concierge called out loudly last week telling me there was an old gentleman downstairs who would not climb the stairs unless he knew I was present. It could only be Rodin, so I quickly fluffed up my hair. The mirror told me I was smart and presentable. It was a shock to see him standing in the doorway; his skin grey, the bags under his eyes puffier, and he was out of breath. Ignoring the bed, he sat down with a thud like a sack of potatoes on a chair, telling me he had returned because Paris was safe from the Germans. I wanted him to discuss art not Paris. All I could think was why does he not ask about my life, about my ideas? He refused an offer of a cup of tea, demanded brandy, and started talking about London. Apparently, the London visit was not successful. Tonks had drawn his portrait in pastels, but the picture had no life. Tonks. His teaching at the Slade used to terrify me but now I can barely recall his face. The days with Ida and Ursula are my vivid memories of Bloomsbury.

'We didn't cuddle last week,' I say to the soldier. 'He had just arrived from London and was tired. We just chatted and he told me how brave the British are. You will be pleased to know that although there have been air raids in London, even a bomb near the Lyceum Theatre, the show continued.'

The soldier smiles as I dry his face.

Rodin preferred to linger on his brandy, and he held out the glass for a refill. After that, it was an effort to encourage him to continue talking.

'There is other good news from London, the Elgin Marbles are safe. Apparently, the authorities stowed them in the British Museum's cellars.'

'Well Paris is safe too,' the soldier says, as if baffled. 'Our tanks are surrounding the city. They're like grey beetles, sliding over every trench. Nothing stops them.'

His eyes are closing. The news is comforting, something I can write to Ruth, persuade her Paris is defended now. Ruth is my lover; Rodin was like a talking newspaper. During his brief visit, he ignored the canvases stacked in the corner of my room, as well as the new canvas on the easel, gave me another hundred-franc note and was out of the door before I could reply. Ruth's naked body on the bed in Meudon is a brighter image.

'You can wash up, Miss John and leave.' Matron's face is kindly. 'Your patient is asleep, and you have been nursing for many hours.'

My apartment is nearby. Although after a morning's work I am always weary, stretching a new canvas restores me. Painting frees my mind to think about Ruth, and about my circle of women artists, all of them free professionals. Even the concierge does not depend on a man for money. The sky is bluer today or is it my imagination?

CHAPTER 41

RUTH MANSON

The sight of Ruth's face on the pillow next to mine each morning is brighter than the sun. When the Germans started retreating, she returned from England with Rosamund, moving into my Meudon house at her suggestion. I am so content. It is a late spring morning, and I am finishing another picture for Quinn. He was delighted when I wrote describing the subject – myself again. The picture in my head is always perfect but resistance begins when I try to convert it into art. Quinn disliked my drawings from photographs, although I told him Walter Sickert often painted using newspaper photographs; so I am returning to oils for the self-portrait in non-naturalistic colours – azure and grey. The texture of the skin and hair is translucent on the surface. Paints, palette, knife, several brushes in a line. All my materials beckon those moments of sweetness, of harmony as I put brush to canvas.

The light in Meudon is clean, unclouded unlike in Paris. Today there are pink tones in the azure, lingering from the sunrise and pushing their way into every corner of the room: sweeping down the wall, across the chaise longue, and into my painting. Last month's self-portrait lacked emotion – flatter, not stiff exactly, but remote from a viewer. This painting will be different. I have a rapture in my heart. The room sings with me; sunlight edges the figure, and the chair from which the figure has risen as if in ecstasy. For an hour, I layer paints, to capture each level of light. I can hear myself breathing rapidly as if I am running towards something heavenly.

'Are you imitating Picasso?' Ruth walks into the room. 'The blue and the oddly shaped hands.'

Her arms circle my waist.

'You tease,' turning awkwardly in her hug to kiss her.

'You are so serious when you work. I love to poke fun.'

These past months, living with Ruth and Rosamund, my house has become so much more than a studio. We have created a home together; I wrote to Gus. He approves our ménage, although I never know with Gus whether he genuinely cares for my happiness, or just admires bohemian relationships.

'This is different,' Ruth releases me and closely examines the canvas.

'The clothes perhaps? It cannot be the colours. I seem incapable of using any other colours.'

'Ah, now I see.' Ruth stares for another moment, her brow furrowing. 'You actually seem happy for once.'

True. I am secure with Ruth, with Rosamund, with the whole sense of a household untroubled by the kind of tension I used to feel waiting in my Paris apartment for Rodin.

'The face is glowing, not worn as usual,' almost tracing the outline with a finger, 'and the figure is relaxed, not taut.'

'Careful, the paint is still wet.'

'Silly. I would never harm your painting. I long to touch you not your art.'

And here it is, the pulse and the shimmer of love like a steady wave. Since Ruth moved in, the world has turned slowly to contentment. Every object in the apartment, every shared meal, the bird calls in the garden, Rosamund shrieking at play, every moment is delightful. I had to find a way of looking at this from a distance because, close-up, the beauty is sometimes overwhelming. The picture records the love – happiness, a life of certainty and clarity – in all the objects and in the figure. Is the painting good? It feels a triumph as if my future as an artist is now secure.

'It is you,' kissing her again on the cheek,' there is no world unless you are in it.'

'Ugh,' Rosamund skips into the room with Pluton. 'You are always kissing each other. What about us?'

Rosamund is taller, her frame filling out, becoming a younger version of Ruth rather than a child.

'We love you,' Ruth says, quickly, 'more than anyone.'

Uncertain whether Rosamund expects me to cuddle Pluton too, I sweep mother and child into my arms, while the dog jumps up at us all.

'Aunty Gwen, do you want me and my friend Elisabeth to pose again for you today?'

They make a good pair with Elisabeth's equally long hair.

'An excellent idea. I will use charcoal and wash, which are quicker than oils. Bring your dolls too. I love the way you place them on your laps as if you are all in conversation.'

'So what will you give us in return?'

'You should not ask for gifts.' Ruth laughs. 'Gwen will soon be a famous artist. We will all live for ever in her paintings.'

Only Gus praises my work so highly. Ruth's warmth and Rosamund's charm sometimes take my breath away.

'I will treat you to the priest's fair in Meudon next week. There will be stalls, donkeys, street performers, even carousel rides.'

Rosamund claps her hands and rushes upstairs with Pluton, calling out, 'Elisabeth, Elisabeth, we're going to the fair.'

'You spoil her.'

'We are a family now.'

In those first months of modelling for Rodin my body dictated everything I thought and felt. Now with Ruth and Rosamund, painting side by side, eating breakfast together without having to converse, is the familiar happiness of the everyday.

∽

On the day of the village fair, Meudon's main street is speckled with lozenges of sunlight. People crowd on the pavements, laughing and shouting to each other, the noise hanging in the air like spent fireworks, and cherry blossoms cluster in pink heaps, waving in the occasional breeze. The fair gives the village an air of joyfulness, as if summer is here and banishing the war. Even the curé makes a little dance as he comes towards us.

'*Bonjour*, Mademoiselles,' shaking our hands and patting Rosamund and Elisabeth on their heads in blessing. 'Welcome to the fête.'

'It seems the whole village is here,' Ruth glances around.

'We are determined to enjoy ourselves, in defiance of the war.'

'Aunty Gwen,' Rosamund pulls at my skirt. 'You promised us a ride on the carousel.'

'So I did,' picking up each girl in turn and settling them on the backs of miniature wooden horses. 'Are you tempted to join them Ruth?'

As she shakes her head, Frère Jacques blares out and the machine rotates before I finish paying coins into the owner's outstretched hand. I am overcome with bliss watching the girls waving their hands at Ruth and me, as they pass her big smile, the fixed point in their slow revolve, as if we are all in a slow-motion film, with me wanting the moment, the day, never to end.

Later with the curé, eating frites with lemonade at tables outside the inn, Ruth's hand is on my knee. Up the street from the fête, nearer the forest, a black figure runs down the hill at full speed. The face is familiar. It is Marcel, Rodin's chauffeur.

'*Monsieur le curé*,' he calls out, '*Monsieur le curé*.'

Villagers immediately look up at the sky as if the man is warning of aeroplanes, but merely a few clouds scud above.

'What is it, Monsieur?' the curé says, as the chauffeur reaches us.

'It is my Master. He needs a priest. Please return with me.'

The light changes from bright blue to grey, I am hot, sweating, about to faint. Ruth's arm is around my waist, propping me up; I cannot speak.

'Monsieur,' Ruth calls out. 'What has taken place?'

'Maître Rodin collapsed, falling down the stairs,' the chauffeur has tears on his cheeks. 'He is in a coma. The doctor attending judged it a stroke. Before becoming unconscious, my Master muttered '*le curé*'. Please be quick.'

The curé retrieves a bible from his pocket, and the two men rush back up the hill. Rodin is not religious, apart from a few masses at Notre-Dame each year; he has never discovered the tranquillity I enjoy, so he must be at death's door. An old dream returns. The one where Rodin and I are at sea, but this time his eyes are unseeing, solid black, and the sea is turning into filthy, muddy water.

'We will return home,' Ruth whispers. 'I will call a hansom cab. You are in no condition to walk.' She turns to the girls. 'Gwen and I must return to the apartment. You can stay longer if you promise to be good.'

'We will, Mama,' Rosamund is too deep in conversation with Elisabeth to notice me.

In the cab, Ruth smooths my hair as if I am her second child. 'You do not have to speak. I know what he once meant to you.'

In the apartment, she tucks me under a blanket on the sofa.

'I will make beef tea,' handing me her handkerchief.

The hot cup warms my cold, aching body. Ruth is stroking my hair again.

It was my dream that Rodin and I would die simultaneously, like visitors who tire of an exhibition and decide to silently leave together. This is probably not what Ruth wants to hear.

'I am here for you, whenever and whatever you need.'

'Your love, and Rosamund's,' taking a deep breath.

Ruth kisses me gently on the lips, and I am asleep in her arms.

∼

I wake and it is dark outside the bedroom window. What day is it? What time? What plans do Ruth and I have for today? – and then a flood of scenes: the chauffeur, the curé, Rodin, and Ruth saving me from being overwhelmed. The house is quiet, everyone must be asleep, even Pluton makes no noise. I dress silently, carrying my shoes to prevent the stairs squeaking, before quietly opening the front door. It is a warm night, and I will see Rodin. Although his house is close, it seems the longest walk I have ever taken just turning the corner. A thin curve of a moon is surrounded by stars but the sky in the countryside has an inkiness about it unlike the sky in Paris. From my old spot, peeking through the hedge, his house is ablaze with lights, while I am in darkness. Rodin's automobile is parked nearby, not in the stable as usual, as if there will be comings and goings and, staring from one window to another, I am a child staring into a doll's house.

There he is in the last window, slumped in a chair, a tartan rug over his knees, a shawl around his shoulders. Rose is sitting alongside, with a bowl and spoon and every so often leans over putting the spoon to his dribbling mouth. He is not drinking, not speaking, but gazing listlessly down at his fingers, moving each in turn as if counting the hours since his stroke. Rose wipes his mouth and sits with the bowl in her lap, crying into the soup and my face is wet too. When the church bell rings out another hour, I walk slowly back home. Dawn is breaking – another day, and Rodin is a shadow behind me.

CHAPTER 42

MEUDON AND FINISTÈRE

When I resume my sketching of the convent girls at Sunday mass, the curé grasps my hands as I leave the church with Ruth.

'My child,' he whispers, 'You seem very troubled. May I assist with prayers?'

'Thank you, Father. Pray for me.'

'I will go ahead to prepare luncheon.' Ruth pats my back and disappears up the hill.

'Will you be painting the prioress this week? We could talk then.'

In a private conversation I can hang my feelings on him like hanging a coat on a peg. It would be a release.

'Yes, Mother Superior is posing tomorrow. I would gladly share the hour.'

On Monday, the afternoon is warm, humid and the prioress's eyelids are closing. A knock at the door and she sits straight up. 'Enter.'

The curé's eyes are on me, not her.

'Miss John, we could talk now, if Mother Superior approves.'

She nods, watching us with her usual beatific expression.

'Thank you,' putting his hands together in prayer. 'May the Lord be with you. What disturbs you, my child?'

'Rodin had a stroke in July, and now it is almost autumn, but I have no information about his health. No one has written to me.'

I cannot tell them about our past affair, or about Rodin's continuing payments for my Paris apartment. 'He gives me so many ideas.'

'I have good news then, Rose, his wife, called on my services. I have been visiting him weekly. He is recovering.'

Rose is not his wife, but they probably need to pretend. I am his companion in art, but she nurses him. Yet it is reassuring. All I desire is for Rodin to live, to be well enough to sculpt, and we can resume our conversations about art, about life. 'Is he sculpting do you know?'

'Yes, he travels to his Paris studio. I cannot remember the name.'

'Hôtel Biron.'

'His mind is not what it was.' The curé seems to read my thoughts. 'One day he is perfectly lucid, then on other days he is unable to do more than count his fingers. We pray daily for him.'

The scene I saw through Rodin's window is so vivid. Rodin's lips drooping, staring listlessly at his hands, dribbling.

'Thank you, you have both given me consolation. Could we finish for today, Mother Superior? I am strangely tired. You must be too; you have been good to pose for so long.'

'Of course. We pray for you too.'

Oddly, I want this version of the Mother Superior to remain unfinished for a while. I like the comfort the convent brings me. The moment of completion is always a moment of loss, a loss of all the images the portrait might have been, and painting extends my life.

On the walk up the hill shadows of the horse-chestnuts creep towards me. The trees are undressing already for autumn as if they have a surplus of leaves and do not quite know what to do with them. Pausing for a moment, lost in the sight, I know that although Rodin and I are no longer together, he will always be with me whenever I paint. The trees continue shedding and leaves stick blindly to my coat. Behind me the convent bell tolls as if calling out for an old friend.

'We should travel to Brittany again,' Ruth suggests at dinner.

'Return to the house in Finistère; and we could also explore southern Brittany together.'

'An excellent idea. We would be further away from the Germans. And Rosamund could see those summer friends of hers – Odette and Simone.'

The curé said Rodin is working and surrounded by old models and hangers-on wanting anything from him – drawings, maquettes, signed photographs. Wrapping up my past with Rodin is like taking off an old, familiar dress to wear one more fitting, more joyful. But it hurts. We cannot remove what has shaped our bodies without pain. Something always endures.

'We will pack tonight,' Ruth lifts her glass, 'to Brittany.'

'To our life,' and I drain my wine.

∾

From the safety of the promenade, waves are tumbling and too frothy to swim today but we all rushed down to the harbour in Finistère as soon as we unpacked, as if the sight of the ocean proves the holiday has begun. Pluton seems to enjoy playing on the beach even more than Rosamund. Immersion in water is good, releases me, my anxieties float away on the surface like fronds of seaweed.

'May we remain in Brittany?' Rosamund asks, 'Pluton loves it here.'

'We can for a few weeks. Gwen and I will paint. The autumn light is perfect at this time of year.'

'Will you pose again, Rosamund?' I say, 'and ask your friends to sit?'

'Do not ask Gwen for anything, Rosamund. We will buy you and your friends ice creams when we are next on the beach.'

I had given Quinn my holiday address and sure enough a letter from him is with the concierge when we return to eat in the evening.

'What does he say?' Ruth asks, smiling, 'He probably wants more paintings from you.'

'He does but this time he will be in luck. I have those paintings of the little girls at mass and portraits keep him happy.' There is an inevitability about working in oils which settles me. 'He admired your landscape as well.'

I had persuaded Quinn to buy Ruth's painting and her smile is my reward.

'Have you ever met Quinn?'

'No, but we write so often to each other it feels like he is a constant friend.'

I avoid the meetings because I prize my independent life in Paris and Meudon, creating whatever art I wish; so although Quinn visited Paris more than once, I managed to be absent. 'I have seen his photograph. Quinn has a kind face. He has asked me to paint Jeanne, his companion when he next visits Europe; so we will meet then.'

Ruth smiles again. My reply seems to please her. 'While waiting for the weather to settle here, why not travel, visit Loctudy again?'

Loctudy is where we first holidayed together, first shared a bed, our bodies.

'Wonderful,' kissing her on the cheek.

∽

The small fishing port is unchanged. The islands in the estuary sparkle in the kinder light of southern Brittany with a glorious view of Loctudy harbour, the seagulls twisting iridescent in the sun, a lighthouse seemingly close enough to touch. We are painting every day. Ruth, with Rosamund in tow, braves the countryside, painting out of doors. The first day, we stood side by side with our easels facing a wide stream flowing down from the forest, but memories of McEvoy in Le Puy surfaced. Those scenes should have faded, and I must not revive the moments. Indoors I settle into a routine – priming, sketching, mixing on the palette and finally the first brush stroke. Often Ruth returns with a whole scene complete before I have even drawn an outline.

'A parcel for you has arrived,' Ruth carries a thick, brown paper shape upstairs.

'I did not hear the concierge knock. I was concentrating deeply.'

'I too but out of doors. It is cold today; I will make tea while you unwrap.'

The parcel is from Ursula. Her name and address are on the reverse. The parcel squashes so it must be the usual clothes package.

'What a marvellous blouse.' Ruth brings in two mugs.

'And a coat and skirt; Ursula is so good to me. She sews everything by hand.'

Ruth glances at my face, with a worried frown, as she hands me tea.

'Ursula and I are old friends from the Slade days. Augustus has been assisting her to exhibit her paintings.'

Ruth puts her arm around my shoulders, and I open Ursula's letter in front of her. There is nothing to hide. As I read, it is impossible not to laugh. Ursula has written such a devastating critique about London art. Ruth is laughing too, seeing my face.

'What is so amusing?

'McEvoy has no less than ten pictures in the Royal Society of Portrait Painters' exhibition. Ursula writes he is deteriorating into a fashionable artist, and I fear Gus will be on the same downward journey.'

'They will be wealthy but lack critical acclaim. Not like you.' And she winks.

What a coincidence. I remember McEvoy while painting in the countryside and suddenly here is news of him from Ursula. What an appropriate place for him to exhibit; I will never show my portraits there, only in contemporary galleries.

'I have discovered a new energy and courage from this holiday, you have renewed my zest for art.'

After dinner, we stand at the shore, without speaking, holding hands, enjoying the mellow night air. The war encourages everyone to go to bed early due to the lack of coals but tonight the wind breathes from the land, warm at our backs. It is not quite night, the sky hazy in the wake of the afternoon's dying sun. There is already a full moon, and the birds begin to fall silent. I study the cliff edges framing the beach, feeling as if I have stood here a hundred times. This was how I felt in Tenby when I would see the beach scene as if it was in galleries admiring Boudin's paintings, or as if I had painted the landscape myself. I have been holding onto my memories of Rodin too much, little dark spaces of limited feelings, cradling my past until it is worn and dim. With Ruth, I am savouring the almost, unbelievable fact she might be my life's love.

CHAPTER 43
RODIN'S DEATH, MEUDON

December 1916 is the harshest winter month I have ever known. The frost turned to heavy snow, and we are wearing overcoats indoors while painting. Yet it seems as if I can paint anything I desire – portraits, spaces, clothes; I love the fluidity of oils but not the multiple glazes. Christmas is too cold to visit Paris and Rosamund is insisting on a Christmas tree here in Meudon.

'We are surrounded by a forest, why do we need an indoor tree?'

Ruth must be concerned about money. Our savings are low, and after years of wartime, coal is expensive.

'A tree will be so pretty,' Rosamund pleads.

'A tree's glass ornaments usually come from Germany.' Ruth is undaunted. 'They will be difficult to find in the war.'

Rosamund seems miserable, and Ruth cuddles her. She can never resist her daughter.

'We will buy a tree then, but you must help with the paper chains, and we cannot have a lavish meal.'

'I will paint walnut shells with my gold paint to hang on the tree.' I always wait for Ruth's final decision before giving an opinion. I learnt not to intervene, or to praise Rosamund too highly without checking first with Ruth. 'I can paint your nails too with gold.'

Rosamund claps her hands. 'There is plenty of snow to decorate the tree.' She points through the window.

'Silly. Snow will melt especially when we light the candles.' Rosamund is almost right. To economise, we light the fire only in the evening and indoors is as cold as the forest, so snow could rest on the tree for a moment.

'I will dot cotton wool balls on the branches instead.' Ruth smiles. 'The scene might fool Santa Claus.'

By Christmas Eve, the sitting room is resplendent. Rosamund's new ribbons and hair grips are in a stocking hanging from the mantlepiece. Beneath the tree there are my sketches of her and Ruth, and one Ruth has made of me. I hope Ruth keeps mine because I will treasure hers. My sketch depicts Ruth as she is – warm and joyful with gold tones in her hair. After Rosamund is asleep, we sit in comfortable silence side by side in front of the grate enjoying the last embers.

'Ursula writes that she saw sacks of Christmas post at Victoria Station waiting to travel to the front. I had been hoping the war would be over by Christmas.'

'The government promised an end to war by Christmas in the very first year, but only to encourage recruitment,' Ruth says. 'Sometimes I wonder if the war will ever end.'

'Well, the Germans are retreating further. We are safe in Meudon and Paris.'

I do not want her to escape again to England. I need her here with me. We hold hands.

After New Year, a few red berries remain on the holly adorning the mantlepiece, and the mistletoe is turning yellow.

'One last kiss?' pointing up at the mistletoe, 'before everything has to be removed.'

The heat from Ruth's kiss travels through my body.

'I feel like a butterfly emerging from a chrysalis. I think 1917 will be a lucky year.' The change from one year to another always makes me optimistic for some reason.

'Again!' Rosamund is standing in the doorway, 'more kissing.'

'You say this to get kisses yourself.' Ruth laughs. 'We are not fools.'

'Why do we have mistletoe and red berries?' Rosamund asks, 'and I have also a question about Santa Claus?'

I cannot tell her red berries symbolise Christ's blood. 'Because it is tradition. What do you wish to know about Santa?'

'His hair and beard are so white. He must be incredibly old. So why does he not die?'

Rodin's hair and beard are stark white, even his eyelashes.

'Santa has eternal life, like the Trinity; as long as we leave brandy and mince pies for him every year.'

Rosamund laughs and glances around the room as if expecting to see Santa arriving down the chimney.

'Look a candle has blown out on the tree.' She points. 'It is bad luck, a concierge told me once. Someone will die this year. Perhaps it will be Santa.'

'Well, not us.' Ruth cuddles her. 'Or Pluton. He is healthier than anyone. He certainly eats more.'

What do they say? A child's eye is far-seeing? But it is a new year, so I am making wishes. Ruth and Rosamund will live with me for ever. I will finish the Mother Superior's final portrait; and send paintings for exhibit to the New English Art Club, as Gus and Ursula keep urging me to do. Quinn will buy another painting. I will become a famous artist. America has joined the Allies so surely the war will be over soon.

※

'The portrait is perfect.' The prioress is standing in front of the painting.

'Lifelike, an uncanny resemblance,' the curé adds, nodding his head.

'Lifelike' is not a term I would choose but at least they are both content. And all the nuns too, apparently, since they want further copies for their cells. I am delighted. Winter slipped unannounced into spring and summer, but it has been a beautiful October, although very cold for the time of year; the months of painting in the convent eased by overlooking its garden trees and seeing shrubs turning auburn, yellow and red.

'We will have a special service to dedicate the painting. A mass to thank you for all your devoted work.'

Little does she know, it is not so much dedication to her portrait, which has taken so long, but my intense need to shape and reshape.

'We will offer prayers too, for those who died in Meudon this year.'

'You may know one of the locals Miss John,' the curé adds, 'since you know Rodin.'

The chair back in front of me is the only solid thing nearby. 'Excuse me. I feel a little unwell.' Sitting down before I faint. 'Which local?'

'Rose Beuret,' and the curé pours me a glass of water.

'Monsieur Rodin's housekeeper?'

'Not housekeeper. Wife. They married in January this year. The Mayor performed the ceremony. And scarcely two weeks after the wedding she died. So sad.'

'Our prayers are with her,' the curé adds, 'and with Monsieur Rodin. He has not been well since she died. Often, he is unaware of his surroundings.'

Why did no one tell me? Surely Rilke might have written even though he is in Germany, or Rodin's assistant who knows me well? I heard nothing. Slowly I sip the water, holding the glass with both hands to prevent any trembling. 'Rose is merely my housekeeper,' he always said when I fell into one of my nagging moods. So many nights I tossed and turned, unable to sleep, wondering what she meant to Rodin. And now she has gone, and no one wrote a word to me all these months. I finish the water.

'More water Mademoiselle?' The prioress picks up the carafe.

'No thank you. I feel well again.'

'You have been working hard. We are to blame. Please rest at home. We will contact you with details of the mass for the painting when it is arranged; and a thousand thanks for the portrait. You have made the whole convent happy.'

The square in front of the convent is full of leaves. Every patch of Meudon used to be swept clean each day but, with the war, few men work on the streets. People are dying and now Rose. Sitting on a bench, scuffing the leaves with my foot, Rose's image is here, grey, and dead. At one time I wished for nothing more; but now Ruth is my life's love as well as my painting. Yet here is a sadness for Rose and for Rodin.

At night after dinner, pleading tiredness to Ruth, I go to bed. My actions are often inexplicable even to me and wanting to stand again outside Rodin's house is impossible to explain to Ruth. Telling her about Rose while we ate, seemed to worry her. A frown appears whenever I mention Rodin, so it is best to remain silent. After checking on Rosamund, Ruth's bedroom door gently closes. The light under her door disappears and I wait a half hour before dressing, until the house is silent.

I tiptoe down the stairs in stockings and lace my boots before stepping out into a freezing night. My breath blows out cloud after cloud until I reach Rodin's house. Last time the house was ablaze, but now it is dark with one candlelit room. Two heads face each other. One is Rodin, nodding repeatedly as if unable to stop, the other is his chauffeur. For thirteen years I have been Rodin's muse and now he is reduced to a bobbing figure with seemingly uncontrollable gestures. His hand, his eye was so precise; every gesture carried an emotion, at one time for me. The candlelit window will be fixed in my memory as if the room possesses the sorrow and happiness of all my unfinished letters. I need to say goodbye, and to all the bushes along the fence surrounding his home, I know so well. I kiss the rough bark of a branch, the damp leaves pressing on my face. My feet are frozen. It is the coldest October I have ever known, and November promises more snow, so I kiss the fence again without staying; it is a quick walk back.

∽

Two weeks later, I am working wearing my overcoat again, and near the fire to keep the paints from hardening. Even oils seem to solidify in this temperature.

'Darling, it is me,' Ruth calls out, stomping the snow from her boots at the door. 'I bought *Le Figaro* today along with our bread.' Rushing towards the fire, she adds, 'I am desperate for news about the war.'

'I will make us both tea,' and clean my brushes, 'warm you after the long hill climb.'

Even a pan of water boils slowly, and are there any biscuits? Suddenly Ruth's arms are around me.

'Gwen, come and sit down,' leading me towards the sofa.

'What is the matter?' Ruth's eyes are dark, troubled.

'*Le Figaro* has a medical bulletin issued by a Dr Stephen Chauvet. It is headed Auguste Rodin.'

'Read it, read it,' and I clutch the arm of the sofa.

'Pulmonary congestion, patient seriously weakened, in a critical condition and died at four o'clock this morning, Sunday 18 November 1917.'

That was yesterday. Through the window snow is falling. In the trees burdened with snow and ice, I see his outline; in the dark shadows I see his eyes. The snow's softness reminds me of his first gentle touch, stroking my breasts, my body. Rodin was once my Master, my lover, my father, my counsel.

'There is more, shall I read it out?'

I nod. It is impossible to speak.

'The funeral takes place on 24 November 1917, in Monsieur Rodin's house in Meudon. A phalanx of territorial soldiers will attend in honour of Monsieur Rodin's position as Grand Officier of the Legion of Honour. A memorial service will be held on the same day in St Margaret's Church, Westminster, England.'

I can watch his funeral from my garden – a comforting thought.

'I am here for you,' Ruth throws her arms around me again. 'Always.'

∾

Next week, I gaze down into the grounds of Rodin's house from my garden wall because no one invited me to the funeral. In the centre of the lawn his coffin is clearly visible – it should be bulkier; he has been in my life for thirteen years. There is such a dense crowd; black top hat after black top hat glistening with drizzle; white faces shrouded in a gloom with flurries of wind drowning out the speakers. Their faces are indistinct, but most must be officials; the thin light picks out insignia stretched across their black frockcoats. The knot of women to the left must be his other models, veils fluttering from lavishly decorated hats; heads moving close together whenever a train passes, horn sounding on its way to Paris. Soldiers are shuffling into a line now around the replica of my Master's *The Thinker* at the head of his grave. The white marble glows through the mist; a single immense figure, head on hand, elbow on knee; the only one without an umbrella, towering above the mourners.

As I watch something is shifting in my body, a tightening of muscles; the same feeling as when seeing my Master drooling and counting his fingers after the stroke. It is over. I will start my memoir at the beginning: winning my first prize at the Slade, the first time Gus spoke to me as if I was a true artist rather than his sister; the first time Rodin admired my ideas not just my body. Those feelings of having a purpose in life, of being a separate person, of becoming a true artist – because I am no longer Marie – but Gwen.

AFTERWORD

Ruth Manson and Gwen soon lived separately, but remained good friends throughout Gwen's life, together with Rosamund and Rosamund's daughter France.

Immediately after Rodin's death, Augustus arrived to care for Gwen. He was Britain's leading portrait painter, with portraits of W B Yeats and George Bernard Shaw although, as Gwen predicted, becoming less critically acclaimed. Later, he took part in CND demonstrations. Notorious for his affairs, Augustus continued to live with Dorelia McNeill, his wife, who cared for their own children and Ida's. Dorelia painted until her death in 1960, a year before Augustus. Ida John (née Nettleship) relinquished painting on having children and died in 1907 in Paris. A collection of her letters *The Good Bohemian* was published in 2017.

Gwen's other Slade friends were lifelong artists. Ursula Tyrwhitt, Gwen's confidant throughout her life, married her cousin and died in 1966. The Ashmolean Museum, Oxford, held a major retrospective exhibition in 1973. Gwen Salmond, 'the other Gwen', also married and taught at Chelsea Art School while continuing to exhibit.

The artist Hugh Ramsay never met Gwen, although it was convenient for my fiction to have him do so. He did study at Colarossi (but earlier in 1901) and had four paintings accepted by

AFTERWORD

the Société Nationale des Beaux-Arts. Returning to Australia, he died of tuberculosis in 1906 aged twenty-nine.

Gwen's solicitor father Edwin supported her financially all her life. After failed attempts to remarry, he remained single, dying in 1939.

Gwen finally met John Quinn in August 1921 in Meudon. As well as supporting Gwen and other artists, Quinn acted as a legal defender of James Joyce and T S Eliot for *Ulysses* and *The Waste Land* respectively and was an active champion of Yeats and Irish nationalism. He died in 1924 and the sale of his outstanding art collection, including Gwen Johns, took place in New York in 1927.

Gwen's friend the poet Rainer Maria Rilke published *Auguste Rodin*, over four hundred poems in French, drawing on Rodin's ideas, as well as many other collections. He aided left-wing causes and died in Switzerland in 1926.

At Rodin's death in 1917, aged seventy-seven, Gwen was forty-one. She became more productive – approximately forty-eight drawings and fifty-eight paintings in the 1920s alone – including the major paintings *Mother Marie Poussepin* (1915–1920) and *The Convalescent* (1923–4). Over sixty-five of her works are in British collections. Her first solo exhibition, at the New Chenil Galleries, London, 1926, confirmed her reputation as a major twentieth-century artist.

Gwen's last relationship was with Véra Oumançoff, her Meudon neighbour and an ardent Catholic, but Gwen spent the final years of her life alone, as she preferred. She died in Dieppe in September 1939. It is said that she was en route to England to escape World War Two. I like to think she also planned one last swim. Her death record, as Mary John, and plaque are at the Janval Cemetery, Dieppe, but the precise location of her grave is unknown.

ACKNOWLEDGEMENTS

After writing my first novel *Talland House*, about a fictional artist Lily Briscoe, I wanted to write about another artist, but in this case, a real person. I also wanted to be braver with the novel form, by writing in the first person, present tense to hopefully make *Radical Woman* more immediate to the reader. Like many people, I knew of Gwen through loving her paintings, but as a woman in the shadows of her brother Augustus John and lover Auguste Rodin. When I became immersed in her archival letters and in books about art and culture at the turn of the twentieth century, I saw how radical Gwen was. This is my story of Gwen John, breaking free of Augustus and Rodin, to become a celebrated artist in her own right.

To do this, I tinkered with Gwen's chronology, for example, simplifying the many house moves she made, omitting members of her family, changing dates and events, to keep a focus on the main themes. I also introduced real-life figures, who Gwen did not know, but were perfect for my narrative.

I am so grateful to novelist Tim Pears (*Gold Dust*) for mentoring me and inspiring new directions, and to TLC before Tim. Thanks to my writing group Edwina, Mary Ann, and Bridget for their expert suggestions. Thanks to my women's book group for their very lively and perceptive discussions about novels: Ann, Ingrid, Jan, Jean, Judy, and Kath. Thank you to others whose support contributed so much at different stages: Annabel Abbs, Anna Falcini, Jill French, Professor Susan Sellers, and Professor Jeremy Thurlow. I am particularly grateful to John and Leigh Spiers of Edward Everett Root Publishers, for being so enthusiastic about *Radical Woman* from day one. John, when Director of Harvester

Wheatsheaf, published my first ever book *Feminist Criticism* (1986) and it feels so appropriate to be returning.

My deepest thanks are to Rodger Sykes for his ideas and support over the years.

More information about Gwen and Rodin lies in archives, including The National Library of Wales, the Barber Institute of Fine Arts, the British Library, the Tate Gallery Archives, Yale University Archives, Musée Rodin, Musée Rodin at Meudon, the British Newspaper Archive.

I drew on many non-fiction and fictional books, these in particular:

- *London and its Environs 1902*, and *Paris and its Environs 1904* – K. Baedeker
- *Gwen John: 1876-1939*, S. Chitty
- *Writing on the Wall: Women Writers on Women Artists* – eds. J. Collins and E. Lindner
- *You Must Change Your Life: The Story of Rainer Maria Rilke and Auguste Rodin* – R. Corbett
- *Gwen John* – A. Foster
- *Keeping the World Away* – M. Forster
- *The Bohemians: The Birth of Modern Art Paris 1900-1930* – D. Franck
- *Rodin a Biography* – F. V. Grunfeld
- *London's Latin Quarter* – K. Hare
- *T. S. Eliot's Parisian Year* – N. Hargrove
- *Gwen John and Augustus John* – D. F. Jenkins and C. Stephens
- *Chiaroscuro: Fragments of an Autobiography* – A. John
- *The Good Bohemian: The Letters of Ida John* – eds. M. Holroyd and R. John
- *Gwen John an Interior Life* – C. Langdale and D. F. Jenkins
- *Gwen John: Letters and Notebooks* – ed. C. Lloyd-Morgan
- *A Wanderer in Paris* – E. V. Lucas
- *Degas and His Model* – A. Michel
- *Auguste Rodin* – R. M. Rilke
- *Letters to a Young Painter* – R. M. Rilke
- *Rilke in Paris* – R. M. Rilke and M. Betz

- *Gwen John: A Life* – S. Roe
- *Vanished Smile: The Mysterious Theft of the Mona Lisa* – R. A. Scotti
- *The Banquet Years: The Arts in France 1885-1918* – R. Shattuck
- *In the Fold Between Power and Desire: Women Artists' Narratives* – M. Tamboukou
- *'If a Young Painter Be Not Fierce and Arrogant – God Help Him': Some Women Artists at the Slade 1895-9* – H. Taylor